*The man was watching her through a pair of binoculars.*

Suzannah stared back, completely confused. He was wearing a baseball cap and nicely fitted jeans. He was also wearing a brown leather bomber jacket exactly like Justin's, but with the binoculars obscuring his features, she simply couldn't tell who it was.

At least, not for sure.

If it were Justin, he would have waved to her by now. Even if he hadn't intended for her to catch him following her, he'd do something now to acknowledge her. Wouldn't he?

She was about to call out to him when the man finally moved. Reaching his hand under his jacket, he pulled out a jet-black, long-barreled firearm. Then, to her shock, he aimed it right at her.

Dear Reader,

Law students learn countless rules governing trial procedure. Most laypeople know the major ones, too, just from reading or watching legal thrillers. Rules like: Don't lead *your* witness. Don't badger *their* witness. That sort of thing.

But Rule #1 overshadows all others: *Don't piss off the judge.*

A good litigator chants it silently before every appearance. No competent attorney wants to test it, much less break it.

It's true that a judge's rulings can be reversed later on appeal, but while trial is in session, he or she is omnipotent. Get on that judge's bad side, and suddenly, you have zero leeway with either your questioning or your arguments. Heck, at that point, you're just trying to survive! Because if you're *really* annoying, you could go to jail for contempt.

Among her other problems, the heroine of *Spin Control* has just broken Rule #1.

Enjoy!

Kate

# KATE DONOVAN

# SPIN CONTROL

Published by Silhouette Books

**America's Publisher of Contemporary Romance**

If you purchased this book without a cover you should be aware that this book is stolen property. It was reported as "unsold and destroyed" to the publisher, and neither the author nor the publisher has received any payment for this "stripped book."

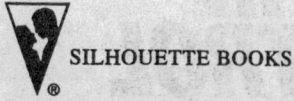

SILHOUETTE BOOKS

ISBN-13: 978-0-373-51419-9
ISBN-10:   0-373-51419-0

SPIN CONTROL

Copyright © 2006 by Kate Donovan

All rights reserved. Except for use in any review, the reproduction or utilization of this work in whole or in part in any form by any electronic, mechanical or other means, now known or hereafter invented, including xerography, photocopying and recording, or in any information storage or retrieval system, is forbidden without the written permission of the editorial office, Silhouette Books, 233 Broadway, New York, NY 10279 U.S.A.

All characters in this book have no existence outside the imagination of the author and have no relation whatsoever to anyone bearing the same name or names. They are not even distantly inspired by any individual known or unknown to the author, and all incidents are pure invention.

This edition published by arrangement with Harlequin Books S.A.

® and TM are trademarks of Harlequin Books S.A., used under license. Trademarks indicated with ® are registered in the United States Patent and Trademark Office, the Canadian Trade Marks Office and in other countries.

www.SilhouetteBombshell.com

**Printed in U.S.A.**

**Books by Kate Donovan**

Silhouette Bombshell

*Identity Crisis* #20
*Parallel Lies* #44
*Exit Strategy* #67
*Spin Control* #105

*Books featuring the S.P.I.N. agency

## KATE DONOVAN

is the author of more than a dozen novels and novellas, ranging from time travel and paranormal to historical romance, suspense and romantic comedy. An attorney, she draws on her criminal law background to create challenges worthy of her heroines, who crack safes, battle bad guys and always get their man. As for Kate, she *definitely* got her man and is living happily ever after with him and their two children in Elk Grove, California. Please visit her Web site at www.katedonovan.com.

This story is dedicated to our dog Murphy,
who was so sweet, so loyal and
so loving for fourteen years,
and who never once complained at the end.
*Good boy, Murf. We'll never forget you.*

# Prologue

Kristie Hennessy's career at the Strategic Profiling and Identification Network required her to excel at three things: evaluating a subject's state of mind, anticipating his next move and designing a strategy to deal with it. She had been doing this sort of thing every day, weekends included, for almost two years, yet had to admit the man she was currently observing was the most fascinating subject she had ever encountered.

He paced back and forth like a wild animal that had just been caged. The fact that he was visibly conflicted was particularly intriguing given his profile. Everything in his file indicated that he was a man of incredible confidence, determination and single-mindedness. And

Kristie's dealings with him up till this point had proved that profile correct.

So why was he suddenly so unsure of himself? So tense? So downright fidgety?

And then it hit her, right between the eyes. This man—SPIN Director Will McGregor—was about to propose to her.

*Finally!*

"As you know," he was saying, his sexy voice resembling an X-rated travelogue as he paced the floor of her Washington, D.C., apartment, "the West Coast office is ready to roll. The last stage in this plan is to assign permanent staff, and then—assuming the President doesn't change his mind again—SPIN will be converted from a separate agency into a division of the Bureau."

"It's like going home for you," she agreed, wistful for the days when he had been an FBI agent in the field, depending on her—his "spinner"—to provide him with undercover identities and support via computer and telephone.

It had been his gorgeous intonation and impressive record that had first attracted her to him. For weeks they had known each other only by voice. Now they were lovers. And if she was reading the signals accurately, they were about to become even more.

"I kind of miss the days when you were an agent yourself," she told him. "But you're such a great director, the change has definitely been worth it."

He seemed disconcerted by the interruption, so she warned herself to stop distracting him from his objective.

McGregor cleared his throat. "Once the transition is

complete, I won't be a director any longer. I'll be an assistant director of the FBI. They've promised me I can choose to be based in L.A. or D.C. And since my sister lives in L.A., that's my preference. But it affects you, too, because I'd want you to permanently relocate there. The good news is, you won't have to find housing. Because obviously you'd be living at my place."

"Then where would *you* live?"

"Huh? Oh. Funny." McGregor grimaced, then joined her on the sofa, taking her hands in his own. "You're not going to make this easy, are you?"

"After fourteen months? Nope."

He chuckled. "Okay. Move in with me, please. I can't live without you."

"Move in with you?" She licked her lips, disappointed. "That's it?"

"For now. I figure eventually we'll make it permanent—"

"Eventually we'll make it permanent?" She pulled her hands free. "FYI, that's the most unromantic thing anyone has ever said to me." She eyed him grimly. "All year long I thought you were waiting until the new office was set up. Then I thought you were waiting to see if Ray would come back to SPIN, which obviously isn't going to happen. Now what? Are you some kind of freakish confirmed bachelor in disguise? Because if you are, you should have warned me."

He gave her a pained smile. "Just the opposite. I'd love to marry you. But our work situation complicates things. If you and I get married…have children…"

"Oh, that." She laughed in relief. "Let me make it

easy for you. You and the kids would come first. Absolutely. But I also love spinning and I love working for you. And I actually think I can run some ops from home, so I can combine business and pleasure. Except when the kids are babies, of course, because I'll be too busy kissing their toes to get anything done."

McGregor grinned. "Sounds great. Unfortunately that's not the complication I was referring to. I'm worried I'll have to fire you someday, and I'm pretty sure the marriage manuals advise against that."

"Fire me?" Kristie scowled. "For what? I'm your best spinner."

"You're great," he agreed. "But you're also a rogue. You've decimated the rules at least three times that I know of—once on my watch, two or three on Ray Ortega's. I figure you and I should live together for a while. See if you do anything else crazy. If I have to fire you, then you can decide if you'll still marry me. And if by some miracle you become a model employee, we can get married next summer. I even bought the ring— Oh, fine!" His blue eyes darkened as the phone on Kristie's desk began to chime. "Is that your operative line? I thought we agreed you'd route it to the backups so we could have an uninterrupted dinner for once."

"I told them not to bother me unless it was an emergency."

"Perfect." He punched the speaker-phone button, his voice turning into a growl. "This is Director McGregor. Identify yourself."

"Hey, McGregor. It's Justin Russo. So the rumors

about you and S-3 are true, huh? You're a lucky guy! Is she as pretty as she sounds?"

"Russo?" McGregor practically spat the name of Kristie's favorite operative. "Not that it's any of your business, but S-3 and I were having an employer-employee discussion. And I wasn't aware we had any ops going with you at the moment."

"We don't," Kristie interrupted. "But we recommended him for the Angel of Mercy investigation. Because of the possible Night Arrow connection. Remember?" Raising her voice, she asked with concern, "Justin? Is everything okay?"

"Sorry, S-3. Didn't mean to get you in trouble with the boss. I know SPIN isn't officially involved with this case, but I was hoping to get some quick advice anyway."

"Don't worry. But hold on, okay?" She pressed the mute button, then prodded McGregor hopefully. "You say you already bought the ring? Do you have it with you?"

"Let's get rid of this guy first." McGregor switched the phone off mute. "Your timing stinks, Russo. Can't you call S-3 tomorrow at the office? It's bad enough when you guys hound her in the middle of the night for SPIN business. But when we're not even under contract for the operation—"

"You're right," Justin admitted. "But I didn't know who else to trust. And Essie—I mean, S-3—hasn't ever steered me wrong."

Kristie sent McGregor a pleading look, and when he frowned but nodded, she said quickly, "What do you need, Justin?"

"The name of a good lawyer."

"A lawyer?" McGregor was growling again. "What's going on out there?"

"I'm not actually 'out there.' I'm in here—a jail cell, to be specific." Dropping the bantering tone, the FBI agent added, "They think I killed a suspect. But I didn't do it. I swear."

"Of course you didn't," Kristie replied, shooting McGregor a warning glare. "How awful, Justin. But don't worry. We'll help you. Right, Will?"

"Yeah, Russo. Don't worry. I've got plenty of contacts at the Justice Department. I'll make sure they fix you up with the best."

"We'll do it right away," Kristie added. "I can't believe they're actually holding you."

"The Bureau will have him out in no time," McGregor promised, his voice ringing with confidence. "Just sit tight, Russo. You may be a pain in the ass, but you're also a federal agent. There's no way anyone at the FBI—or here—will let you down."

"Thanks, McGregor. And Essie? Just for the record, I didn't kill anyone—"

"I know you didn't," she murmured, although in the back of her mind warning bells were beginning to clang.

This was sounding a little too familiar. The last time a close friend—former SPIN director Ray Ortega—had assured her he was innocent, she had believed him without question, and that misplaced trust had almost gotten her killed.

She licked her lips. "You said it was a suspect? You don't mean the Masterson heiress, do you? I read about that shooting."

"Yeah, and believe me, when I get my hands on the guy who did it, I'll make him pay." Justin's tone grew brisk. "I've gotta go. McGregor? Give Essie a kiss for me."

As the line went dead, McGregor muttered, "That guy is nothing but trouble."

"Like me?"

He laughed warily and reached for her. "At least you have some redeeming qualities."

She backed away. "You're supposed to be calling your friends at the FBI, remember? To make sure they get a great lawyer for Justin." Then she jutted her chin forward defensively. "He and I may use unorthodox tactics at times, but we each have excellent success rates."

McGregor snorted. "Russo's unorthodox tactics usually involve fooling around with some female when he's supposed to be working on a case. Big surprise that there's a woman behind this murder charge, too."

"At least he knows how to be romantic. Maybe you should ask for a few pointers."

McGregor winced. "I probably should have mentioned this earlier, but if I ever *do* have to fire you, my next official act would be to resign as SPIN director."

"*Assistant* Director," she reminded him drily.

McGregor seemed about to respond but ended up just shaking his head instead. Then he pulled out his cell phone, punched in a number and was soon lobbying the FBI to find the best attorney the Justice Department had to offer for Special Agent Justin Russo.

# Chapter 1

"Thanks for coming with me today, Suzannah. I can really use the moral support."

"If half of what we've heard about Judge Taylor's temper is true, you don't need moral support. You need a flak jacket." Suzannah Ryder gave her colleague Tony Moreno a wry smile. "You're pretty brave taking on this case, knowing how angry he is about it. Can you believe he hasn't ever had a ruling reversed on appeal before? They say he threw a huge fit when he got the news."

She paused to wince, knowing that Judge Taylor's anger had actually been focused in *her* direction. After all, she was the attorney who had successfully appealed the judge's ruling. And since he was known throughout Northern California as "Taylor the Jailor" because of his habit of throwing attorneys into jail for contempt of court, she was glad it was Tony rather than she who was handling the Driscoll case from here on out, including this morning's appearance.

"You're sure you don't want to be my co-counsel?" Tony asked, his expression hopeful.

"I don't have a death wish. Plus, I don't really know anything about criminal cases, remember? I only got roped into taking the appeal because Driscoll is my best friend's sister's boyfriend." She shook her head. "I don't know how you guys do it. An appeal is one thing, but here at the trial-court level, it's complete anarchy. Hobnobbing with criminals. Kowtowing to hostile judges like Taylor every day. I'm glad my firm only accepts civil cases. Give me a nice safe stack of contracts any day of the week."

"Yeah." Tony sent a worried glance toward the heavy double doors that would soon admit them to Taylor the Jailor's courtroom. "A stack of contracts sounds pretty good right now. Excuse me, will you? I've gotta go to the restroom and puke my guts out."

"You really do look a little green." She patted his shoulder. "There's a water fountain over there—"

"Nope. When I get this nervous, there's only one solution." Tony was already edging toward the men's room. "If I'm not back in five minutes, tell Driscoll to find another lawyer."

Suzannah grimaced as her friend lurched away. Apparently he really was going to be sick. And she could hardly blame him. The thought of facing Judge Taylor would be enough to scare anyone. But to deal with him on this particular case, the one that had caused the judge so much embarrassment—

"Suzannah Ryder?" a voice asked from behind her.

She turned to find herself staring into the warm blue eyes of a truly gorgeous guy who was extending his hand toward her. The man had it all—a tall, athletic build, a smile with a provocative blend of sincerity and mischief, and wavy brown hair that was just shaggy enough to suggest he'd been marooned on a desert island for a while, which would also explain his golden tan.

"My name's Justin Russo," he told her, his voice clear and confident. "Congratulations on the big win. My colleagues were just telling me about it. Very impressive."

She accepted the handshake, shamelessly enjoying the R-rated tingle it induced. "Thanks. Do you have an appearance before Judge Taylor today?"

"Yeah. Now that you've got him all riled up," Justin complained.

She bit back a smile. "Sorry."

"You must be one helluva defense attorney."

"Actually, I only took that appeal as a favor for a friend. I'm totally out of my element here. And I'm no longer involved with the Driscoll case. I just tagged along today to give the real defense attorney some moral support."

"I like that. You know your stuff. You're modest. And you're loyal to your friends."

"Hey, Russo. They're ready for us," a nearby man announced, motioning to the courtroom doors, which were being opened.

Justin's associate was a grim-faced man who appeared to be in his early forties, with dark hair and dark eyes. Not as good-looking as Justin by any stretch but still attractive, as was a third man hovering close by who also seemed to be part of the entourage and who had curly hair the same shade of dark blond as Suzannah's.

*You should come to the courthouse more often,* she teased herself. *These litigators are kind of sexy. Either that or you've been out of commission for way too long.*

"Gotta go," Justin murmured. "Maybe we can hook up later for some coffee? Assuming the Jailor doesn't lock me up, that is."

Suzannah hesitated, but this was supposed to be a fun, relaxing week, wasn't it? What harm could one cup of coffee do?

She pulled a business card out of her purse and handed it to him. "That's my office number. I'm on vacation this week, but I'll be checking voice mail regularly, so...yes, definitely call me if you survive Judge Taylor."

He flashed a killer smile, pocketed the card and said, "See ya." Then he trailed his companions into the courtroom.

Suzannah hung back for a moment, enjoying the unfamiliar sensation of being a little weak in the knees over a guy.

*This is going to be the best vacation ever,* she told herself with an embarrassed laugh. Then she remembered that this week wasn't completely about fun. She had to prepare for an upcoming conference in Hawaii, where she was slated to make a presentation—a presentation that was quite possibly the last step in the rigorous timetable she had set for herself and her career.

She called it her "Twelve-Year Plan," a blueprint she had designed at the age of eighteen to help her attain certain professional goals. Four years of college, three years of law school and enough time with a prestigious law firm to establish a reputation and develop a marketable specialty, which could then translate into a house-counsel job with a corporation. It was now year ten and she was way ahead of schedule.

Reminding herself that her rapid progress had been the result of working hard and *not* dating lawyers—especially not towers of sex like Justin Russo!—she decided it would be best if he didn't call her after all. There would be plenty of time in year twelve for romance—wasn't that the plan, after all?

Resolving to resist Justin if he should call, she pulled out her state-of-the-art PDA to check her calendar, messages and task list, which was a mile long. Forty separate entries for this "vacation." And so far she had only accomplished three—*Paint the bathroom, Clean the refrigerator,* and *Go with Tony to court on Monday.*

Tony...

She was worried about him, not just because they were friends but because if he failed to appear, Suzannah might have to take his place. And since the Driscoll case had only been remanded by the appellate court for resentencing, rather than for a new trial, the option of moving for automatic disqualification of Judge Taylor wasn't available, no matter how angry he was at Driscoll's attorney.

To her relief, Tony finally emerged from the restroom, his face pale but his shoulders squared, ready to do battle.

"Are you okay?"

"Yeah. Bring it on," he said with a wry smile.

*Ritual vomiting,* she realized in relief. *All the great trial lawyers do it before a big case. He's going to be just fine.*

"I'll just grab a seat in the back row, if you don't mind," she said, pulling out the oversize, tinted glasses she had brought with her in case Judge Taylor had caught a glimpse of her face on TV the day the news story about the appeal broke. "But I'll be up there with you in spirit."

"You're the best," Tony told her, giving her an unexpected hug. "Driscoll didn't deserve you, and neither do I."

Touched, she followed him into the courtroom, but when he proceeded to a row near the front, she hung back, settling into a seat right by the doors so that she could escape quickly if the judge began hurling expletives in her direction.

Then she sank low in her chair, fixed her glasses firmly in place and prepared to enjoy a little free entertainment, courtesy of the Jailor. It might not be as much fun as a hot date with Justin Russo, but it would be much, much safer.

Apparently Justin and his two associates were first on the docket, because they made their way directly to the defense table. To Suzannah's dismay, her hot date seated himself in the chair usually reserved for the defendant, while the other two men sat in the counsel chairs.

*This can't be right,* she told herself nervously. *What if he's a freaking ax-murderer? That's worse than a lawyer!*

The bailiff instructed everyone to rise, then announced that Judge Nathaniel Taylor would be presiding. Grateful for the distraction, Suzannah turned her attention to the massively built, wild-haired jurist who strode into the room, his black robes flapping. He seated himself without so much as a glance at the crowd that was watching him with a mixture of fear and anticipation, but she suspected that he was well aware of the effect he was having on them.

The man had made quite a name for himself in one short year on the bench. Passionate about his calendar of felony prosecutions, he reportedly brutalized any attorney who dared to appear before him unprepared or otherwise unprofessional. And according to some reports, he often berated them even if they had done absolutely nothing wrong. He had sent three lawyers to jail for contempt already—two assistant district attorneys and one defense attorney from a private firm. And he had sent countless others running to the restrooms with their stomachs tied in knots after a session with him.

Grateful that she was beyond his radar, Suzannah was still tempted to flee for her life, especially when the bailiff announced the first case for the morning: the People *versus* Justin Russo.

*Okay, Judge Taylor,* Suzannah insisted as she slunk down in her seat and tried to become invisible. *I'm counting on you. Do what you do best. Lock up this creep and throw away the freaking key before he ends up stalking me.*

After introductions were made, the defense attorneys and the prosecutor sat down, but Justin remained standing, shocking the courtroom by announcing in a loud voice, "I'd like to make a motion, Your Honor."

Suzannah watched with fascinated dread. Maybe he really *was* going to get himself thrown into a jail cell.

Judge Taylor scowled. "Don't you watch Court TV, Agent Russo? *You* don't make motions. Your attorneys do." Turning his blistering gaze to the lawyers, he instructed them, "Control your client. Or else."

"Your Honor?" Justin walked around the counsel table and approached the bench. "That's what my motion is about. I don't want these gentlemen as my attorneys. I didn't choose them and I'd like to fire them right away."

"Is that so?" The judge's voice dripped with sarcasm. "Let me guess. You think that means we're done here today? You just get to run around loose indefinitely while you find another lawyer? That's not quite how it works."

"I've already chosen another lawyer, sir," Justin told him. "And she's sitting right here, so we won't lose any time at all."

*Oh, God...*

Suzannah tried to believe that he couldn't possibly be talking about *her*, but just to be safe she began calculating how quickly she could run for her life. The door to the hall was just a few yards from her seat. If only she could count on her legs not to buckle....

"Her name is Suzannah Ryder, Your Honor."

She heard herself whisper, "No," like a child pleading with a nightmare in the dark. Then she shook herself, determined to keep some semblance of poise.

Judge Taylor stared at Justin in disbelief. Then he slowly turned his gaze toward the audience. "Are you saying the infamous Suzannah Ryder is here with us today? *E*xcellent. Join us, won't you, Ms. Ryder?"

A dozen or so people turned to stare at her, and she realized they recognized her from the unfortunate interview she'd given after news of her successful appeal had hit the airwaves. She hadn't said more than a few words—mostly *No comment* and *Judge Taylor is one of our finest judges*—but she imagined it had been memorable, if only because of her futile attempts to duck the cameras.

She knew she had to do something fast to salvage this situation, so she took a deep breath, pasted a confident, slightly bemused smile on her face and stood up. Thankfully her legs held her weight, so she walked slowly toward the bench, ignoring the piteous stares of the attorneys she passed, including Tony, who winced expressively.

Justin Russo, on the other hand, was ready with an encouraging smile, which actually helped Suzannah a little because it allowed anger to surpass embarrassment as her dominant emotion. This was all *his* fault. And she was going to find a way to pay him back just as soon as she got beyond the contempt zone.

"So," Judge Taylor said with a drawl. "The victorious appellate warrior in person. What an honor. I didn't think you'd be here today. Did you change your mind about handling Mr. Driscoll's resentencing?"

"No, Your Honor," she assured him, her voice hoarse but steady. "Tony Moreno is taking over. I'm just here as a spectator."

"According to Agent Russo, you're his new attorney."

She grimaced. "I assure you, Your Honor, that's a misunderstanding on Defendant Russo's part. I barely know him and I certainly never agreed to represent him. It would be malpractice for me to even try. I just don't have the experience."

"You had enough experience to get *me* reversed on appeal. Are you saying my ruling was so wrong *any* attorney could have gotten it reversed? Even an incompetent one?"

"No, Your Honor." She took a deep breath to calm her nerves. "What I meant was, I don't have much trial experience and absolutely no *criminal* trial experience. I have a corporate practice. Contracts, mostly. E-contracts, actually. It's all transactional, except for the occasional hearing, and even those are few and far between—"

"Fascinating," Judge Taylor interrupted with a growl, "but would you mind if *I* talked for just a moment?"

"Sorry, Your Honor." She forced herself to maintain eye contact with him despite the smoke visibly pouring out of his ears. "I'm just pointing out that I'm not a trial attorney. This situation with Agent Russo is all a big mistake."

"That is abundantly clear," the judge agreed. "Agent Russo? Could you enlighten the court on this bizarre motion of yours?"

Justin nodded. "I trust her, Your Honor. She's smart, she's got class and she's got guts. And quite frankly I don't trust the lawyers the Bureau supplied for me. They're nice guys, but I'm concerned they'll put the government's reputation and interests ahead of mine. I'm hoping Ms. Ryder can devote herself to my case without dividing her loyalties. Especially because she's on vacation this week—"

"Wait!" Suzannah sent him a death glare, then told the judge, "It's a working vacation. I've got a very important presentation to prepare for. On electronic signatures and Internet contracting. I'm attending a conference in Hawaii next week and I have to be fully prepared. I don't have time to do anything else. And I don't have the skills either! I've never handled a jury trial—"

"Counselor?"

"Yes, Your Honor?"

"Are you familiar with the concept of a gag order?"

The audience laughed at the play on words, knowing that a gag order involved statements about the case made *out*side the courtroom, not in it. Still, there was no misunderstanding Taylor's meaning.

He was saying that Suzannah was babbling. And it was true, but she couldn't seem to make it stop.

"That's pretty funny, Your Honor," she admitted. "I'll be quiet now. I promise."

"Thank you." He arched a stern eyebrow. "The last thing I want to do is interfere with your little junket to Hawaii, but some of us have real work to do. Did you happen to take a criminal-law course when you were in school?"

"Of course, Your Honor. But—"

He held up his hand to silence her, then continued. "Did you take criminal procedure?"

"Yes, Your Honor."

"Evidence?"

"Yes, Your Honor."

"And last but not least, did they teach you anything about your ethical obligations? To this court, for example? Are you aware that I have the power to appoint you to represent Agent Russo?"

She nodded, too miserable to argue. "May I ask what he's charged with, Your Honor?"

A hint of a twinkle invaded Taylor's green eyes. "That would be murder."

"Oh, God..."

"I didn't do it, Suzy," Justin assured her. "I swear I didn't."

"Suzy?" The judge's scowl had returned. "Just what is your relationship with the defendant, Ms. Ryder?"

"I don't *have* a relationship with him, Your Honor."

"Well, you do now." Taylor turned his attention to the two defense attorneys who had been hovering nearby, clearly too intimidated to speak. "I want you gentlemen to assist Ms. Ryder, since by her own admission she's borderline incompetent. But she's Russo's choice, and I'm going to respect that. At least for the moment. Agent Russo? Are you comfortable allowing these men to remain involved?"

Justin pursed his lips, then nodded. "As technical advisors, sure. But I want to be able to talk to Ms. Ryder in complete confidence. And I want her to make all the decisions about my representation."

"Agreed." Judge Taylor squared his shoulders. "Now, if you don't mind, I have other cases on my docket. Unless Ms. Ryder wants to regale us with more irrelevant tidbits about her vacation plans, I suggest we move on to the issue of bail."

"Your Honor?" The assistant district attorney, a petite brunette in a severe black suit, spoke for the first time, her tone guarded. "The People strongly feel that Agent Russo represents a flight risk."

"A flight risk?" Suzannah rolled her eyes. "Are you kidding? *Look* at him. He's too cocky to run."

"That's a novel defense," Taylor muttered. "Care to throw in any traditional arguments, just for fun?"

Suzannah shrugged. "Obviously, Your Honor, the fact that he's standing here right now shows that he intends to cooperate fully. I mean, he could have gotten away from these two clowns any time he wanted." She grimaced in quick apology toward the defense attorneys, then continued. "It's not like my client could get out of the country even if he wanted to. As an FBI agent, there has to be a file on him a mile thick. Prints, DNA, photos, and a list of all his relatives, friends—assuming he has any—and travel patterns."

The prosecutor was shaking her head. "The fact that he's a federal agent doesn't lessen his flight risk, Your Honor, it contributes to it. You've seen his file. Working undercover—in disguise—is one of his specialties! In fact, he has made a career out of seducing and conning people."

"He did all those things for his country," Suzannah reminded her. "And this is the thanks he gets? Just because of one little…well, misunderstanding?"

"A second-degree misunderstanding," the prosecutor retorted.

"Forgive the interruption, ladies, but could I get a word in here?" Judge Taylor fixed a stare in the prosecutor's direction. "I can understand Ms. Ryder's exuberance, because she's obviously still giddy over her appellate triumph." He paused as the audience laughed nervously, then he growled again. "From you, Ms. Armstrong, I expect better. In fact, I demand it. Is that clear?"

"Yes, Your Honor." The brunette slunk backward until she was flush against the counsel table.

"Agent Russo?"

"Yes, sir?"

"This is your lucky day. Thanks to Ms. Ryder's innovative arguments on your behalf, I've decided to place you in her custody."

"Thanks, Your Honor."

"Wait!" Suzannah shook her head frantically. "I never consented to that. *My* custody? I don't even know what that *means*. I mean, I know what it means generally, but in this context—"

"It means you're vouching for him," the judge explained. "And I don't need your consent. This is still my courtroom, is it not? Which means I'm in charge. And from now on you're going to listen, not talk, while I walk you through this, step by baby step. Is that clear?"

She nodded.

"I want you to spend some time with your client today. Listen to his story. Evaluate its strengths and weaknesses. Consult with his former counsel as appropriate. Then come back here—all of you, Ms. Armstrong included—tomorrow morning. I'd like an update at that time."

"And at that time, if it's clear I can't effectively represent Agent Russo—"

"My God, Ryder! Do you *want* me to hold you in

contempt?" The judge snorted. "I'm starting to believe your claim that you're incompetent."

"Your Honor?" Justin interrupted. "I'm going to have to insist that you treat my attorney with respect."

*Oh, God...* Suzannah stared down at her hands, silently warning him that he was only making things worse.

When Judge Taylor finally managed to respond, his voice was soft with anger. "In case you're not clear on the rules, Agent Russo, you're not supposed to talk unless I instruct you to. Ms. Ryder will do your talking for you from now on, and according to the Court of Appeal, she's a legal genius. So be quiet and let her work her magic. Unless you'd prefer to represent yourself, because that can definitely be arranged." His green eyes flashed. "What's it going to be?"

"My client understands now, Your Honor," Suzannah assured him, concerned that Justin was hopelessly prejudicing himself in Taylor's eyes by his misguided hero routine. Didn't the agent understand that this angry jurist was going to decide his fate on a *murder* charge? They didn't dare alienate him more than they had already done.

So she added with a respectful smile, "Thank you for your patience, Your Honor."

The judge exhaled slowly, eyeing each of them in turn. "We're all clear, then? We'll meet back here tomorrow for another round of fun and games? Fine. You're dismissed. Bailiff? Next case, and make it snappy. We're already running behind, thanks to Suzy the e-lawyer."

She clenched her fists at her sides, forcing herself to

give the judge one last humble smile before she turned and stalked past a wide-eyed Tony and down the aisle, bursting through the double doors to the hallway before the guard could open them for her. She knew she was being trailed by Justin and his former lawyers. She just hoped they had the good sense to keep their heads down and their mouths shut indefinitely.

But as soon as the doors had closed behind them Justin dared to address her. "Hey, Suzy! Wait up."

She spun around and stuck her finger in his face. "Not a word. Not—one—word. Is that clear?"

"Ms. Ryder?"

She sent Justin's former attorney her most frustrated glare. "That goes for you, too. *All* of you. Just be quiet and let me think."

"But—"

"Do you have a freaking *death* wish?" she demanded. But it was clear the government lawyers weren't going to back down, so she assured them soberly, "We've got a huge problem on our hands. That judge has it in for me, which means we can't possibly get a fair shake from him. But we don't dare piss him off any more either. At least not until I'm sure how to handle it. So give me a little time. And space. I'll get in touch as soon as I figure a few things out."

"We can help," the attorney insisted.

"Really? Because so far you've been a big fat zero." She pressed her fingers to her temples. "I've got to talk to my senior partner. Maybe he'll have some ideas. And at least my secretary can start drafting up a fee agreement, because believe me, Russo, you're gonna pay through the nose for this."

"No problem," Justin replied. "I'm just glad to have you on my team."

"Cut the crap. I'm not in the mood to be conned. *Or seduced.* Those are your two specialties, right?"

"I have more than two," he assured her with a playful smile.

She folded her arms across her chest to stop herself from reaching out and strangling him. Then she told the attorneys, "Give me a number where I can reach you later today. Will you be available?"

"Anytime, anyplace," the dark-haired one assured her, handing her his card. "Good luck."

"Yeah, good luck," the blond man echoed. "Here's my card, too. We'll be waiting."

When they had hurried away, Suzannah gave Justin a weary sigh. "Are you staying in a hotel?"

"Yeah, the Charlton. They've got a coffee bar in the lobby, if you want to meet there. Or if you want me to come to your office, that's fine, too. Whatever you say."

Suzannah hesitated, imagining the commotion if she showed up at her dignified law firm with a sexy, swaggering FBI agent when she was supposed to be on vacation. The women would be impressed. Her senior partner? Probably not so much. At least not without some well-executed preparation.

"The coffee bar sounds good. I'll meet you there. Take a few minutes to gather up whatever you need to brief me. And to change out of your suit if you want." She arched her eyebrow for emphasis. "If you're smart, you'll cooperate with me. If I'm lucky, you'll run, and I'll be off the hook."

"I'm not a flight risk. Not just because I'm cocky," he added with a wink, "but because I'm innocent."

Biting back an expletive, she told him between gritted teeth, "Just do what I say, okay?"

"I need to tell you something first. Something important."

"Fine. Make it quick."

His smile warmed. "I'm honestly grateful to you for taking this on. I know it's not how you wanted to spend your vacation, but I really need your help. Those two guys Justice found for me are probably fine lawyers, but they can't possibly be one hundred percent on my side. That's why I need you. So...thanks."

She closed her eyes and sighed in exaggerated martyrdom. "Fine. You're welcome. Whatever. Now let's just go to the hotel so you can *freaking* brief me."

"Sure, Suzy," he said fondly. "Whatever you say. You're the boss."

"This is S-3. Please identify yourself."

"Essie? It's me. Got a minute?"

Spinner Kristie Hennessy smiled with relief at the sound of Justin's voice. "I was hoping you'd call. How did things go in court today? Are you comfortable with the attorneys the government supplied? Director McGregor says they're the best."

"It went great, but not because of those stiffs. I hired a new lawyer this morning. That's why I called. I was hoping you could check her out for me."

"You hired her on the morning of your court appearance?"

"Yeah." He chuckled. "Luckily she's a quick study. Her name's Suzannah Ryder. Every bone in my body tells me she's clean, but if you could run a check—"

"I'm on it." Kristie's fingers flew across her keyboard.

"I drew a hard-ass for a judge," Justin was explaining, "so I figured I'd better call in reinforcements if I wanted to stay free pending trial. Suzy just won a big victory against this particular judge, so I figured she could come through for me. And she did."

"Suzy?" Kristie grimaced. "I'm guessing she's attractive?"

"Are you jealous?" he said, his tone teasing. Then he added more seriously, "It's her attitude that sold me, Essie. She effing *radiates* confidence, but with enough vulnerability to keep things interesting."

A recent photo of Suzannah Ryder flashed across Kristie's computer screen. Honey-blond curls, huge blue eyes and cheekbones so striking that Kristie made a note to incorporate them into one of the composite pictures she sometimes built for SPIN ops.

"She's darling."

"Yeah," Justin confirmed. "But I hired her for her guts. My question to you is, is she as good as I think she is?"

"Her reputation's spotless, at least on the surface." Kristie scanned Suzannah's credentials, noting that she had graduated at the top of her undergraduate class at Notre Dame, then came out comfortably in the middle of her law-school class at Princeton before landing a job at a well-respected civil law firm. Again Kristie made a note to use Suzannah's profile in a fake ID some day soon. She had just the right blend of excellence and normality, almost as if she had engineered it that way.

"She doesn't practice criminal law, Justin."

"Yeah, I know. The win against Taylor was an exception. Something she handled for a friend."

"That makes sense." The spinner continued to search her favorite agency and Internet sources. "I'll keep digging."

"Okay. I'll call again tonight."

"Actually—" The spinner hesitated before suggesting, "If I find something, I'll let you know. Otherwise, just assume she's clean, okay?"

There was a long silence, then Justin asked her, "What's wrong?"

"Nothing. I'm on probation again. It's seems like I always am, doesn't it? But this time McGregor means it. In more ways than one," she added with a self-conscious laugh.

"Unbelievable," Justin muttered. "They should be kissing your feet, not trying to control you. Don't they know how great you are?"

"To be fair, they've given me a lot of slack."

"They don't deserve you," Justin retorted with unexpected vehemence. "Maybe we both should just chuck it all and run away together."

"Huh?" Kristie's stomach knotted. "Are you that worried about the verdict?"

"Nah. I'm innocent, so it'll come out fine. But meanwhile..." His tone grew pensive. "The thrill has gone out of this gig for me, Essie. I never thought I'd say that, and it's probably temporary. So just forget I said anything."

The spinner bit her lip. Until now, Justin Russo had loved his work more than anyone she knew. He thrived on the danger, the heroic opportunities, the romantic possibilities....

"Obviously I screwed up this time," he was admitting. "But *you* haven't done anything wrong. The fact that they don't appreciate you—"

"They appreciate me. They just want me to start following protocol. And I've decided they're right. And," she added, trying for a lighter tone, "I'm not just saying that because I know the monitors might be listening to this call."

Justin's chuckle sounded forced. "Don't get in trouble on my account. I'm doing fine here. Just forget I called. I won't bother you with this anymore."

"I'll keep looking at Suzannah Ryder's background," she assured him. "If I find something negative, I'll call. And if you need anything—anything at all—*please* let me know."

"Sure, Essie. But for now I'd better get going. I don't want to keep my new lawyer waiting."

"Right. Okay, good luck."

She winced when he said, "'Bye" and hung up without giving her a chance to say anything further. She was actually tempted to call him back and make him promise to contact her at least daily.

Then a video popped up on her monitor, distracting her completely. It was a recent film of Suzannah Ryder handling—or rather, attempting to politely terminate—

a news conference on her recent appellate court success. Even with the graininess of the footage, the attorney's smile was amazing, just as Justin had described—confident yet vulnerable.

"The Court of Appeal's opinion is pretty blunt in its criticism of Judge Taylor," a male reporter was observing. "Do you think there should be an investigation of his heavy-handed tactics? Maybe even a recall?"

"Judge Taylor is one of our finest jurists," Suzannah assured him. "I don't think there's a member of our legal community that doesn't respect and admire him. The appellate court's comments are specific to this particular trial and shouldn't be taken as a general criticism. Or even as a criticism at all. These things are complicated," she added with another, warmer smile. "It's the reason I don't generally practice criminal law. I leave that to the real pros, like Defendant Driscoll's new attorney, Tony Moreno."

A barrage of questions erupted, but Suzannah held up her hand and insisted, "That's all, folks. Have a good afternoon." Then she dismissed them with a friendly wave, and while a few reporters made halfhearted attempts to ask follow-up questions, most of them cooperated.

Kristie nodded, pleased with what she saw. This Ryder woman had poise as well as brains. In fact, she was the consummate professional in her perfectly tailored suit and medium heeled shoes, not to mention the casual, easy-care style in which she wore her chin-length curls. If the rest of her background check came out as well as this, Justin had definitely picked himself a winner.

Assuming, of course, that he was able to keep his hands off her.

And assuming, further, that he was innocent...

Kristie tried not to think about *that,* but it was too late. The knot—a cruel blend of spinner instinct and bitter experience—had returned to her stomach.

## Chapter 2

They took separate cars to the Hotel Charlton, giving Suzannah a chance to adjust to what had happened. It was obvious that Judge Taylor saw this as an opportunity to punish her for getting his ruling reversed on appeal. If she made any further attempts to resist, he might even hold her in contempt. She had to be very careful, not just for her own sake but for Justin's.

She knew why the FBI agent had chosen her. He thought she was a great criminal-law attorney because of her success in the Driscoll case. Poor guy—not only was he wrong about that but he simply didn't understand how much Taylor hated her or how much all that resentment would work against him now, too.

Like it or not, their best strategy for the short run was to cooperate completely with the judge. Hopefully

Suzannah's role in the case wouldn't be too taxing. She really had only two responsibilities: the first, to make sure the defendant didn't skip town, which made her a glorified babysitter; and the second, to make sure the government defense attorneys didn't sell Justin down the river to protect the FBI's reputation.

She could do both of those things while also working on her Hawaii presentation. The government lawyers could handle the big defense issues, do the footwork and keep her informed so that she could make the final strategy decisions.

It didn't sound so bad, assuming Justin cooperated. And assuming he was innocent. Not that it really mattered, because if he wasn't, she was going to strangle him. So either way justice would be done.

Once she reached the hotel, she found a seat in the coffee bar adjacent to the lobby, rejecting any thought of going to his room to check on his progress. There was a slight risk that her new client might ditch her and dash for the border, but in the long run, that would be a *good* thing, wouldn't it? In any case, she wasn't ready to be alone with a suspected murderer who had a reputation as a charmer. Better to stick to public places for the moment.

Keeping one eye on the elevator, she ordered a mocha, then checked her office voice mail to see if any messages had come in. Then she sent some brief e-mails to her colleagues, just in case they heard rumors about what had happened with the Jailor. And finally she attacked the job of reorganizing her obsolete calendar and task list.

*Forty things to do in two short weeks, all of them trumped by a murder case. Ugh!*

Justin finally appeared, ambling toward her in tan slacks and a sexy black polo shirt. And she had to sigh, right out loud. He had looked so good just two short two hours ago, with his shaggy hair, sexy smile, golden tan and great body. Now he just looked like a pain in the ass.

"That was fast," she told him, tucking her PDA into her purse.

His tone was warm as he settled into the seat across from her. "I know you're mad, but—"

She held up her hand to stop him. "I've adjusted, actually. Let's just get started, shall we?"

"Great." He motioned to a nearby waitress, who almost tripped over two other customers getting to him right away, then breathlessly introduced herself as Janet.

Gracing her with one of his sexiest smiles, he ordered a latte with an extra shot, plus a refill for Suzannah.

"Should we get something to eat, too?" he asked his new attorney. "It's almost lunchtime."

She hesitated but then remembered her policy of making him pay through the nose for ruining her vacation, so she nodded. "The quiche looks good. And a small salad?"

Justin nodded, then told the waitress, "I'll have grilled cheese if you've got it."

"It's not on the menu, but I'm sure I can talk the cook into it."

"That would be great, Janet. Thanks."

Suzannah watched the woman hurry off on her mission. "I guess you get a lot of that?"

"Pardon?"

"Females falling all over themselves to do your bidding?"

"She's just trying to do a good job. Anyway..." He exhaled sharply. "I know I screwed up your morning, to put it mildly. And I realize criminal law isn't your specialty, even though you kicked some serious judicial ass on that appeal. So I just want you to know you're off the hook as of now."

"Pardon?"

"You earned your fee by getting me released on bail. That was my big concern this morning. Now I can take it from here. After tomorrow's court appearance, you can just do whatever you were already planning to do this week."

When Suzannah glared, he laughed and said, "I know, I know. The judge wants me to brief you, and I will. But take my word for it—this thing will never go to trial. I'll conclude my investigation and find the real perp long before that happens. I promise you that."

"Oh, you *promise*? Well, *that's* a relief." She glared again. "I'm the attorney of record in a murder case. I take that very seriously. I take *everything* very seriously—a fact you'd better start respecting. I've spent ten years building a sterling reputation and I don't want this case to torpedo it."

"I told you, it'll never go to trial."

"Because you'll solve it first? No offense, but I'd rather not count on you. Especially considering you're an accused murderer."

He leaned back in his chair and studied her for a

moment, then nodded. "Fair enough. So how do you want to approach this? I can give you details or just the big picture."

"Let's start with the punch line. Who is it you're supposed to have killed?"

"A woman named Gia Masterson. She was a witness in a case I've been investigating."

"Gia Masterson?" Suzannah bit her lip. "In that case, I already have the big picture. From reading the newspapers. Not that I've kept up with it faithfully, but she was shot a couple of weeks ago, right? And a few weeks before that, she inherited a huge fortune from her father when he was murdered by the Angel of Mercy serial killer."

When Justin nodded, Suzannah rubbed her eyes, acutely aware of the ache forming behind them.

The Angel of Mercy, as the papers had dubbed him, had been in the headlines for a couple of months. He apparently thought he was receiving psychic signals from vegetative patients who were begging him to free them so that they could go to heaven. Unable to resist, he had finally begun infiltrating nursing homes, using his position and training as a licensed vocational nurse to put the patients out of their misery once and for all.

Rallying herself, Suzannah asked carefully, "Any chance the Angel of Mercy killed Gia, as well? I mean, I know he usually goes after people in comas, but..."

Justin shook his head. "I'm not even sure the Angel of Mercy killed the father, much less the daughter."

"Ooh, that's new. The papers made it sound like a slam dunk."

He nodded. "We tried to keep it quiet while we investigated. Horace Masterson was the fourth in a series of patients supposedly killed by the Angel—by lethal injection—in nursing homes. But given Masterson's enormous wealth and the fact that his company handles top-secret government research, the possibility of a copycat killing with financial or political motives couldn't be discounted."

"Hmm... And since Gia inherited her father's money, she was a suspect in his murder, even though the Angel of Mercy was the prime suspect?"

Justin hesitated. "Putting aside the whole mercy-killing angle, the Masterson case is pretty complicated. For one thing, Gia could have pulled the plug on her father any time she wanted. He's been brain-dead and completely dependent on life support for more than three years because of a massive stroke and a slew of complications. Gia had a durable power of attorney over his health decisions. But she worshipped her father, almost to a perverse degree. She swore she'd never—*ever*—order life support removed, even though doctors said there was no hope of his regaining the slightest awareness. And since Gia had full authority to handle Masterson's financial affairs, she was able to pay for endless excellent care."

Suzannah frowned. "So that's why you called her a witness, not a suspect, in her father's murder investigation?"

"It's complicated," he repeated. "But yeah, I don't think Gia killed her father. On the other hand, I don't think the Angel of Mercy did it, either. My instincts are generally pretty good in these cases. That's why the

Bureau sent me in the first place. And right from the start I was sure a huge chunk of the puzzle was missing. Unfortunately I went off in the wrong direction."

"How so?"

He hesitated, then explained. "Like I said, Masterson Enterprises handles top-secret government projects. At the time of Horace's murder, his company was being considered as the contractor for a project known as Night Arrow. Night Arrow," he added reverently, "is an amazing phenomenon. I'll fill you in on the nonclassified details later, but take my word for it. It's probably the biggest find—scientific or otherwise—of our lifetime."

Taking a deep breath, he visibly checked his enthusiasm. "The point is, I focused on Night Arrow as the motive. I figured someone wanted to get their hands on the research—even take over Masterson Enterprises to do so—and the first stage was killing the old man."

"But now?"

"Now I'm not so sure," he admitted. "If Night Arrow was the motive, killing Gia was counterproductive. Because Masterson Enterprises lost any chance of getting the contract when Gia was murdered. Scandal and government research don't go together. So," he finished with a shrug, "I've put Night Arrow on the back burner for now."

Suzannah wasn't fooled. She had caught the gleam in his eye when he'd first mentioned the project, and it was a look guys usually reserved for sex and sports. There was no way he had truly abandoned his theory, but for the moment she would play along.

So she asked him, "Are you sure the same person who killed the dad killed Gia?"

"I'd bet my ass on it."

"Okay..." She pursed her lips. "Gia was Horace Masterson's sole heir. But Gia must have an heir, as well, right? So *that* person would have a motive to kill them both, right? First kill Horace so Gia would inherit his fortune. Then murder Gia and get everything—the whole Masterson estate—for himself or herself." She gave him a hopeful smile. "So? You're not Gia's heir, are you?"

He laughed. "Hardly. She recently changed her will, but not to give it to me. Her sister, Mia, is her sole heir."

"Mia and Gia?" Suzannah winced. "Cute. If they're sisters, how come Mia didn't get half of Masterson's estate in the first place?"

"Horace Masterson disowned Mia about eight years ago. Kicked her out of the house, out of his life and out of the will—all for having an affair with the son of his archenemy."

"He had an archenemy?"

"Cool, huh?" Justin grinned. "William Seldon and Horace Masterson were partners. Then William had an affair with Horace's wife, Julia. Needless to say, the partnership ended. William is long since dead. So is Julia, for that matter."

"But Mia had an affair with William's son?"

"Correct. William's son, Derek."

"And then Horace disowned Mia."

"Right. And since big sister Gia was such a slave to her father's affection, *she* turned her back on Mia, as well. So Mia went to live with a cousin named Cynthia on the East Coast. Even after Horace Masterson had his stroke, Gia didn't thaw out about her estranged sister. But then…" He gave an apologetic wince. "Can you handle more or are you overloaded?"

"You're kidding, right? What finally made Gia thaw out?"

He chuckled. "Like I said, Mia had been living with their cousin. Apparently this Cynthia was something of a bridge between the sisters—she had visited them often as a child, and they both loved her. When Mia went to live with Cynthia, Gia turned her back on both of them. After Horace's stroke, Mia wanted to come home to visit her dad at the nursing home. When Gia said no, Cynthia decided to intercede. She drove across the country and appeared on Gia's doorstep to plead for a reconciliation between the two sisters. Gia sent Cynthia away. But Cynthia—who was exhausted and in tears—never made it home. She crashed her car into a power pole."

"Oh, no."

Justin nodded. "That's when Gia came to her senses. She told me she finally realized how isolated she had allowed herself to become, physically and emotionally. So she contacted Mia and they reconciled as sisters. Mia moved back home and started visiting the old man—and since he was in a coma, he didn't object, obviously. The sisters became genuinely close again. Closer even than regular sisters in some ways. I can't imagine Mia killing Gia. But someone did it, and it sure wasn't me."

"So besides you, the Angel of Mercy, and Mia, are there any other suspects? In Gia's murder, I mean."

"Well, like I said, it's always possible—although less

likely now—that some outsider wanted to gain control of the company for political or economic reasons. But, ironically, the series of scandals hitting that family has probably ruined the company's reputation, at least temporarily. So if someone killed Gia for wealth or secrets, they grossly miscalculated."

"Okay." Suzannah held up her hand, palm forward. "I can't absorb much more for the moment. But there's one last thing I need to know up front. Why would anyone suspect *you* of murdering Gia?"

He gave her a pained smile. "Promise not to get upset?"

"Oh, God, let me guess. You *slept* with her? A *suspect?*"

"A witness," he reminded her with another, weaker smile. "Anyway, no one really thinks I had a motive to kill her. She was found alone in her bedroom, shot by a gun with my prints on it, about an hour after I had dinner with her. The circumstances indicated that there was a struggle, so the consensus was that I must have shot her in self-defense." His blue eyes clouded. "They offered me a deal right away. If I would admit that she tried to shoot me and that I just acted to protect myself, there wouldn't be any charges. I'd keep my job after a perfunctory investigation. That's what everyone wanted, because my career's been solid up till now. No one wanted to see it end over this."

Suzannah gave him a sympathetic smile. "But you didn't shoot her, so you didn't take the deal."

"Right. Someone shot her, and I'd be damned if I was going to let them get away with it. Or have that kind of crazy shit on my record. Unfortunately the evidence against me is fairly strong."

"Like the fingerprints on the gun?" she murmured.

"I helped her load it before I left that night. She was getting nervous—about the Angel of Mercy coming after her next. Poor kid."

"That makes sense. About the fingerprints, I mean, not the Angel."

"Right. But it ticked the D.A. off big-time when I wouldn't take his deal. So he slapped a murder charge on me. I think they all thought that *that* would make me cave and admit it was self-defense for sure. But I didn't shoot her. End of discussion."

"And those two guys the Bureau got to defend you?"

"They wanted me to take the deal, too. To save everyone the embarrassment."

She bit her lip, acknowledging to herself that Justin had done the right thing firing those guys. But hiring her was still wrong, wrong, wrong....

"You believe me, don't you, Suzy?"

She rolled her eyes. "Yes, I believe you."

"Good." He gave her a confident grin. "You've already been such an incredible help, making sure they didn't lock me up pending trial. I knew the D.A. was going to make Armstrong go for the jugular on that. But you handled it like a pro. Now I can solve Gia's murder, see? Not just to clear my own name but to get that last piece of the puzzle I need to solve the father's murder, as well."

Suzannah shook her head in protest. "I'm guessing you're on some sort of administrative suspension, aren't you? I don't think they want you running around trying to solve *either* case. You need to stay out of trouble, especially because you're in *my* freaking custody. I'll handle any investigating from here on out."

"Just like I told the judge—you've got guts." He reached across the table and grabbed her hand. "We'll solve it together, then."

"Are you nuts?" she demanded, pulling free, then glaring. "I don't need to *solve* anything, and neither do you. The burden of proof is on them, and they don't have a strong enough case to convict a respected federal agent. Fingerprints? A couple of hot dates? None of that adds up to motive, and jurors need a motive, not just evidence. Besides—" she settled down enough to give him a sheepish smile "—all I really have to do is load that jury with females and you're as good as acquitted."

To her surprise, the compliment seemed to rankle Justin. "I'd like to think it's my professional accomplishments—not my sex appeal—that will give me credibility."

"You're charged with murder. We'll use anything we've got. That's my first strategy decision as your incompetent e-lawyer."

He laughed. "Fair enough. Looks like we both have something to prove." Pulling out his wallet, he dropped a handful of bills on the table. "So where do we go from here? Your law office?"

She studied him carefully, impressed by his enthusiasm, openness and clear desire to get to the truth. He was innocent—she'd stake the Twelve-Year Plan on that. And he needed more than a quick consultation under the dubious eyes of her senior partner.

He needed a lawyer.

"We'll go to my apartment. I'll wait while you get

what you need from your room, then you can follow me in your car."

His blue eyes widened. "You want me to move into your place?"

"I'm not *that* convinced you're innocent," she said, shaking her head in amusement. "Just bring what you need for the rest of the day. We can work at my kitchen table. It's not as ritzy as this place, but it's comfortable."

"I'll bet it is. And this hotel isn't so great, believe me. The only thing it has going for it is a state-of-the-art fitness center."

"You'll be able to get a good workout in my bedroom," she assured him, then she grimaced when he arched a playful eyebrow. "There's a treadmill in there and some free weights, smart-ass."

"Nice to know you're getting some action at least," he said teasingly. Then his smile softened. "Thanks for the vote of confidence, Suzannah. I promise you won't regret it."

He followed her to her redbrick apartment house, parking in one of the visitor spots behind the four-story building, then catching up with her at the elevator. In some ways, it felt more like a date than a business meeting, which made a certain kind of illogical sense to Suzannah. Justin was sexy and charming and single, and while she rarely brought men home with her for any reason, she definitely never brought clients or associates to her apartment.

The reason was simple: this place was her sanctuary.

Her refuge. An integral part of the Twelve-Year Plan. Knowing from the start that her decision to focus on her career might get out of hand, she had done virtually all of her law work downtown, even though it meant late nights and weekends at the office, returning home only when she was exhausted and depleted. Home was reserved for relaxation—watching movies and reading.

Fortunately her firm's building had a guard in the reception area for anyone working late, and the office parking lot was well lit, courtesy of the all-night market adjacent to it. So all in all, the system had worked well for her.

Until today.

Opening the front door, she entered the apartment ahead of him and smiled proudly, reminded of the other reason she loved coming home to this tiny place. It was simply beautiful, with its gleaming hardwood floors, built-in shelves and cabinets and magnificent bay window in the eating area.

She had kept the living room furniture simple—two overstuffed chairs facing a matching sofa in front of a small brick fireplace, a brass trunk that served as a coffee table and additional storage and a pair of stained-glass floor lamps. Everything else, from the TV to the small desk accommodating her laptop and household files, was hidden behind cabinet doors.

"Nice place," Justin murmured. "Sorta like a hideaway."

She bit her lip, pleased by the description. "You can set up camp in the kitchen. I don't have an office here, unfortunately." Remembering the jigsaw puzzle scattered across the tabletop, she added quickly, "I'll just clear my stuff away first."

"I can work around it. Plus, when I want to take a break, I'll do some of the easy pieces." Still scanning the environment, he set his briefcase and duffel bag on a kitchen chair. "You've got yourself a busy schedule for a girl who's supposed to be on vacation."

"Pardon?"

He pointed to the large wipe-off board next to her refrigerator, where she had scribbled the date followed by a list of chores and appointments:

Court with Tony
Research, two hours
Confirm HA reservations
Reread P&P
Bubble bath
RS marathon
Call M&D

She knew her cheeks were flushed as she grabbed an eraser and got rid of the evidence. "Thanks to you, this list is irrelevant now."

"M and D? Mom and Dad, right?" When she nodded, he smiled. "P and P?"

*"Pride and Prejudice."*

"Are you running a marathon this week?"

Suzannah wasn't about to admit that she had planned on watching at least a dozen episodes of *Remington Steele.* "RS is a guy I know. I wanted to remember that he was involved in a marathon."

"And you actually schedule your bubble baths ahead of time? That's kind of sad." Justin's finger tapped a piece of paper attached to her refrigerator by a magnet. "What's this? More chores?"

"Not that it's any of your business, but that's my shopping list."

"Looks more like an anti-shopping list." He began to read aloud. "'*No* cookies, *No* candy, *No* ice cream.'"

"Never mind." She snatched the page, crumpled it and threw it into the trash. "I'm going to change out of this suit. Make yourself comfortable, but no snooping. I mean it," she added over her shoulder as she strode into her bedroom.

"I'll just work the puzzle," he promised.

She closed the door behind herself, then leaned against it and sighed. He was a little too observant and *way* too intuitive. What was it the prosecutor had said? That he had "made a career out of seducing and conning people"?

She definitely needed to stay on her toes. And she didn't dare leave him alone for too long, so she quickly peeled off her clothes and wriggled into a pair of soft, faded jeans. Then she added a hooded sweatshirt of soft pink cashmere, zipping it halfway to partially obscure a white lace camisole.

Her pink fluffy slippers seemed a little much, so she put on pale blue socks instead. After checking her hair and makeup, she opened the bedroom door and stepped back into the living room, then froze as the sound of her best friend's recorded voice greeted her.

"...and she says the killer's *gorgeous*, but the little creep didn't give me any other details. So call me! I'm supposed to be your best friend, but you'd never know it from the way *you* act. Sheesh!"

Sprinting for the answering machine, Suzannah punched the stop button, then turned to glare at her houseguest. "What's your problem?"

"She sounds like fun. What's her name?"

"Never mind." Suzannah grimaced. "Was that the only message?"

"She left two. The first one was about the Sperminator. You'll never guess what he did."

Suzannah stared into his laughing eyes, muttered, "You must have a death wish," then rewound the recorder and pushed Play.

The machine announced, "Message number one," then Noelle West's voice began again: "Hey, it's me. You'll never guess what the Sperminator did last night, so I'll just tell you. He proposed again. For real this time. He said, and I quote, 'I know we were only getting married because we thought you were knocked up, but I got kind of used to the idea.' Romantic, huh? So where the hell are you? *We need to talk.*"

There was an emphatic click, then the machine announced, "Message number two."

It was Noelle again, saying, "Hey, what's going on? Why aren't you answering your cell? I'm *dying* over here. First the Sperminator, now this hot new rumor about *you*. My cousin was in the courtroom and she said the hanging judge almost locked you up. But instead he *hooked* you up. With some killer. And she says the killer's *gorgeous*, but the little creep didn't give me any other details. So—"

Suzannah stopped the tape again, shaking her head in amused disbelief. The Sperminator had actually re-proposed? That was big, *big* news. It was a little embarrassing that Justin had heard about it and downright mortifying that he had heard himself described as a gorgeous killer, but it could have been worse.

"If you're going to be spending time here, you need to respect my privacy."

"The light was flashing," he explained. "So? What's your buddy's name?"

"Noelle. And obviously I need to call her right away. Excuse me, please? Just for a few minutes?"

"Sure. She sounds great. Best friends? For how long?"

Suzannah hesitated but could see he wasn't going to let it go. "Her family lived next door to my grandmother. Every time my parents got divorced, I went there to live for a while. So we've been friends, off and on, forever."

She liked the fact that he was speechless, at least for the moment. Not that she blamed him. She didn't usually share her parents' bizarre marriage history with strangers, but she had a feeling Justin would run a background check on her anyway, so he'd eventually find out about the divorces.

"How many times—"

"Twice. Which means I got to attend two of their three weddings." She smiled in wry amusement. "If my mother were here, she'd tell you it's romantic. That's how nuts my parents are."

"But they're set now?"

"God, I hope so." She rolled her eyes in mock

frustration. "Anyway, living with Grandma next to Noelle's family was crucial to my sanity, so in a way, it's a good thing they were so…so whatever. They're fun," she added quickly. "And lovable. But they got married when they were just crazy kids and they've somehow managed to keep that childlike quality right into their fifties. Anyway…" She backed toward her bedroom. "I've got to get the details on this Sperminator development. And *you* need to work on clearing yourself of murder charges. So why don't we both get busy?"

True to form, Noelle had Suzannah laughing within seconds as she recounted the Sperminator's beer-induced but still amazing proposal. More stunning still was the fact that Noelle seemed to be considering it!

"We'll have to start calling him Steve, you know," Suzannah told her friend. "Just in case you guys go through with it."

"Speaking of men, I need details. About the murderer."

"I told you, he's innocent. An FBI agent with a spotless record. He was framed, and hopefully I can help *un*frame him without getting myself charged with contempt in the process. Wish me luck. I'd better get back in there before he starts rummaging through my files."

"Is he as good-looking as my cousin said?"

"Yep. Picture a blend of Highlander and a young Obi Wan."

"Which Highlander?" Noelle asked, her tone challenging. "Yours or mine?"

"There can be only one," Suzannah reminded her

with a laugh, wondering for the umpteenth time how Noelle could prefer Christopher Lambert's Highlander to Adrian Paul's. "Anyway, I'd better get back to him. I'll call you when he leaves."

"Are you sure he'll be leaving? He sounds pretty sexy. Maybe he'll sleep over."

"He's a client. And a murder suspect. Plus, he's not my type."

"Give me a break," Noelle drawled. "You said yourself he's a cross between your two favorite heroes. Does he have an accent?"

"Well, not Scottish, that's for sure. If anything, he's got the tiniest hint of a cowboy twang." She expected Noelle to react strongly, but she said nothing, so Suzannah prodded her. "Noelle?"

"Sorry, I just drooled all over myself."

"You're such a nut." Suzannah grinned and repeated, "I'll call you when he leaves. Don't elope or anything before then. 'Bye."

She hung up the phone, then braced herself for another round with Justin. She was getting used to the idea of being his attorney, but having her privacy invaded was something else.

*He cons and seduces people for a living. So be careful....*

Taking a deep breath, she returned to the living room and found him dutifully working the jigsaw puzzle, just as he'd promised.

He had draped his leather bomber jacket over one kitchen chair and had slung his shoulder holster over another. Just those few subtle touches, along with his not-so-subtle sexuality, had given her home a strong infusion of masculinity that she found disorienting.

*So this is what it's like to have a man around the house,* she teased herself nervously. *Next he'll be opening jars for you and taking out the trash.*

Shaking off the confused mood, she walked over and sat at the table. "I've got more questions about the case."

"Shoot."

"Speaking of shooting…" She eyed the shoulder holster, which was empty. "They confiscated your gun and your badge, right? I mean, temporarily. So…?"

"Force of habit. I can put it away if it bothers you."

"It's fine." She arched an eyebrow. "Don't you guys usually have backup weapons? Something with the serial numbers sanded off or whatever?"

"Are you sure you want me to answer that?"

"Good point. Never mind."

"What about you?" he asked. "A pretty girl, living alone. How do you protect yourself?"

"I use the dead bolt whenever I'm home. And I have a can of mace in my purse whenever I'm out."

"You should keep the mace by your bed at night, too."

She hesitated, then nodded. "Good advice. Thanks."

Her attention was attracted by a group of yellow self-adhesive notes he had attached in a row to the nearby wall. It appeared to be some sort of timeline.

His gaze tracked hers. "That's my system. Must look pretty lame to an organizational genius like you, but it works for me."

"Those look like Angel of Mercy notes. Shouldn't we be concentrating on Gia's murder?"

"They're interrelated."

"So you admit it's possible that the Angel of Mercy killed Gia?"

Justin shrugged. "Anything's possible. But it's more likely that Horace Masterson's murderer tried to capitalize on Charlie Parrish's crime spree by committing a look-alike murder and hoping Charlie would take the rap."

"Or—" Suzannah met his gaze directly "—Charlie killed them all. The three nursing-home residents out of a sincere but deranged belief that they wanted him to kill them. Then Horace. And then Gia because she publicly announced she'd never honor her father's wish to have the plug pulled. Maybe Charlie found her attitude so arrogant and repugnant he wanted to punish her for it."

"Gia said the same thing to me," he mused. "The night she died."

*"What?"*

Justin nodded. "She was nervous that night. More than usual. She kept saying she thought the Angel would come after her next because of the videotaped statement by her that was shown on the news after Horace was diagnosed. She said that was the kind of thing a truly insane man would never be able to forget."

"Wow. What did you say?"

He shrugged. "I comforted her. Told her that wasn't Charlie's MO. He uses drugs, not guns. And he truly believes he's helping the victims, not hurting them. He's the Angel of Mercy, not Vengeance."

"You talk about him like he's rational. But I agree with Gia. He's a nut. And probably getting crazier by the minute. All that killing—it might have made him feel powerful. Validated. Almost godlike."

Justin grinned. "Very cool analysis. You remind me of a friend of mine." He began digging in his briefcase and pulled out a manila envelope. "I meant to give this to you earlier. Don't open it. Just put it somewhere safe."

"It's not a confession, is it?"

He laughed. "No such luck. It's my friend's phone number. If something goes wrong—if I get killed, for instance—"

"Killed?" Suzannah bit her lip. "You think the murderer might come after you?"

"I'm a loose end. Plus, I'm determined to solve Horace Masterson's murder. And now Gia's, too. The real killer would be smart to get rid of me."

"Oh, God, I never thought of that."

Justin flashed a reassuring smile. "The good news is, he's also got a strong incentive to keep me alive. If he kills me, then everyone will know I was innocent. Right now the evidence against me is so strong the authorities aren't looking anywhere else."

"But *you're* looking."

*And so am I....*

He must have heard her thought, because he patted her hand and assured her, "The bad guys don't have any reason to come after you. As far as they know, you're handling the legal angle, not the investigation. And it was clear in the courtroom today that you were a reluctant participant. So I'm pretty sure you're safe."

She held up the envelope. "But if something happens...?"

"Right. If something goes wrong, call that number. It'll connect you to SPIN. Have you heard of it?" When Suzannah shook her head, he explained. "It's a backup agency for agents like me. The Strategic Profiling and Identification Network. They call themselves spinners and they're effing geniuses. Literally."

"Wait! Are you sure it's okay to tell me all this?"

He laughed. "Yeah, it's okay. The only confidential info is the actual identity of the spinners. Their whole system is based on anonymity. They use aliases, and our only contact with them is by phone."

"So you have a friend, but you don't know his name?"

"*Her* name."

"Oh, right." Suzannah rolled her eyes. "I should have guessed."

"Her code name is S-3. I nicknamed her Essie." He hesitated, then admitted, "I've known her real name for a while now, but I never use it. Anyway, she can get you any information you need. Plus, her instincts are stellar. Downright eerie, really. No matter how bad things get, she can always figure out a solution. So..." He squeezed Suzannah's hand. "If something goes wrong—if I get killed or you get scared or start to doubt my innocence, anything like that—call S-3. Got it?"

"I've got a better idea," she told him, pulling her hand free. "Let's call her right now."

"Huh?"

"She's your friend. And she's brilliant. We'll brainstorm with her. Three heads are better than two, right?"

His eyes clouded. "It's not that simple, Suzy. She's not

assigned to this case, so she's not supposed to work on it. I've gotten her into trouble a couple of times over the last few years. I've promised myself I won't do that anymore."

"Too bad. We could use the help."

"She's got a tendency to go rogue, especially when her friends are in trouble." He cleared his throat, then admitted, "I rely on her too much sometimes. It's not fair to her. So I've gone cold turkey. I won't call her. But if things go really wrong, I want you to."

Suzannah studied his forlorn expression. "Are you in love with her? Even though you never met her in person? That's so romantic."

"I love her like crazy, but I'm not *in* love with her," Justin said, chuckling. "I like my girlfriends to have bodies."

"Like Gia?"

"Gia had one helluva body," he agreed, fishing in his briefcase again until he found a folder containing a dozen or so photographs. "Here, see for yourself. The best rack money could buy."

"Good grief." Suzannah bit back a smile, wondering how such a tall, skinny woman had managed to carry herself upright with the giant breasts she had apparently bought for herself. "You said she was sweet. I'd say she was a little vain, too."

"You'd think so," he murmured. "But you'd be wrong. The boob job wasn't because she wanted to look better. She just wanted to look different."

"Pardon?"

"Look at this. It's Gia nine years ago. Before she started having plastic surgery."

Suzannah stared at the second photo, shocked to see a girl who only vaguely resembled the busty woman in the first picture. "She didn't just have her breasts enhanced. She had—what? Her eyes? Her cheeks?"

"Eyes. Cheeks. Jaw. Bust. Six surgeries over a seven-year period."

"She changed her hair color, too."

"And wore blue contact lenses so her eyes wouldn't look gray."

"I don't get it." Suzannah shook her head. "She was so pretty."

"So was her mother. So was her sister Mia." His tone grew pensive. "Do you remember what I told you? That she was desperate for her father's approval? But unfortunately she looked just like her mother and sister, the two females that had made him so angry. He apparently told her more than once that he could barely stand the sight of her."

"Oh, my God. She actually did all this for him? And he didn't try to stop her—his own daughter!—from mutilating herself? I mean, the end result was attractive, I suppose...."

"But it wasn't *her* face. Or *her* body. She said that to me more than once. That she felt like a stranger to herself when she looked in the mirror. But at the same time, she kept having surgery. Breast implants. Then her eyes. Then the cheek implants—she had those *after* Horace went into the coma, by the way."

Suzannah gasped. "Why?"

"She said she was sure he'd regain consciousness one day, and when he opened his eyes, she didn't want the first face he saw to remind him of his unfaithful wife."

Suzannah grimaced. "No offense, but that was one sick chick."

"One sick father," Justin corrected her. "The more I found out about Horace Masterson, the less sorry I was that someone had offed him. If it hadn't been for the fact that his company did top-secret research, I would have considered his murder a petty crime."

"Poor Gia."

Justin nodded. "She was a lonely, frightened, sweet girl. It was pitiful. And it made her bizarrely irresistible. Not sexually but emotionally. I wanted to make her feel better. Feel loved. I screwed up, but it wasn't what it looked like. Not lust, Suzy. Just..."

"Compassion?" Suzannah slid the photos of Gia back into the folder, then buried her face in her hands and peeked through her fingers. "What a mess."

"Yeah, it's rough. Maybe we should change the subject."

"Okay." Suzannah gave him a hopeful smile. "You said you'd give me more details about the Night Arrow project. Maybe now would be a good time for that."

He beamed. "You're fascinated by it, too?"

"Nope. Just fascinated by your obsession with it. There's a difference."

Justin's cell phone began to ring, and he winced as he asked, "Do you mind if I take it?"

"No, please do." Suzannah jumped up and went to the refrigerator for a bottle of water, glad for the chance to digest the information he had given her about Gia

Masterson. The idea that any father could be despicable enough to contort his daughter's affections the way Horace had done made Suzannah sick.

Then she scolded herself, remembering that Gia Masterson had been a wealthy, powerful woman who had turned her back on her little sister just when the girl had needed her most.

*So get a grip, will you? Worry about Justin, not some crazy dead heiress.*

He was arguing softly with someone, but his eyes were on Suzannah, and she realized he was looking a little guilty around the edges, which told her the caller was probably one of his girlfriends.

Did he really think she'd be bothered by that? What an ego!

"Okay, I'll come over," he muttered into the phone. "Just don't do anything crazy. And don't expect me to stay long. I'm not kidding, Mia. So...huh? Oh, okay... See ya."

He closed the phone and laid it on the table, then gave his attorney a sheepish grin. "Hi."

"Mia? As in, Mia Masterson? You're in touch with her?" Suzannah eyed him sternly. "Do you *want* to go to prison?"

"I tried to get rid of her. But she's freaked out about some premonition she had. She thinks whoever killed Gia is coming after her next."

"Tell her to call 911."

"I did. But she was crying...." He shrugged as if to say, *Consoling beautiful rich girls is what I do. Don't ask me to stop just because I'm on trial for murder.*

Pushing back his chair, he stood and reached for his jacket. "I'll be back in two hours, tops. I know we still have a lot to talk about—"

"We can talk in the car. You drive, I'll lecture."

"Huh?" He laughed warily. "You're sure you want to come along?"

"Do you have rocks in your head? Or just in your pants?" Suzannah demanded. "Can't you see what's going to happen? You'll go over there. Get your prints all over her and her house. Then after you leave, the Angel will swoop in and murder her, and Taylor the Jailor will lock *me* up. He released you into *my* custody, remember? You aren't going anywhere without me except to your hotel room at night, and that's only because I'm afraid to sleep with an accused murderer in the house."

"In other words, it's all about you?"

"Believe it."

Justin laughed. "This is actually a great idea."

Suzannah had to admit she liked it, too. Getting the facts of the case through Mia's eyes, rather than just through Justin's, made sense. And aside from Charlie Parrish, aka the Angel of Mercy, Mia was the prime suspect, at least in Suzannah's mind. The younger Masterson daughter was inheriting millions of dollars from Gia, not to mention control of their billion-dollar corporation. Talk about a motive!

"Give me five minutes to change back into my suit—"

"Don't do that," Justin interrupted. Then he explained carefully, "Anyone can look professional in a suit. But you carry it off in jeans. Let Mia see that. It'll drive her crazy and keep her off balance."

"I don't play games."

"Trust me on this, okay? Sometimes a game is the best strategy."

*Because he cons and seduces people for a living,* Suzannah reminded herself. *And obviously he's good at it, so...*

"Can I wear heels at least?"

"Absolutely. The higher, the better." Justin's blue eyes began to twinkle. "You and Mia—man, this should be good."

## Chapter 3

During the hour-long ride to the Masterson estate, which was located in the rolling, grapevine-covered hills outside the city, Justin insisted upon hearing about "the divorces." Suzannah didn't put up much of a fight, reminding herself that even though he was on administrative leave, he probably had access to multiple sources of information. Or he could contact the supergirl whose phone number was in the manila envelope. What was it he had called her? A spinner? Not to mention a genius with answers to any and every question.

Suzannah didn't really mind discussing her parents' bizarre courtship anyway. As ambivalent as she was about most of her childhood, she loved this part of the story.

"To really appreciate the divorces, you have to know how they met in the first place," she told Justin as she settled into the soft leather seat of his BMW convertible. "My mother is a talented poet. When she was a freshman in college, she entered a contest and won, and as a result, one of her poems was published in an anthology with some pretty famous folks. Meanwhile, my dad—a college dropout with an ear for languages— was making a good living in Mexico as a translator. He was hired to translate Mom's poetry anthology into Spanish and supposedly fell in love with her just by reading her poem. So he sent her a letter saying he'd like to meet her. She and some friends decided to go to Cancun for spring break, partly to meet Dad. They hooked up there and then got married two weeks later. Mom never went back to school. It was a huge scandal in Mom's family, believe me.

"Anyway..." She took a deep breath. "They lived from job to job. Dad got translating gigs. Mom published an occasional poem and made money on the side with these great charcoal sketches she does."

"Like the ones on your dresser?" Justin interrupted. "You're right. Those are really terrific."

"When did you see my dresser?" she demanded.

"I checked it out while you were in the bathroom. Force of habit," he explained. "Go on with the story. They lived from job to job and..."

"And then one day Dad was offered a plum assignment. But he turned it down. When Mom wanted to know why, he admitted that the poet was a woman he'd had an affair with once, before he married Mom. He figured the old girlfriend had arranged for him to get the job because she wanted to rekindle things, and of course he wasn't interested." Suzannah gave Justin a fond smile. "Can you guess what happened then?"

"Your Mom was so jealous she divorced him? That's a burn considering your old man did the right thing and turned down the job."

"Actually, Mom took it as a sign that Dad didn't trust himself with this woman. Why else was he afraid to work with her? Unresolved lust. She wanted him to get it out of his system once and for all, so she divorced him and brought me here to live with Grandma for a while. She told Dad to call us when he was ready to get married again."

"You're kidding." Justin grinned. "Did he have an affair with the old girlfriend?"

Suzannah shrugged her shoulders. "Who knows for sure? He says he did. And he got paid a *lot* for that particular job, so Mom was convinced. He promised it was definitely over this time and that Mom was the only woman in the world for him now, so they got remarried."

"Makes a lot of sense, actually."

Suzannah rolled her eyes. "It was ridiculous. But it worked for me because I got to be friends with Noelle, who lived next door to Grandma. It was a great year, actually. But of course I missed Dad, so I was glad when they got hitched again."

"But then...?"

"Divorce number two? That was strictly financial. My great-grandma—the only person on either side of the family with any significant wealth—was at death's door. She told my grandmother that the worst day of her life was the day my mother met 'that awful man,' aka my father. She claimed that if Mom would divorce Dad, she'd leave half her money to her. But if not, she'd get nothing. So, long story short, they got divorced again. I was twelve, and it was kind of freaky, but it gave me a chance to renew my friendship with Noelle. And they bought me off by getting me a horse, which I had always wanted. So all in all, everyone was happy."

"Then they remarried after Great-Grandma died?"

Suzannah nodded. "Welcome to my childhood."

He chuckled. "Did you grow up in Mexico?"

"Mexico, Brazil, Italy, France and Australia, with lots of pit stops in the U.S., mostly Santa Fe and Seattle."

"Sounds amazing."

"It was fun," she admitted carefully, "but it had its downside. My education was a disaster. Constantly switching schools and getting lots of homeschooling from my mother, who didn't believe I needed to learn any math beyond simple arithmetic. I had to really scramble in my senior year just to get into college. I moved in with Grandma again and took math and science courses in the evening at the junior college, just to shore up my transcript." She grimaced. "While everyone else was at the prom, I was stuck at home, cramming for an algebra final. Stuff like that. But it was nice spending time with Grandma, especially because she was getting sicker around that time. She died the next year." Suzannah cleared her throat. "Anyway, that's the story."

"Sorry about your grandmother. But still, very cool about your mom."

"Pardon?"

"Ordering your dad to have an affair," he explained.

"That's my idea of an outstanding wife. Great-Grandma, on the other hand, is scary. And I've gotta say, you've done a great job incorporating the best of both of them in that dominatrix routine you use."

"*Excuse* me?"

"You know. Sexy but controlling."

When Suzannah arched an annoyed eyebrow, he crowed, "There! That's the look I'm talking about. Domineering but in a fun way."

"Be quiet." Suzannah struggled not to smile. "Anyway, talking about divorce number two reminds me why I consider Mia Masterson the prime suspect in her sister's murder. In a way, she did the same thing my parents did when they went through a charade to get their rightful inheritance. Mia pretended to reconcile with Gia, but it was just an act. A way to position herself to inherit all the money. But she never really forgave Gia for siding with Horace when he exiled her."

"You're wrong about that," Justin told her quietly. "I saw them together, remember? No way would either of them have hurt the other one. Not for any amount of money."

Suzannah started to debate the point, then stopped herself, deciding instead that she would use the impending visit to Mia's house to judge the heiress's grief level for herself.

The guard who waved them through the gate at the Masterson mansion had absolutely no expression on his face, which to Suzannah seemed ominous.

"Friend of yours?" she asked Justin.

"He was on duty the night Gia was killed. He obviously thinks I did it."

"Didn't he notice that you left an hour before the time of death?"

"Apparently not." Justin motioned toward a second gate in the distance. "The exit is way over there, and he doesn't control that gate. It's triggered automatically when a car approaches from the inside. He says he was reading a magazine that night and didn't see me or anyone else leave."

"Do you believe him?"

"Yeah. He's a decent guy. Retired cop. He probably thought I was going to spend the night, so he wasn't paying a lot of attention, especially at that hour. I left at nine. She died at nine forty-five or so. For all I know, he could have been sound asleep."

Suzannah scowled.

"He's okay," Justin insisted. "It's not like there's a lot of traffic here. And there's an elaborate security system for the actual house, so he doesn't have to pay attention to anything but his gate."

Suzannah turned her attention to the mansion, a gigantic stone box of a building with about as much warmth and personality as the guard had demonstrated. The grounds were equally severe—more concrete than lawn, with hedges and trees that had been pruned into complete submission.

"Noelle would love to get her hands on this place," Suzannah murmured. "She's a landscape designer."

"Yeah? Very cool." Justin eased his convertible into a parking spot near the front steps. Then he gave his passenger a wary smile. "There's something you should know about Mia."

Suzannah groaned. "Please don't say what I think you're going to say."

His face reddened slightly. "It's not as bad as it sounds. More like a near miss."

"What does *that* mean?"

"I was in bed with Gia. Just talking. That's usually all we did, by the way. Talked. Or cuddled. Because, as I mentioned, she was a basket case. Anyway, there was a knock at the door, then Mia comes in wearing this flimsy little getup. And the next thing I knew, it was a party."

"You're kidding."

"I got the impression this wasn't the first time they'd teamed up, if you know what I mean. It was weird. And I put a stop to it before it went too far." He gave a sheepish grin. "I figured it was bad enough I was sleeping with one witness, let alone two."

"You're a pillar of strength," she assured him sarcastically.

"So?" He cleared his throat. "How pissed are you?"

"Not at all. Once again, you're just the victim. Right?" She gave him a teasing smile, honestly relieved that he hadn't slept with sister number two. "What's Mia like?"

He shrugged. "Spoiled. Selfish. Not the brightest woman I ever met, but she knows how to get her way. She's probably okay, deep down inside. And like I said, her grief over her sister's death is genuine. I don't know about her fear that she'll be the next victim. But she sounded pretty scared on the phone."

"I still say she never really reconciled with Gia. It was all an act to get the money." Suzannah started to open her door, then asked drily, "Anything else I need to know?"

"Nope, that about covers it." His blue eyes warmed. "You're a good sport, you know that?"

"A good sport who charges by the hour," she reminded him, trying not to be impressed by the tingle of excitement he could send through her at a moment's notice. "So let's get going."

Unlike her dreary surroundings, Mia Masterson was colorful and expressive, throwing her tall, skinny body right into Justin's arms the moment he and Suzannah crossed the threshold into a cavernous receiving hall.

"Thank you, thank you, thank you for coming," she told him, wrapping her arms around his neck, then pasting a full-scale kiss on his mouth.

As Justin tried to extricate himself, Suzannah took the opportunity to study their hostess. She was wearing a hot-pink-and-green tube dress that was slit high on her thigh. No shoes. No jewelry. Quite possibly no underwear. She had waist-length, straight blond hair, and her pretty face was almost identical to the one Suzannah had studied in the "before" pictures of Gia.

One thing appeared certain. Mia trusted Justin completely, which seemed odd in light of the fact that he was accused of murdering her sister. How could she be so sure he didn't do it?

*Because she did it herself*, Suzannah reminded herself. *Why am I the only one who sees that? Mia ended up with the millions. And she had another motive, because Gia and the father treated her like shit for years. Plus, she's got a thing for the victim's boyfriend. Case closed, folks.*

"Cut it out, Mia." Justin grabbed the heiress by the waist and planted her a safe distance from himself. Then he looked her up and down, not with lust but with clear disapproval. "You said you were afraid you were being stalked. So what's with the sexy outfit?"

"You think *this* is sexy?"

"In other words, that phone call was just a con? That figures. Good thing I brought my lawyer."

Mia turned slowly, as if reluctant to acknowledge that she and Justin weren't alone. Then she gave Suzannah a quick appraising glance. "Hello."

"I'm Suzannah Ryder. Nice to meet you, Ms. Masterson."

Mia turned back to Justin. "My company has dozens of high-powered attorneys you can use. No need to hire one. No one really thinks you did it, anyway."

Intrigued, Suzannah asked her, "Who do *you* think did it?"

"The Angel of Mercy. Obviously. And *I'm* probably next," Mia added with a pout. "Not that anybody cares."

Justin shook his head. "If you're really worried, try putting some clothes on. And hire some additional security."

"Why can't *you* be my security? You could move in here and protect me. So I don't wind up like Gia."

"Under the circumstances," Suzannah interrupted, "I think my client's right. You need to hire your own security. He's busy working on his defense."

"With you? Cozy."

"That's it," Justin muttered. "We're leaving."

"No! Don't go. I'll be good."

Suzannah sighed. "Do you mind answering some questions, Ms. Masterson? Agent Russo just hired me this morning, so I'm not quite up to speed yet."

"It's simple," Mia assured her. "The Angel of Mercy killed my father because those were Daddy's wishes. Then he killed Gia for keeping Daddy alive against his will for all those years."

Suzannah arched an eyebrow. "How can you be so sure my client didn't do it? The evidence—"

"Justin loved Gia. He'd never hurt her. Right, Justin?"

"I cared about her," he corrected Mia carefully. "And yes, I never would have hurt her."

There was an awkward silence, then Mia murmured, "Come on. Let's go have a drink."

She led them into an elegant living room and motioned for them to be seated. Then she walked over to a freestanding bar.

"Miss Ryder—it is Miss, isn't it?" Without waiting for a response, she continued, "Do you want ice with your scotch?"

"I'll just have a glass of water, thanks," Suzannah told her as she sat on a navy-blue velvet sofa.

Justin took a seat next to his lawyer. "Just water for me too, Mia."

"Oh? Since when?" Mia flashed a teasing smile. "Don't bother trying to impress your new attorney. I can tell she already has a crush on you. Right, Miss Ryder?"

"I can't afford to have a crush on him, Ms.

Masterson. Luckily yours seems big enough for the both of us."

Mia scowled. "I'm genuinely in love with him. Not that it's any of *your* business."

"Jeez, Mia. That's a stupid thing to say." Justin stood and walked over to the heiress, then looked down into her eyes. "What are you doing?"

"I'm just being honest." Glancing toward Suzannah, she lowered her voice to a mock whisper. "When Gia was alive, I had to back off. But now that she's dead, is it so wrong to tell you how I feel? I'm not asking you to do anything about it yet. But once the charges are dropped—and I know they will be soon—you and I need to talk. About our future. Together." She sent another glance in Suzannah's direction as she added with quiet insistence, "Alone."

Justin seemed frustrated but didn't respond. Instead he brought the two glasses of water back to the sofa. "Here, Suzannah."

"Thanks." She set hers on a coaster on a side table, then picked up a framed portrait. "Is this your mother, Ms. Masterson? You look just like her."

"So Daddy always said." Mia took a long drink of scotch, then strolled over and sat in a wingback chair. "How much do you know about our family melodrama?"

"I'd like to hear it from you, if you don't mind."

Mia sighed. "It's pretty simple. When Gia and I were little, my father was mean to my mother and ended up driving her into another man's arms. She paid for that mistake the rest of her life. And after she died, *I* paid for it. And so did Gia, but in a different way. She got plastic surgery so she wouldn't look like us anymore. And I had an affair with the son of the guy Mom had *her* affair with. The shrinks say that that was my way of begging for Daddy's attention. Instead I got the boot. It wasn't until the old fart was brain-dead that I got to come home. Then Gia and I mended fences and things were perfect until...well, you know the rest."

"Yes. I'm so sorry." Suzannah took a sip of water. "So by the end, you and Gia were close? That's good, at least. Especially because those other years must have been rough. I mean, you must have really resented her in those days. Anyone would have."

"It wasn't her fault, it was Daddy's. He's the one I hated. Not Gia. And just for the record," Mia said, her tone unexpectedly defiant, "those years weren't so bad. My cousin Cynthia took me in. She was my only family for years. Everyone was so sure I wanted to be here in this big, cold house, but I was happy *there*. Cynthia was exactly like my mother. Sweet and loving and nonjudgmental. I would have gladly stayed with her forever. But when Daddy had his stroke, she convinced me I should try to come home. To say goodbye to him before he died.

"It's funny," Mia added softly. "Cynthia tried to make us a family again, but Gia refused. It could have been so easy. But instead Cynthia had to die a horrible death before everything could be right again. Strange, don't you think?"

"It's a sad story," Suzannah agreed.

"And *I'm* the biggest victim. My parents are gone. My sister's gone. My cousin's gone. I've got no one. Except Justin, of course," she said, scooting out of her chair and onto the agent's lap, then giving him a hug. "Thank God."

"Cut it out, Mia," he warned, standing to dump her off himself.

"It's okay. Anything she hears is privileged. Right, Miss Ryder?" Mia eyed Suzannah coolly. "Justin's in an awkward position. He knows how I feel, but he can't even *think* about me that way. Not while he's on trial for Gia's murder. People might think he and I conspired to kill her and get all the money for ourselves. But *you* don't think that, do you? And even if you did, since you're his attorney, you'd have to keep it to yourself. Wouldn't you?"

Justin scowled. "No one wants to hear this, Mia, so just cut it out."

"Miss Ryder wants to hear it." Mia gave Suzannah a knowing smile. "Don't you?"

"I actually have a different question, if you don't mind," Suzannah told her carefully. "How did you feel about your sister's plastic surgery?"

Mia pursed her lips as though pondering the question. Then she said simply, "I felt sorry for her."

"Really?"

"Of course. Everyone knew Daddy preferred small-breasted women. He married Mother, didn't he? And *she* was flatter than *I* am."

Suzannah bit back a smile. "That's why you felt sorry for Gia? Because she wanted your father to love her *more*, but the surgery actually made him love her less?"

"It turned him off. I'm sure of it," Mia insisted.

*Ugh, thanks for the visual,* Suzannah complained to

herself, wondering if Mia could possibly be as shallow as she seemed.

She decided to test the depths. "So your father would have preferred *your* body to Gia's?"

"He married my mother, didn't he? And she looked just like me. So obviously he would have chosen me over Gia. If we weren't his daughters, I mean."

*This is the best sibling rivalry ever,* Suzannah decided. *Justin's crazy if he thinks these gals really reconciled.*

"Any other questions?" Mia prodded her.

"Actually, yes. I'm curious about Derek Seldon. He's the man you had the affair with, right? But when you talk about the people who cared about you back then, he isn't on the list?"

Mia seemed flustered for a moment, then rallied. "At the time, I thought we were in love. But like I said, the shrinks explained that it was just my way of getting Daddy's attention. And a way for Derek to get his hands on Masterson Enterprises, which he really, really wanted."

"You two aren't friends anymore at all?"

She shrugged. "We've chatted once or twice since I got back. Nothing serious. Why?" Her eyes narrowed. "You think Derek killed Gia to get the company? He's not that kind of guy. Tell her, Justin."

The agent shrugged. "I only met him a couple of times."

"I'm not accusing anyone," Suzannah explained. "Just trying to get the facts straight. Thanks for being so cooperative."

Mia gave a light, victorious laugh. "See, darling? Your lawyer and I are getting along great. Maybe I should give her a tour of the house. You'd like to see where Gia was killed, wouldn't you, Miss Ryder? I mean, Suzannah?"

Suzannah winced. She had completely forgotten that this was more than just a monstrosity of a mansion. It was a crime scene. Somewhere in this cold building Gia Masterson had been shot.

Suzannah had never actually been to the scene of *any* crime before, much less a murder. But she'd have to see it eventually—or at least detailed photos—if she wanted to represent Justin properly. So she braced herself and said, "If you don't mind, yes. That sounds like a good idea."

"Justin, make yourself a drink. And find some sports on the television. Suzannah and I won't be gone long."

"I hope you're kidding." Justin's voice had descended into a growl. "She's not going anywhere without me."

"That's silly. We want some time for girl talk, don't we, Suzannah?"

Suzannah nodded. "I'm sure we'll be fine, Justin."

To her surprise, he stepped close to her, then stared down into her face, his expression deadly serious. The normally twinkling blue eyes had gone completely gray—the color of cold, hard steel. "I don't tell you how to run your law practice. Don't tell me how to do *my* job. I'm not letting you out of my sight. Not until we're out of here."

"Because you think this house is dangerous?" Mia demanded. "But you're perfectly happy leaving *me* here all alone?"

"Mia, please don't interfere," he suggested quietly. "I'm talking to my lawyer."

Suzannah licked her lips, completely speechless at the abrupt change in attitude. His tone was serious to the point of being intimidating. And those dark eyes. They were so unexpected. So commanding.

And sexy as hell.

She finally managed to semi-arch an eyebrow. "Maybe we should just go. I don't need to see Gia's bedroom. At least not today."

Justin nodded in emphatic agreement. "There's nothing to see, anyway. Once forensics finished up in there, Mia had it cleaned. Right, Mia?"

The heiress winced. "The police said I could."

"That's perfectly understandable," Susannah assured her. "Thanks for the hospitality, Ms. Masterson. You've been very informative. If I think of any other questions, do you mind if I call you?"

Mia pouted. "It's not just Gia's room, you know. We have a bowling alley. And a huge greenhouse. And an infirmary. How many houses have you ever seen with one of those? And I just redecorated my bedroom. It's the prettiest room in the house now." She grabbed Justin's hand. "You can come with us. We were just kidding about leaving you behind, weren't we, Suzannah?"

"We need to go, Mia," he explained, his voice gentle and completely back to normal. "Suzannah's had a rough day."

"And I haven't?" the heiress demanded. "Will you at least call me later? To check on me? See if I'm alive or dead—"

"I agree with my client on this one, Ms. Masterson," Suzannah interrupted. "If you're worried about your safety, you need to hire more security. Or move into a hotel. He's not in a position to protect you right now, as much as he might want to. It could get him into more trouble. You don't want that, do you?" Before Mia could respond, Suzannah turned away abruptly and headed for the entry hall.

Justin trailed Suzannah to the car, then reached out and grabbed her by the wrist just as she was reaching for the handle of the passenger door. "Wait a sec, Suzy."

This time she managed to fully arch her eyebrow. "Something wrong?"

"I shouldn't have talked to you that way. I'm sorry. I just didn't like the idea of you going alone with Mia to that bedroom. I mean..." His voice grew pensive. "The last time I saw Gia, she was alive and well, lying there in her bed, seemingly safe but also completely vulnerable. When I heard she had been murdered—well, let's just say I don't ever want to feel that way again. But I shouldn't have been so harsh. I apologize."

"Just don't do it again," Suzannah advised. Then she turned and got into the car, hoping he couldn't see that she was still a little flustered from the way her body had responded to his overprotective take-charge attitude.

*The boyish-charm routine is tough enough to resist, but—whoa—there's a whole other layer there that you'd* really *better watch out for,* she warned herself as they rode back to her apartment in silence.

Then she forced herself to think about the rest of the visit—specifically Mia's proclamation of love for Justin. It had seemed uncomfortably sincere. But maybe it was just what he had said—that she was spoiled and selfish and used to getting her way. The more Justin resisted her, the more she wanted him, even if he was the man who had been sleeping with—and was accused of murdering—her dead sister.

*Or she really is in love with him...*

Suzannah had to admit that was a possibility. She herself was proof that he was devastatingly attractive. With Gia gone, maybe Mia really might want Justin for herself, not just as a conquest but permanently.

What was it the heiress had said?

*Justin's in such an awkward position. He knows how I feel, but he can't even think about me that way. Not while he's on trial for Gia's murder. People might think we conspired to kill her and get all the money for ourselves.*

Suzannah glanced at him, then quickly looked away, realizing that that was exactly what people *would* think if he showed the slightest interest in Mia Masterson. Yet he had been more than willing to rush over to her house today and would have done so alone if Suzannah hadn't intervened.

He was either stupid or noble or reckless...

Or he cared about Mia after all, despite his protestations to the contrary.

*Wouldn't that be the biggest burn of all?* she decided glumly. *You give up your vacation and jeopardize the Twelve-Year Plan just to save his hide. Then he runs off and marries that skinny brat? What kind of crappy karma do you have going today, anyway? Sheesh!*

Annoyed all over again at having been saddled with such an impossible client, she dug in her purse for the business cards of his other attorneys. She had intended to meet with them eventually, and tonight seemed like the perfect time.

"I still think you should go back to your hotel," she told Justin as he followed her into her apartment. "I might be gone for hours."

"I was listening to your phone conversation with Johnson, remember? You're just meeting them for drinks. Not dinner. I'll rustle up some takeout while you're gone, and we'll eat together. Then I'll go home."

"What's the point?"

His tone grew wistful. "I can't believe you're this mad. Just because I didn't want you wandering around the scene of a murder without me?"

"I'm not mad. I just need time alone to process everything I've heard today." Suzannah kicked off her heels and flopped onto the couch. "What a mess."

"Want me to rub your feet?"

"I hope you're kidding."

Justin sat next to her and patted her arm. "If you're overloaded, postpone your meeting with those stiffs. They'll just make it worse. Stay here and relax instead. We'll order a pizza and work on the puzzle."

"That's like fiddling while Rome burns. Believe it or not, I still want to save you from prison. Which means I've got to hear what the experts have to say."

"I already *know* what they're going to say. That I killed Gia. And in this mood, you're probably going to buy it."

Suzannah gave him a rueful smile. "It's not that bad. Close, but not that bad."

He seemed to relax a little. "I just realized something. I haven't filled you in on Night Arrow yet. Things will become clearer once you have the details."

Suzannah smiled again, reluctantly admitting to herself that Justin had chosen the perfect way to lure her back into his corner. "I don't think our attorney-client privilege is the same as security clearance. Are you sure this won't you get into trouble?"

"It's mostly compromised information. Not exactly launch-code-level stuff. Just promise to keep it to yourself and we'll be fine." He jumped up and walked over to her stereo system. "I would have told you at the hotel, but someone might have been listening. Even here we need to take precautions."

"Precautions?"

He selected a CD from her collection and slid it into the player. "We could take a shower together and let the sound of the water drown out our conversation, but you don't seem in the mood to get wet with me. So…" He pushed the play button, and as the soft, romantic sounds of Madonna's "Crazy for You" filled the air, he held his hand out to Suzannah.

The twinkle in his blue eyes confirmed that he wasn't really concerned about eavesdroppers or listening devices. He was simply offering her a way to indulge her curiosity—to discover what might have been had their encounter in the courthouse hall led to a date rather than a professional relationship.

And since she really *was* curious, she stood and crossed over to him, trying not to look like a lovestruck idiot. Or any kind of idiot at all, in fact.

*He's your client. He's your client* she told herself.

But the chant wasn't working, so she bumped it up to *He almost had a threesome with Gia and Mia*.

Which worked fairly well until she was actually in his arms, swaying with the music while completely and hedonistically enjoying the feel of his lean physique.

She had expected groping hands—or at least a tight embrace—but his touch was loose and casual, as though he knew his chest and torso would supply all the magnetism he needed to imprison her.

*Mmm...you're going to get me disbarred, Justin Russo. But it just might be worth it.*

She knew she would wonder later that night how he had found this particular CD so quickly. Entitled "Prom Night Love Songs," it had been a joke gift from Noelle, who'd claimed she was sick and tired of hearing Suzannah whine about missing the big night. But Suzannah had ended up loving the gift, which contained many of her favorite songs.

She played it often, and therefore kept it at eye level in the stack of CDs next to her stereo system. Of course, *her* eye level wasn't the same as Justin's. But he was a trained investigator, so he'd notice that sort of thing.

*He's either mocking you or manipulating you. Remember what the prosecutor said? He seduces for a living. Have some pride, Suzannah.*

Reluctantly opening her eyes, she found him gazing down at her, his expression hopeful as he suggested, "You're not mad anymore?"

"Just tell me about Night Arrow. I have to leave in five minutes."

"Yeah, okay." He slid his hand under her sweater and rubbed her back lightly. Then he lowered his head until his lips were against her ear. "I need to say this very softly. In case they're listening."

She shuddered with delight but forced herself to say, "I'm losing patience."

"Right. Night Arrow. It started thousands of years ago. In a jungle far, far away."

"Justin! I thought you were serious about this."

"I am." He pulled her back against himself. "All we have now are scattered legends with conflicting elements, but they all agree on the basics. There was a ferocious tribe that hunted their enemies at night. They were successful because of a potion they used to anoint their arrows—arrows that never missed their intended victims, even in the dead of a moonless night. We call these guys the Ankasi, based on the most reliable version of the legend."

Suzannah stared up into Justin's eyes and noted in amazement that they had again turned color—dark blue this time, not that steely gray of her fantasies or the bright blue that usually twinkled with mischief. This appeared to be full-fledged arousal, and while she wanted to take credit for it, she had a feeling it flowed as much from his romantic story as from the swell of his body against hers.

"Night Arrow," she murmured without thinking.

He nodded. "The potion made the arrow seek its victim. Or at least that's what the legends say. But the secret—the formula—died with the last of the Ankasi. Or so we thought."

Suzannah licked her lips. "But then...?"

"But then, a few months ago, a friend of mine broke into a research lab in South America. She was looking for something else but found documentation of a provocative experiment. And samples of a liquid. The company called it HeatSeek—"

"Because it was heat-seeking?" Suzannah flushed and added more coherently, "I mean, did they verify that it had heat-seeking properties?"

Justin's eyes were positively glowing. "The results were inconclusive. For every test that failed, another one seemed to indicate that the potion worked. Can you imagine, Suzy? With all of our technology, all of our supposedly advanced knowledge, Night Arrow comes along and turns everything on its head.

"If it works the way we think it does," he continued eagerly, "it can be used with any type of projectile. Bullets, missiles, you name it."

The song ended at that moment, but he reset it with a touch of his finger without letting Suzannah out of his grasp. Pulling her closer, he assured her, "There's more."

"Mmm, I love this story," she admitted.

"Okay, this part isn't from the file. It's not exactly classified, but it's definitely a secret." He cleared his throat, then told her in a voice still hoarse with excitement, "My friend Miranda—the one who found the research—actually tried it out. And she thinks it might have worked."

"She tried it? You mean, on an arrow?"

"Right. But she's a fantastic shot, so it's tough to say—"

"Did she kill someone with it?"

Justin winced. "What difference does that make?"

"You have a friend named Miranda who breaks into laboratories and steals research and kills people with arrows. And I suppose she's beautiful? And of course," she added with a surge of irrational jealousy, "you have had—or *are* having—an affair with her?"

"Hardly. Her husband would gut me like a fish if I laid a hand on her. But yeah—" he gave a fond laugh "—she's beautiful. Almost as beautiful as you are when you get crazy like this."

Suzannah stepped back from him and folded her arms across her chest. "You know what I hate about you?"

"Everything?"

"Bingo." She strode over to the coatrack and grabbed her purse. "I'm late. Thanks for the story. I won't bother asking how much of it is true."

"Would I lie to you?" Justin was laughing again as he followed her to the door. "Hey, Suzy. Wait a minute."

She turned back to him, arching her eyebrow as sharply as she possibly could. "What now?"

"Don't believe a word those guys say about me. Promise?"

She grimaced, then nodded.

Without warning, he cupped her chin in his hand and tilted her face up. Then he brushed his lips across hers.

"Justin!" She wiped her mouth with the back of her hand in exaggerated disgust. "Are you nuts?"

"No, just crazy," he told her softly. "Hurry back. I'll have dinner waiting."

She struggled for a zingy retort, but her brain let her

down. Plus, she needed to get away from him before he tried to kiss her again—or dance with her or tell her bedtime stories—so she pushed past him and hurried out into the hall, slamming the door behind her.

Then she stared at it, imagining him on the other side. Sexy, confident, irresistible.

*Threesome with Gia and Mia, threesome with Gia and Mia...* she reminded herself again and again. *And he probably slept with that Miranda woman, too! And the one with the code name. What is it? S-3 something. And now he's going to sleep with you and there's nothing you can do about it. How's that for screwed? I mean, freaking* literally *screwed!*

She shook her head in defeat. A part of her had known she would eventually fall for this guy, at least around the edges. But in less than twelve hours? That had to be some sort of record. The only remaining question was, how long was she going to pretend to resist before she gave in?

Because she was definitely going to cave. It was just a question of time. But meanwhile, she had to go see the two stiffs so she'd be ready for another round with Taylor the Jailor in the morning.

By the time she found attorneys Johnson and Wiley at a corner table in the penthouse bar of the Hotel Charlton, she had recovered her composure completely. "Thanks for meeting me on such short notice."

"Are you kidding?" Wiley shook her outstretched hand vigorously. "We were worried you wouldn't call at all. Our asses are on the lines with this case, too—"

"So we're all in this together," Johnson interrupted, his smile broad but clearly forced. "Have a seat, Ms. Ryder. What are you drinking?"

"White wine spritzer, thanks." She slipped into an empty seat across from him. "Light on the wine, heavy on the bubbles, please."

"You'll need something stronger than that if you're going to have Russo for a client," Wiley said with a laugh.

Johnson handed Suzannah a stack of folders. "We made copies of all our files for you."

"Thanks." She scanned the folders, selecting the one marked with Justin's name to leaf through first.

"We know you have a million questions," Johnson told her. "And we're sure Russo has been filling your head with wild stories. But facts are facts. He was having an affair with the victim. He admitted as much to the D.A. He had dinner with her in her room—the scene of the crime—that very night. And his prints were found on the weapon. It was probably self-defense. If he had just confessed to that right up front, there wouldn't have been any problem. But he torqued off the D.A. by refusing to admit it."

"The good news," Wiley interrupted, "is if you can convince him to admit it now, we think we can still get the charges dropped. He'll get a reprimand from the Bureau for lying, but we'll say he had an honorable motive, i.e. he didn't want to be transferred to another case before he solved Horace Masterson's murder."

Suzannah had only been half listening as she pored over the details of Justin's brilliant service record. Glancing up, she said quietly, "He says he didn't do it."

"Yeah, we know. But—"

"Lots of other people had motives. Mia Masterson for one. She's rich because of Gia's death."

"True, but—"

"And the Angel of Mercy is still at large," Suzannah continued stubbornly. "Maybe *he* did it."

"That's doubtful." Wiley held up a hand to discourage further interruptions. "Russo's prints were on the weapon."

"Because he helped her load it. So she could protect herself."

"So he says." Johnson leaned forward, his expression grim. "Think about it, Suzannah. He was sleeping with a suspect. He got too close to the truth—or, more likely, they had some sort of lover's quarrel—and she pulled a gun on him. He panicked, grabbed it, and it went off, killing her *and* his career. The truth is, he's a screwup, pure and simple. It was only a matter of time before it caught up with him."

"What are you talking about?" Suzannah asked, honestly stunned. "Have you looked at this?"

"Huh?"

"Look at his file! The things he's done. My God, he's freaking amazing."

Johnson turned to his friend and said quietly, "It didn't take him long to get to her. You were right."

"Yeah." Wiley gave Suzannah an apologetic smile. "No offense. We actually thought you'd last a little longer than this. But the guy apparently has one talent, and he uses it wisely."

"One talent?" Suzannah jumped to her feet, just so she could glare down at them. "*One?* I've only *glanced* at his file and I already know he's a sharpshooter with a photographic memory who solves serial murders when all the experts throw up their hands."

"He's lucky," Johnson retorted. "And he's gotten some great publicity. But take my word for it, he's a hot dog. Completely undisciplined. He would have self-destructed long ago if he didn't have a guardian angel."

"Pardon?"

"She works at SPIN. Have you heard of it?" Before Suzannah could respond, he assured her, "Most civilians haven't. It's a support agency for field operatives. The spinners do the behind-the-scenes research. You'll see in his file that he works with them a lot. And with one in particular. She makes sure he gets plum assignments and lots of commendations. Probably in exchange for...well, never mind."

Wiley gave a knowing chuckle.

"Wow, you guys really are jerks." Suzannah scowled at each man in turn. "Did you even bother to read the details? You *couldn't* have, because if you did, you'd know he's the guy who saved that little Rodriguez girl last year. Remember her from the news bulletins? A pervert kidnapped her, and an FBI agent saved her. My God," she added, her voice hushed. "If I'd known a guy like that—a hero!—was coming to my house, I would've baked him a freaking cake! You two are just jealous because he's superior to *either* of you in every single possible way that counts."

The men stared at her, clearly flabbergasted.

"I'll tell you something else." She leaned down to ensure that the wide-eyed waiter hovering nearby couldn't hear her. "If I *ever* catch one of you saying a disrespectful or slanderous word about our client again, I'll report you to the State Bar. You've got a duty of loyalty and you'd better start honoring it. And while you're at it, you might try becoming better human beings as well as better lawyers. Because right now, quite frankly, you suck at both." Picking up her purse, she pulled out a wad of bills and threw it on the table. "Agent Russo was right. You really *are* a couple of stiffs."

"Hey, Suzy," Justin greeted her from the living room. "I hope you're hungry. I had Chinese delivered."

Suzannah hung her purse on the coatrack. Then she instructed her houseguest sternly, "Sit down."

"Huh? Oh, shit, what did they tell you?"

"Agent Russo, would you *please* sit down and listen to me?"

"Sure." He settled down on the sofa, visibly dejected. "Go ahead. Let's hear it."

She folded her arms across her chest as she'd done earlier with Johnson and Wiley. "I know why you picked me as your attorney. To psych out Judge Taylor so he'd be sure to release you on bail. That was a smart move."

"It's more than that now," Justin protested.

"You bet your ass it is. You thought I was a one-note lawyer. And a pushover. But I've got news for you. I'm neither. Lucky for you. Because—" she paused to give him a confident smile "—whether you know it or not, I'm the perfect lawyer for you. I might even be the *only* lawyer in the whole *freaking* world that can give you the kind of representation you deserve. Do you know why?"

He shook his head, his expression wary.

Suzannah spread her hands in front of her as though explaining something obvious. "Men can't properly represent you. Either they'd feel inadequate or they'd feel threatened or just plain jealous. So that eliminates a huge percentage of the attorney population right off the bat. And guess what? Women can't represent you either! You're too freaking sexy."

Justin chuckled. "Thanks for the compliments. I just have one question. Aren't *you* a woman? 'Cause if you're not, you do one hell of an impression."

"That's right, funny boy. Laugh it up. Hit me with your best routine. It just doesn't work on me anymore. Because this is what I do best. I resist temptation. You may be the world's sexiest apple, but trust me, I'm no Eve."

"What the hell are you talking about?" he demanded, still laughing but now with some impatience.

"I grew up in chaos. Why do you think I make crazy lists all the time? Why do I keep everything around here so nice and tidy? Do you think I'm naturally that way? It's just the opposite! I came from a gene pool that doubled as Party Central. I'm programmed to be irresponsible, flighty and spontaneous. I've had to fight it, to learn to overcome it. Lucky for you, I succeeded."

"Man," he said reverently. "Do you have any idea how much I want to kiss you right now?"

"Again with the flirting?" Suzannah eyed him in frustration. "Do you remember this morning? When I said all I had to do was stack the jury with women and I could get you acquitted? And you said you hoped it was your record, not your sex appeal, that counted?"

Instantly subdued, Justin nodded.

"So? My grandmother always said, 'If you don't respect yourself, you can't expect anyone else to.'"

He was quiet for a moment. Then he murmured, "Fair enough."

Suzannah gave him an encouraging smile. "She had another expression. My all-time favorite. Want to hear it?"

He nodded.

"She used to say, 'Someone has to be the adult.'"

He cocked his head to the side. "What?"

"I told you a little about my parents, but there's more. They weren't just eccentric nomads. They were—*are*—hopelessly immature. It was fun for a while—I mean, according to reliable reports, my very first word was *candy*. Do you *love* that? What kind of crazy-ass parents feed so much candy to an eight-month-old that she actually says *that* before she says *Mama* or *Daddy*? Anyway..." She paused for a deep breath. "When I was sixteen, something inside me snapped, and my inner adult took over. I embraced discipline like a religion. Studied my ass off and got into a great college on SAT scores alone. Then I plotted out my entire future, year by year. I learned how to defer gratification in ways you can't possibly imagine. And I learned how to resist temptation."

"Like sex with clients?"

"Exactly." She gave him a confident smile. "And just in case you think I'm bluffing, I'll tell you a little story. Last week I was picking up my dry cleaning and they had a box of abandoned puppies there. These were the cutest puppies ever born. Absolutely, positively precious little mixes of who-knows-what breeds—just the kind I love the most. The clerk persuaded me to hold this tiny black one. He had soft, floppy ears twice as big as he was. And big brown eyes. And he wiggled and waggled and kissed my nose, and my heart melted. And then—" she folded her arms across her chest again "—I put him back in the box. Then I walked away and never looked back. Do you know why?"

"Because you're not Eve?"

She arched an eyebrow. "Right. I'm not ready for a puppy yet. I plan to get one when I'm not working for a firm anymore. When I have a normal-ish job—let's say, fifty hours a week instead of seventy. When I have a house with a backyard. When I'm ready. Everything I do is built around my plan—"

"The Twelve-Year Plan," he said, nodding admiringly. "Noelle told me all about it and I think it's great. Like you said, you're amazingly disciplined. I can't even plan my next—"

"Wait!" She stared in disbelief. "You talked to Noelle? When?"

"She called while you were out. We had a great chat."

Completely deflated, Suzannah walked over to the sofa and sat down beside him. "Just when I think I'm in charge, the loonies take over the asylum again. Talk about a childhood flashback."

He patted her knee. "The point is, you really are the right lawyer for me. Just like you said. You're disciplined. Goal-oriented. Passionate. And dedicated. I saw *that* today. Even when you were mad at me, you were loyal. It's cool. I appreciate it. Really."

She sighed. "So? No more flirting?"

"I'll do my best."

"And tomorrow in court? You'll let me do all the talking?"

"Yep. That judge terrifies me."

She rolled her eyes. "Joke all you want, but in court, be serious. Those stiffs are convinced you and I are either having an affair or headed in that direction. If the judge thinks that, too, he might decide I can't be your lawyer. So don't call me Suzy in front of him. That sort of thing."

"What did those assholes say? If they insulted you—"

"They insulted us both. But I gave it right back. To the point where I'm pretty sure they had to change their pants and call their mommies."

Justin burst into laughter. "You've got a definite mean streak."

"Believe it."

"So?" He patted her knee again, then stood up and asked her, "Any chance you love cold chow mein?"

Over dinner, Justin filled her in on the latest in Noelle's Sperminator-proposal saga, explaining that the romance had hit a wall when the prospective groom told his feisty girlfriend he expected her to give up her landscaping business and help him run his accounting practice instead.

"He must have a death wish," Suzannah murmured when the meal had ended and she was walking her client to the door.

"Yeah, sounds like she gave him hell over it."

"She should. She's really talented, Justin. People are

beginning to notice. Like, she just got a job over on Sea Shell Drive. I don't know how well you know this city, but that's considered posh digs. Not Masterson posh but pretty ritzy. All the movers and shakers—including the mayor—live in that neighborhood. I think even Judge Taylor has a place over there."

"Good for Noelle. I can't wait to meet her in person."

Suzannah grinned, imagining how much Noelle West would love this guy. Who wouldn't?

For the first time since her outburst with Johnson and Wiley, she questioned her ability to resist Justin Russo. And even if she *could* do it, why should she?

*Because someone has to be the adult,* she reminded herself. *It's just too bad it always has to be you.*

Gathering her wits, she told him briskly, "I'll pick you up at eight sharp. Right in front of your hotel."

"Sounds good." He opened the door and started to step into the hall, then abruptly turned back, grabbed her by the waist and planted a quick kiss on her lips. Then he explained cheerfully, "I can only be so good."

"Just go," she advised him with a halfhearted glare.

As she watched him amble down the hallway to the elevator, she sighed in wistful frustration over what might have been. Then on impulse she called after him, "Agent Russo?"

He turned back, clearly surprised. "Yeah?"

"I'm really proud to have you as my client."

He hesitated, then gave her a respectful wave. "Thanks, counselor. See ya in the morning."

## Chapter 4

"Well, here we are again. The whole gang. Good morning, Suzy e-lawyer. Agent Russo. Ms. Armstrong. Nice of you all to join me."

Suzannah stood and smiled directly into Taylor the Jailor's smirking eyes, wondering how long it would take for him to discover that she wasn't the same woman who had appeared before him twenty-four hours earlier. That lawyer had been caught off guard. Out of her depth. Blindsided.

But now she was ready for him. For one thing, she was wearing her dark gray pin-striped suit—the most powerful of all her power outfits. It had cost her a week's salary but had proven its worth again and again. In it, she looked and felt invincible.

More important, she had true confidence in two

facts—her client was innocent, and she was the right attorney to help him prove it. In fact, her only concern this morning was that the judge might try to remove her from the case.

*What a difference a day makes....*

"Good morning, Your Honor," she said, flashing a confident smile.

"You're very chipper this morning, Ms. Ryder. Any particular reason you slept so well?"

She had thought she was prepared for anything, but the directness of his suggestion caught her off guard, and she sent a quick accusatory look toward Johnson and Wiley, suspecting they must have said something to him. But they each gave her a tiny shake of the head to indicate that they weren't to blame.

She imagined Justin was offended by the remark, as well, but to her relief, he was keeping his promise to stay silent. He had been wonderful all morning, greeting her outside his hotel promptly at eight with a steaming double mocha for her and a latte for himself. Sharply dressed in a light gray suit, he had complimented her appearance without actually flirting, then had chatted about the weather as though he sensed she needed to concentrate on keeping her head clear, her nerves steady.

Now it was time to put those steady nerves to work, so she cocked her head to the side and murmured, "I'm not sure I understand the question, Your Honor."

He scowled. "I'm asking you if there's any reason I should reconsider this appointment, beyond your self-professed incompetence."

She pursed her lips, wondering when he would realize that he was helping her build a record of prejudice that would result in reversal of any conviction that might befall Justin. Not that she thought it would come to that—he was innocent, and they were going to prove it. But if the worst happened, the attorney who took the case on appeal could simply point to the well-developed theme—that Suzannah had "proclaimed" herself unable to properly defend Justin, and the judge had refused to listen. In fact, given the history between them, Taylor had quite possibly used this entire case as a means of getting back at Suzannah for her success in the Driscoll appeal.

*As Justin would say, very cool.*

She gave the judge another, warmer smile. "You asked us to report back to you today on our progress, specifically on whether Agent Russo had thoroughly briefed me on the facts of his case. He has done that, and I've consulted with his former counsel, as well."

"I see." Judge Taylor licked his lips, visibly confused by her unflappable confidence. Then he asked carefully, "How long will your Hawaii trip take?"

"I leave on Sunday the fourteenth. My presentation is on Wednesday the seventeenth. The conference ends on Friday the nineteenth, and I fly home the following morning."

"Fine. Since I'll be anxious to hear all about it—and to see if you're ready to proceed with this pesky murder trial—I'd like to see all of you here again on the twenty-second. Do you think that can be arranged?"

"Yes, Your Honor."

He turned to the assistant district attorney. "Ms. Armstrong, does that work for you?"

"It's fine, Your Honor," the petite prosecutor assured him. "But in the meantime, the People have a request, if it please the court."

He frowned. "A request?"

"Yes, Your Honor." Armstrong tried to smile, apparently in hopes of duplicating Suzannah's easygoing manner, but the expression was too tense, too unnatural.

Suzannah almost felt sorry for her, knowing that Taylor would sense weakness and go after her, just as he had done to Suzannah the previous day. Unless of course he was so fixated on the Driscoll embarrassment that he wasn't interested in hitting any secondary targets, no matter how obviously they presented themselves.

Armstrong continued. "Agent Russo is no longer assigned to the Angel of Mercy investigation. But that investigation is still active, and we don't want him meddling in it. We have reason to believe he still wants to crack that case in hopes of redeeming himself. Unfortunately it's no longer his business, and the detectives are concerned that his interference will undermine their strategy."

"I see." The judge arched an eyebrow in Suzannah's direction. "Can you control your client? Or do I need to lock him up?"

"No problem, Your Honor. We're not interested in the Angel of Mercy killings except to the extent that those incidents intersect with Gia Masterson's murder. We'll confine ourselves to matters directly related to *our* investigation."

"But, Your Honor!" The prosecutor was shaking her head frantically. "The two cases are completely interrelated!"

"I believe that's Suzy's point," the judge told her quietly. "So here's what we're going to do. Agent Russo? Are you listening?"

"All ears, Your Honor."

Taylor scowled but continued. "In preparation for your defense, Suzy will examine any and all leads that might help you establish your innocence. You, in turn, will confine your participation to those leads. And you will act under her supervision. As a civilian. Is that clear?"

"Crystal. Thanks, Your Honor."

"If you step out of line, your attorney will answer for it."

"Understood, sir."

Taylor turned back to the prosecutor. "Anything else on your wish list, Ms. Armstrong?"

"No, Your Honor. Just so it's clear. If he impedes or obstructs the State's investigation—"

"He won't. Isn't that correct, Suzy?"

"Yes, Your Honor. And meanwhile..." Suzannah took a deep breath. "We have a request of our own, sir."

"Doesn't anyone make motions around here anymore?" he grumbled. "Go on. What can I do for you?"

"I've had the feeling since yesterday that I was being watched. Can you remind the prosecutor that all communications between me and my client are protected by law? In the same way that they don't want us interfering in *their* investigation, we don't want them intruding on our preparation of Agent Russo's defense."

"Ms. Armstrong?"

"We've had them under surveillance, Your Honor, but nothing intrusive—"

"It ends now," he interrupted. "Is that clear?"

"But, Your Honor—"

"You are dangerously close to contempt at this moment, Ms. Armstrong. I suggest you choose your next words carefully."

The prosecutor's chin tipped up, showing a respectful defiance that Suzannah couldn't help but admire. Then Armstrong said simply, "The People still consider Agent Russo a flight risk."

"Noted." Taylor's tone softened. "I'll take full responsibility for that. As Suzy pointed out yesterday, he's still here, isn't he? If he had wanted to run, he surely could have gotten away by now. So tell your people to back off. Understood?"

"Yes, Your Honor."

"Ms. Ryder? Anything else I can do for you?"

Suzannah bit her lip, impressed that for once he hadn't called her Suzy. Either he was beginning to respect her or, more likely, was wising up, realizing that his demeaning comments would be red flags for any appellate court reviewing these proceedings.

"We're fine, Your Honor. Thank you."

He stared at her for a long, uncomfortable moment, then nodded. "See you on the twenty-second then. Try to stay out of trouble in the meantime. And Agent Russo?"

"Yes, sir?"

"Contrary to popular belief, I don't enjoy being made a fool of. Don't make me regret trusting you."

"You have my word, Your Honor. I'd never let you—or Ms. Ryder—down."

"Fine then." Taylor waved his hand in dismissal, then instructed the clerk to call the next case.

Justin was right on her heels as they exited the courtroom and proceeded down the hall, so she turned her head enough to instruct him bluntly, "I know you're jazzed. So am I. But *don't* touch me."

From his chuckle, she knew she was right. He had been just about to grab her and swing her through the air. And as much as she might have enjoyed it, they had to watch their image carefully.

"At least slow down a little. I want to say something."

"When we get to the car. Not before."

She maintained her pace all the way to the parking lot, but as soon as they were seated in her silver Lexus, she grinned and said, "Okay, what did you think?"

"You were amazing. Not only do you get me released on bail, you get them off our backs completely!"

"It was such a rush," she admitted, fanning herself playfully with a file folder. "I guess this is why those crazy litigators put themselves through all this."

"You had that judge eating out of your hands. The same guy who wanted to lock you up yesterday." He gave her a proud smile. "You're good at this, Suzy. Really good."

"Thanks. But I couldn't do it for long. Too nerve-racking."

"Because you like things neat?" He shook his head. "Just because your parents gave you a couple of pieces of candy—"

"Not a couple. A ton of it." She smiled wistfully. "My father admits it, by the way. He says, and I quote, 'it didn't seem fair' for them to eat candy in front of me, so they 'always shared.' And believe me, they eat it a lot. Chocolate in particular."

"You were irresistible, even then," Justin said, adding quietly, "I knew you were going to kick ass today, just by your attitude when you picked me up. Calm. Centered. Completely recovered from yesterday's madness."

She smiled in agreement. "It's amazing what a good night's sleep can do. Plus, I talked to Noelle again, which always helps."

"Did you take your bubble bath?" When she nodded, he grinned. "And you read *Pride and Prejudice*?"

"One chapter."

"And watched the *Remington Steele* marathon?"

She groaned. "Big-mouth Noelle strikes again? Yes, I watched one episode."

"You're hilarious. So? What's on today's list?"

"You tell me."

He cleared his throat. "Actually, I have a lead on Charlie Parrish. But I need to follow that up on my own. So just drop me at my hotel. I'll take care of it, then head for your place."

Suzannah shook her head. "Weren't you listening to the Jailor? If we follow leads, we do it together."

"Not this one. It's in a crummy area." He cocked his head to the side, then asked, "When you told the judge you had a feeling you were being watched, did you mean it? Or was it just for theatrical effect?"

"A little of both," she admitted. "It's not like the hairs

on the back of my neck have been standing up or anything. But ever since you told me the D.A. has it in for you, I've been assuming they were keeping tabs on us." She arched her eyebrow. "Which is another reason for me to come along when you follow up on leads. So? Shall we go right now?"

He grimaced but nodded. "Okay, but I'll drive. And when we get there, *you'll* stay in the car. Understood?"

"Yuck, I didn't even know we *had* an abandoned factory this close to town. It looks like rodent central. Are you sure this is where you're supposed to meet the guy?"

"I'm sure. Just stay put—"

"I'm coming. Judge's orders." Suzannah eyed the building grimly. It had burned almost to the ground decades earlier, according to the information her client had given her during the drive from the courthouse. Now it provided a home to various vagrants, one of whom had left a message for Justin at his hotel. Hand delivered by a little girl, the scrawled note stated that the anonymous writer had heard Justin was offering a reward for information about the Angel of Mercy, and if he came to the burned-out factory with the money, they could do business.

"Stay close behind me, then." Justin reached into the duffel bag he had stowed in the backseat, calmly pulling out his shoulder holster, which this time contained a black pistol. "And let me do the talking. If I tell you to go back to the car, do it. Understand?"

"Okay."

Wishing she had been warned so that she could have

brought a pair of tennis shoes, she gingerly stepped over chunks of concrete and other assorted rubble.

"There he is." Justin nodded in the direction of a solitary figure. "Poor old guy. He really looks down on his luck."

"Or criminally insane," Suzannah muttered, digging in her purse until her fingers located and curled around her trusty can of mace.

"He's probably harmless, but stick close."

"Don't worry. I will."

She could practically hear the moths chomping on the old guy's faded tweed jacket as they approached him. He was toothless except for a few brownish-yellow broken remnants. The only good news was that he looked to be nearly as apprehensive as Suzannah was.

To her surprise, Justin greeted the man with warm respect, extending his hand to him as though oblivious to the dirt and grime. "I'm Justin Russo, sir. Thanks for contacting me."

The old man wiped his palm on his worn pant leg, then accepted the handshake. "They said you'd pay me twenty dollars."

"Yes, sir. That's the arrangement. Is there somewhere we can sit and talk?" When the informant glanced at Suzannah, Justin explained, "This is my attorney."

The old man started to wipe his hand off again, and Suzannah gulped, not thrilled about touching him but also slightly ashamed of herself, given Justin's respectful behavior. Luckily her client solved the problem for her by insinuating himself discreetly but definitely between Suzannah and the informant, so that no handshake was possible.

"Let's sit," Justin said again, gesturing toward a long crumbling brick wall that stood about knee height. "What should we call you, sir?"

"I don't want no one knowing my name."

"Fine. If it's okay with you, I'll call you Mr. Jones."

When Justin again placed himself between her and the old man, Suzannah was able to relax a little, promising herself that the only danger here was a little dust that the dry cleaner could easily get out of her power suit.

After they were seated, Justin took out his wallet, extracted a twenty-dollar bill and handed it to Mr. Jones. "Your note said you met Charlie Parrish, sir. When and where did that happen?"

"I don't know 'bout no Charlie. The fella I met was that Angel they're all talking about."

"The Angel of Mercy?"

"He killed a lot of folks, but only 'cause they asked for it. Nice fella."

Justin pulled out a photo from the inside pocket of his suit jacket. "Is this the man you spoke to?"

Jones studied it closely. "Could be. Differ'nt, though. Had a beard. And black hair. Prob'ly dyed, don't ya think?"

"I imagine you're right, sir." Justin smiled encouragingly. "What did he say to you?"

"Said he heard a voice telling him what to do."

"Was it God?" Suzannah asked.

The old man shook his head. "He said it was the sick folk begging him to help. I didn't like the way he looked at me. Like he thought I was sick, too. I couldn't sleep when he was here."

"I don't blame you," Justin said sympathetically. "How long ago did this conversation take place?"

"'Bout a week. Maybe more. He slept here two nights. Then he moved on. When my buddy heard about it, he said we could've got twenty dollars. He still had your card from when you gave it to him at some bar."

"I remember. Please be sure to thank him for me." Justin smiled. "What else can you remember?"

"He was a spooky fella. Sad, too. Needed a friend. I don't need no more friends, though. And I don't like folks who hear voices. They scare me."

"They scare me, too," Justin admitted. "Can you show me where the Angel slept?"

"Sure. Right behind this wall." Jones watched as Justin stood and wandered around, poking occasionally, then shaking his head. "You won't find nothing. He didn't have nothing."

"Where do you get your food from?" Suzannah asked softly.

"I manage."

She winced. "What about the Angel? Did he have food with him?"

"He had a car."

"Oh?" Justin walked back. "What kind?"

"I never seen it. Just know he had it. Could hear his keys a-jingling. Then he took off in the night. I figure the car was here all the time. Just hidden a ways away."

"That was very observant of you, sir," Justin assured him. "Do you remember what he was wearing?"

"Pants. Sweater. Stocking hat, but I could still see that dyed-black hair of his. Sorta long, more long than yours."

"He didn't say where he had been? Or where he was going?"

"All he said was he'd been killing folks 'cause they asked him to. Said it was his duty. But he was too tired to keep on with it. And too scared. I felt sorry for him. He was a mess," Jones added sincerely.

"I'm sure he appreciated your hospitality, sir." Justin stood and extended his hand again. After Jones had shaken it, the agent pulled out his wallet and handed him another twenty along with his card. "You've done a service to your community today, Mr. Jones. Thanks a lot. And if you think of something else, give me a call."

The old man stared at the money, then looked up at Justin and murmured, "Thanks, son."

Justin nodded. "Nice meeting you." Then he took Suzannah by the elbow and inclined his head toward the car. "Shall we?"

"Wait." She felt her cheeks flush a little as she held her hand out to Jones just as Justin had done. "Thank you for your help, Mr. Jones."

"My pleasure." He touched her fingers gently, barely making contact. "You have a nice day now, young lady. You hear?"

"Can I buy you lunch?" Justin asked as they drove back to town.

She glanced at him, still impressed by the way he had treated the homeless informant. "I actually need to stop by my office just to check on a few things. Do you want to come with? Or I can drop you at my place."

"Drop me at the hotel. I'll get my car and meet you at your apartment."

"Okay." She bit her lip. "Do you really think he saw Charlie Parrish out there by the factory?"

Justin shrugged. "He could have gotten all of those details from the newspaper and/or word on the street. But he seemed sincere."

"So did you."

"Pardon?"

"Nothing." She gave an inward sigh, succumbing for a moment to the borderline hero-worship she had felt the previous evening when she had turned off *Remington Steele* in favor of an even hunkier hunk—Justin Russo—and his exploits, which were nicely detailed in the files Johnson and Wiley had given her.

"Did you always want to be an FBI agent?" she asked him.

"Nah. My old man was our county sheriff. I watched him work long hours for low pay while people took shots at him and I figured law enforcement was for chumps. My plan was to become a stockbroker or financial consultant. I'm good with numbers and people trust me."

"So what happened?"

"I went away to school. My old man had a friend at the Bureau who was investigating a fraternity on my campus. They asked me to infiltrate it for them, and I figured why not? It never occured to me—" He hesitated, then explained. "They knew the fraternity was into drugs and grade-fixing, but nothing could have prepared me for what I found. These assholes were blackmailing female students with...well, let's just say, it was ugly."

His jaw tensed visibly. "We brought them down, and it was such a rush. I switched my major to criminal justice the next day and went straight into the FBI when I graduated."

"For a life of low pay and long hours."

"The pay's not that bad," he assured her. "And the hours are only long when something's just about to break. Believe me, that's not work. That's pure fun."

Suzannah smiled. "Your father must be so proud of you."

"Yeah. I'm glad he lived to see me follow in his footsteps. Especially because he died in the line of duty. A few years ago."

"Oh, no. What happened?"

"A crazy survivalist took a local woman hostage. Dad didn't wait for the professional negotiator. He just offered to trade places with the woman, and since she was having heart problems, the nutcase agreed. My Dad was pretty persuasive," he told her sadly. "He must have gotten through to the survivalist somehow, but it backfired. The jerk shot Dad, then shot himself."

"Oh, Justin."

"Yeah, it was rough. But in some ways I think he always wanted to go out that way. Like a hero. Which he was. Plus, we lost my mom to cancer the year before, and they were pretty close, so..." He shrugged as if to say, *They're together now.*

Then he flashed a reassuring smile. "Now look at

*you,* doing some investigative work of your own. If you're not careful, you'll get the bug."

"That's doubtful," Suzannah told him. "But we really did make some progress today, didn't we? We now know that Charlie was in town recently. And since none of the other victims, other than Gia and her dad, were within a hundred miles of here, that indicates he could have some connection to the Masterson killings."

"Yeah," Justin admitted. "His presence here blows my original theory out of the water. But then again, *everything* blows my original theory out of the water."

"Your theory that Horace Masterson was killed because someone wanted to gain access to the Night Arrow project?"

He nodded. "My idea was that the killer believed he could manipulate Gia better if her father was out of the picture completely. Either he planned to infiltrate Masterson Enterprises or buy it outright."

"That's kind of far-fetched. Especially now."

"Yeah. But part of me still believes it. The attraction of Night Arrow...well, let's just say, once someone hears about it, it stays with them. Captures their imagination. The excitement is contagious."

"I must be immune," Suzannah drawled.

"Because it's the apple and you're not Eve," he reminded her mischievously. "You're intentionally resisting it. But give it time. I'll bet you start thinking about it and asking me questions."

"Don't hold your breath." She pulled up to his hotel, then fished in her purse for her apartment key. "Here, in case you get there before me. I'll get my spare from the office."

He licked his lips. "Thanks for trusting me, Suzy. It means a lot."

She felt her cheeks redden. "I meant what I said last night. It's an honor to be your attorney."

"Don't forget to pick up a fee agreement for me to sign."

"It's on the list," she assured him, deciding not to mention that she wasn't going to charge him after all. She was fairly sure she could talk her management into allowing her to work this case pro bono, especially after they heard about Justin's amazing history of public service. And since she was willing to give up her vacation for it, how could they really object? Still, it was prudent to talk to them first.

"Go straight from the hotel to my place, okay?" she reminded him. "We don't want to give the judge a reason to throw either of us in jail."

"Sure. We're a team."

She put her hand on his arm as he began to exit the vehicle. "One more thing, Justin." She cleared her throat, but it still sounded a little froggy when she murmured, "I know the partners will ask me about the gun. About your fingerprints on it, I mean. Of all the details, that's the most—"

"Incriminating? Yeah, I'd say so," he agreed with a laugh. "Just tell them the truth. She was afraid someone was going to hurt her, so she bought a gun. I helped her load it. Showed her how to use it. But I didn't really think she was in danger."

"Who was she afraid of?"

"Isn't it obvious? She thought whoever killed her father would come after her next."

"I thought she was afraid of the Angel of Mercy specifically. That's what you said yesterday, when you first briefed me."

"Man," he said with a chuckle, "I'd better get my story straight, right?"

She flushed. "Stop clowning around. I wasn't implying anything. But actually…" She bit her lip. "It's true, you know. At some point, we need to go over exactly what you said to the authorities. To your superiors, et cetera. And then yes, you should stick to that. Unless you think of something else, of course. But even then—"

"Hey, counselor?"

"What?"

"I'm innocent, remember? I don't need a story. I just have to tell the truth."

"I know that." She closed her eyes and sighed. "Sorry if I implied otherwise."

"Hey, are you worried?"

"No." She opened her eyes and smiled. "Not at all. I promise."

"That's better." His eyes twinkled. "That pretty smile of yours is your second most sexy expression."

"What's the first? Oh!" She felt her cheeks burning again, remembering his comment about her dominatrix eyebrow. "Be quiet and get out. Don't talk to strangers. And go straight to my apartment. Got it?"

"Whatever you say, mistress. I mean, counselor." He was chuckling again as he jumped out of the car.

\* \* \*

Two hours later, Suzannah turned the key in the lock on her apartment door, eager to see her obnoxious client again. She had good news for him, relatively speaking. The partners had been more than happy to take the case pro bono, although Suzannah's own willingness to handle yet another criminal case had clearly shocked them. The only condition they had placed on her was that if things grew any more serious, she should allow a more senior member of the firm to assist her.

She didn't want that, and she was pretty sure Justin wouldn't agree either. But for now it didn't matter. Things were going well for two reasons. The first and most important, Justin was innocent. And second, they made a great team. Justin had experience, intuition and instinct. And she had the organizational abilities and discipline to complement him perfectly.

Opening the door, she groaned aloud, her optimism fading at the sight of Justin sitting in the middle of the floor, trying to wrestle a sock away from a tiny ball of black fur.

"What the...? Justin!"

The ball of fur turned toward the new voice and immediately bounded over to her as Justin scrambled to his feet, grinning and announcing, "Look who I ran into on the way over here."

"Oh, wow." Suzannah scooped up the puppy, which immediately began licking her face as he'd done a week earlier at the dry cleaner's. "Look how big you've grown! Such a sweetie." She buried her face in his soft coat.

"Am I a sweetie, too?" Justin asked.

"No. But you've got a lot of other doglike qualities." She eyed him sternly. "What were you thinking?"

"I was thinking a can of mace wasn't enough protection for a hot-bodied female living all alone."

"This is my new protector?" She laughed in spite of herself as the puppy continued to plaster her with love. "What's he going to do? Lick intruders to death?"

"I was just teaching him the 'kill' command when you showed up."

She laughed again, then cuddled the puppy against her chest. "I love him. But he has to go back. I know you think I'm not tough enough to do that, but I am. That's the point I was trying to make last night. I'm not ready for a dog yet. But if I were," she admitted, raising the wiggly creature back to her face for another round of kisses, "he'd be my choice. Wouldn't you, you sweet little thing?"

"I think he's hungry. We can give him the leftover broccoli beef. Or if that seems too spicy, the dry cleaner gave me a starter can of puppy food."

"I can't believe you went there," she told him, shaking her head. "How did you even know which cleaners I use?"

Justin walked over to her refrigerator and tapped a receipt held in place there by a magnet. "I tried to pick up your stuff, too, but it won't be ready till tomorrow."

She placed the puppy on the floor, and Justin tossed a tennis ball into the breakfast nook. In an instant, the little ball of fur was racing after it.

"He has to go back, Justin. We're not allowed to have dogs in this building."

"Sure you are, as long as you pay a two-hundred-dollar damage deposit. I already took care of it."

"What?"

"I asked your landlady. She was very cooperative."

Suzannah rolled her eyes. "You're officially a Casanova. That woman hates everyone! But she loved *you*, right?"

"What's not to love?" He stepped closer, his grin softening. "Try him out. If you don't like him, *I'll* keep him. But don't make me take the poor little guy back. Those dry-cleaning fumes are bad for his lungs."

Suzannah grimaced. There weren't any fumes. She happened to know that the clothes were shipped to another location to be cleaned. But still, the idea of sending the puppy away...

"It's like Murphy's Law has taken over my vacation," she murmured. "Everything that can go wrong... Except in this case, it's everything that can go sideways."

"So you're naming him Murphy? I like that. Hey, Murf!" When the puppy dashed over to Justin and jumped into his arms, the agent beamed like a proud father. "He's pretty smart. Already knows his own name."

"I'm glad you like him. Because when you leave, he goes with you," she reminded him, but in her heart she was already weakening. "I'm gone twelve hours a day, practically every day during a normal week. He'd be too lonely and neglected here."

"It's better than the pound, aka Puppy Death Row. Which is where he was headed. I have that on good authority."

"Be quiet." She rubbed her eyes. "Didn't you hear a word I said last night?"

"You mean, someone has to be the adult?" He slipped his hand behind her neck and massaged it gently, sending a slow thrill of arousal through her. Then he insisted, "That's why I brought Murf to you. Because I knew you'd take good care of him."

She stared into his vibrant blue eyes. "You're sabotaging the Twelve-Year Plan, you know."

"Nah, just accelerating it a little. You were going to get a dog someday, remember?"

*And I was going to fall for a big, brave, hunky guy, too,* she told him in wistful silence. *But it can't happen now, and we both know why.*

Pulling free, she arched a disapproving eyebrow, then headed for the kitchen, announcing over her shoulder, "I'll heat up the broccoli beef for us. Murphy will have the puppy food."

"Okay, here's what we know so far." Suzannah stood in front of her wipe-off board while Justin and Murphy watched intently. "We have five victims. The first three were comatose residents of two different nursing homes where Charlie Parrish worked. We're pretty sure he killed those three, at least."

"There's a videotape of him killing at least one of them, and fairly incontrovertible evidence on the other two."

"Okay." She made a column labeled Victims, and filled it in with Victim #1, V #2, V #3, Horace M., Gia M. Then she made a second column labeled Suspects, where she wrote: Charlie, Gia, Mia, Derek, N-A Spy. "That's Night Arrow Spy," she explained.

"I call him Agent X."

"Ooh, I *love* that." She grabbed the eraser and quickly made the correction.

"You forgot to list my name," Justin reminded her.

She knew from his tone that he wasn't joking, so she added his name to the Suspect list, as requested.

"Okay, now... We know Charlie killed the first three." She crossed off each of those. "His motive was probably benevolent."

"Probably?"

"Unless he was in cahoots with Agent X."

"He wasn't." Justin held up a folder. "Read his file. He's a nice young guy with mental problems who genuinely cares about people. That's why he went into nursing years ago, long before our government came into possession of Night Arrow, so that couldn't have been his inducement. Plus, his mental deterioration is fairly well documented. Arguments with staff. Suspended from one facility for counseling a patient's family to pull the plug. He's just what the papers called him—an angel of mercy. No hidden agenda. No selfish motive."

"Okay." She pursed her lips. "You have to admit, he's a prime suspect in the Horace Masterson murder, as well. Horace was just as brain-dead as they were and he was killed by lethal injection, too."

"The other victims spoke directly to Charlie."

"Maybe Horace spoke to him, too."

Justin put the puppy, who had dozed off, onto the pillow Suzannah had fitted into a cardboard box. "Maybe so. If Mr. Jones told the truth—if Charlie *is* here in town—then he's more of a suspect in Horace's murder than I ever thought."

"Okay. Pretend for the moment we have proof that Charlie killed Horace. Then the question becomes, did he kill Gia?"

"No."

"You said Gia was afraid Charlie saw that videotaped statement on the news. Is that possible?"

"Sure. Horace was the poster child for euthanasia on some of the more radical Internet sites. And Gia was the evil daughter, prolonging his agony. Keeping him from peace or heaven or take your pick. There's no doubt Charlie saw it."

"My God." Suzannah walked over and laid her hand on her client's arm. "Why are you fighting this, then? It works for us in every conceivable sense."

"Because my gut tells me Charlie didn't do it."

"Because of Night Arrow?" She bit her lip. "You know, Justin, I'm beginning to think you really are a little obsessed by that story."

"I freely admit it. Like I said, it's infectious. Not just to me. To lots of people. My friend at SPIN, for example. Remember?"

"The girl in the envelope?"

He chuckled. "Let's hope not. But yeah, the girl whose number is in the envelope. She's hot about Night Arrow. And so is my friend Miranda. I guarantee you there are other people out there jonesing for it, too, and not all of them are good guys like us."

"Still..."

"You said it yourself yesterday," he reminded her.

"The prime suspect in Gia's murder is Mia, because Mia stood to inherit the fortune. Charlie is a possibility, but he's a long shot for several reasons, the big one being he probably never held a gun in his life. And had no way of accessing Gia's bedroom." Justin took a deep breath. "Once we start admitting it probably wasn't Charlie, then we have to consider the possibility that both deaths—Gia's and Horace's—were connected to the secret projects handled by Masterson Enterprises."

"I disagree. Given Mr. Jones's statement, we can safely say that Charlie probably killed Horace. He knew Horace wanted to die. He wanted to help people like Horace. And he didn't have any other connection to this town—no reason to be here except to kill Horace."

Justin rubbed his eyes. "I'd agree with that if Gia were still alive. But Gia dying within weeks of her father's death? Doesn't that tell you something? It can't be a coincidence."

"True." Suzannah sifted through a stack of Masterson family photos. "You said yesterday Gia was depressed. Felt like a stranger in her own skin. And she had lost the great love of her life, aka Daddy Dearest. Is it possible she shot herself?"

"The gun was fired at very close range, but she would have had to hold it at a truly weird angle for the bullet to enter the way it did."

"But still…?"

"The coroner ruled out suicide. And I agree with him."

"Wow, déjà vu," Suzannah murmured, distracted by a picture she had just found of Horace Masterson and his wife Julia in each other's arms on their wedding day. "Do you know who these two remind me of? You and Mia, yesterday at her place."

"Huh?" Justin took the photo from Suzannah and studied it. "I get how Mia looks like Julia—that's a given. But I don't look anything like Horace."

"It's the pose. See how Julia has her arms around his neck? But he's barely touching her? Even then, she was the loving one, he was aloof. Like you two yesterday. Plus—" she gave her client a teasing smile "—you look more like him than you think. The same long, lean body. The same confident posture. If I needed any more proof that the Masterson girls had a crush on Daddy, this would be it. They both wanted to sleep with you because you reminded them of Horace."

"Okay, *stop* saying that. You're creeping me out."

Laughing, Suzannah hoisted herself up onto the counter to sit, dangling her legs. "Okay, back to the Charlie-killed-Horace scenario. As long as Dad was still in a coma, Mia didn't dare make a move against Gia because she would be the prime—and *only*—suspect. But after Horace was killed by the Angel, Mia felt she could get away with killing Gia, thereby inheriting the Masterson fortune. But just in case Charlie surfaced and had an alibi for killing Horace, Mia also framed *you* as a backup suspect."

Justin grinned. "So you can prove categorically that Mia did it? Yet five minutes ago you proved beyond a shadow of a doubt that Charlie did it?"

She laughed. "That's right. No jury in the world could find you guilty beyond a reasonable doubt when there are two other prime suspects with actual motives running around loose."

His eyes clouded. "You keep trying to come up with a defense for me. But I don't care about *any* of that. I want to solve the murders, not defend myself."

"What if we can *never* solve them? At least you'll be free to save the world in future cases. Not to mention flirt with its women."

He scowled as though completely frustrated. Then he surprised her by saying, "Do Derek Seldon now."

"Hmm?"

"Let's hear you analyze him. Motive, opportunity, et cetera."

"That's easy. Derek and Mia secretly got back together—or never really split up in the first place. They were just biding their time, hoping Horace would die. In the meantime, Mia used Cynthia's accident to get back into Gia's heart. To become the beneficiary of her will. Then the Angel of Mercy came along and advanced their timeline. So they framed Charlie for Horace's murder, then framed you for Gia's. They'll wait a decent time, then pretend to rediscover each other, get married and remerge the companies. That way Derek vindicates his own father, and Mia gets the ultimate revenge against *her* dear old dad."

"Sounds plausible," Justin admitted. "Except for the fact that I've interviewed Derek a couple of times. He's pretty bland. Not my idea of a mastermind."

"Maybe *she's* the brains," Suzannah suggested, adding with a laugh, "Just kidding."

Justin grinned. "She's no genius, that's for sure. Neither is Charlie, though."

"But Agent X is?" Jumping to the floor, she walked over to her client and stroked his handsome cheek. "Give it up, Justin. Your theory doesn't work anymore. If Agent X is so smart, he would have known he'd lose any chance of getting Night Arrow if he killed Gia. Her murder and the resulting scandal ensured that the government would never award the project to Masterson Enterprises."

Justin rested his hands on her hips, pulling her to within inches of himself. "Yeah, I know. But maybe that's why he framed me. To discredit me. I'm the one who kept insisting that Masterson's murder was something ominous, instead of the benign act of a misguided angel. Agent X was hoping that I'd get arrested and would confess to self-defense just to save my job. Then all the scandals would evaporate—just a mercy killing and a justified homicide. And Night Arrow would go to Masterson Enterprises."

"And then?" Suzannah murmured, trying to ignore the nearness of his body yet also unwilling to pull away from it. "How does that put the spy closer to obtaining it?"

Justin shrugged. "He's in league with Derek? Or with Mia? Or he has someone on the inside at the company but needed Gia out of the way because she was so involved and aware? I don't know. It doesn't fit. Not exactly."

"It doesn't fit at all," Suzannah insisted. "Not compared to all the other models we've come up with. Especially the sibling-rivalry scenario."

Justin shook his head. "No way did Mia kill Gia."

"So we're back where we started."

"Yeah, I guess so." He locked gazes with her. "Okay. Now for the pièce de résistance."

"Pardon?"

"You've done all the other suspects. Now do me. And keep in mind," he added solemnly, dropping his hands from her waist, "Mia claims to love me. Wants to get together with me someday, maybe permanently. I'd say that gave me a helluva a motive to kill Gia, wouldn't you?"

## Chapter 5

"Justin..." Suzannah sighed, wishing she could banish the frustration in his blazing blue eyes. "No one thinks you murdered Gia. Not even the D.A. You said yourself, he's just prosecuting you to force you to admit it was self-defense."

"Until he talks to Mia and she tells him how she feels about me. And implies that she and I have a future together. If I were the D.A.—or a juror—I'd find that pretty damning."

Suzannah pursed her lips, impressed. "Maybe that's why she said it."

"Huh?"

"We both assumed she was being sincere. But maybe she was just trying to frame you again. Right? To give you a financial motive for murdering Gia, since the self-defense frame didn't work out like she planned."

Justin's expression brightened. "How did I miss that? You're right! She was trying pretty hard to—what?—alienate you from me? Or just flat-out frame me? But wouldn't that implicate her at the same time?"

Suzannah covered her face with her hands. "Now I'm totally confused."

"Me, too," he admitted. "I think we need a break. Less talking, more touching," he added, reaching mischievously for her waist again.

"Don't make me call Judge Taylor on you," she warned, jumping backward, then eyeing him sternly. "Play with your dog for a while. I'll go buy some more puppy food. Do you want me to pick up anything for you at the grocery store?"

"Candy, cookies and ice cream?"

"Troublemaker." She flashed a fond smile. "I was wrong when I called you the apple to my Eve. You're actually the devil himself, trying to tempt me every way you can."

"How'm I doing?"

"I'm a rock, remember?" She grabbed her purse off the coatrack, then turned and gave him another stern look. "Don't let your dog destroy my apartment. Don't snoop. And *don't* answer my phone. I'll be back before you know it."

Puppy food and teething biscuits for Murphy, sub sandwiches for herself and Justin and ingredients for root-beer floats...

"I guess you *are* Eve after all," Suzannah taunted herself as she exited the market and headed for her car, which was parked in the lot that served both her law firm's building and the grocery store. The monthly fee she paid for this spot was a bargain compared to a covered space in the adjacent four-story parking structure where most of her colleagues parked. And it worked better for her, given her habit of hitting the market nightly after work.

Setting her two overstuffed grocery bags on the hood of her car, she began digging in her purse for her keys. "So what if you gave in to a little sweet-tooth temptation? That's better than jumping into bed with a client, right?"

She laughed at herself, remembering how close she had come to buying a bottle of champagne to celebrate the conclusions they had reached about the case on the wipe-off board. Suzannah was now convinced that there were so many other suspects running around with strong motives to kill Gia, no jury in the world would convict Justin. Of course, her client wouldn't be satisfied until they had actually solved the case. But for Suzannah, acquittal was the victory that counted.

*And then what?* she asked herself warily. *You and Justin hit the sheets? Isn't that what you really want to celebrate? The way he makes you feel? It's crazy, Suzannah! Not to mention dangerous. So snap out of it, will you?*

Just as she located her key chain, a pinpoint of bright light flashed across her eyes, as if a mirror had caught a sunbeam and redirected it straight at her. Startled, she looked up and saw a man standing on the rooftop of the parking structure. For just an instant she thought the guy was Justin, so much so that she started to wave.

But she stopped herself because she knew it couldn't be him. He was at her apartment playing with the dog.

Wasn't he?

The man was watching her through a pair of binoculars, and she stared back, completely confused. He was wearing a baseball cap and nicely fitted jeans. He was also wearing a brown leather bomber jacket exactly like Justin's, but the binoculars obscured his features so completely she simply couldn't tell who it was.

At least not for sure.

If it were Justin, he would have waved to her by now, wouldn't he? Even if he hadn't intended for her to catch him following her, he'd do something now to acknowledge her.

Wouldn't he?

She was about to call out to him, when the man moved. Reaching his hand under his jacket, he pulled out a jet-black, long-barreled firearm. Then, to her shock, he aimed it right at her.

Shrieking, she dived to the pavement just as two bullets whizzed overhead, hitting the grocery bags. The giant bottle of root beer exploded all over the hood of her car. Suzannah scrambled for the cover of a nearby pickup truck, her chest tight with fear, her blood pumping with adrenaline. There was no one else around—just her and the shooter—and a squeal of tires from the direction of the parking structure told her *he* was already fleeing the scene.

Digging into her purse again, she found her cell phone. Then she dared to peek around the corner of the truck, just to be sure the man was no longer in sight.

*He thinks you're calling 911,* she told herself shakily. *So do it! He's getting away!*

Her hands were trembling, so she allowed herself a moment to close her eyes, lean against the truck and calm her racing heart. She hoped that in the meantime a witness would come running to her assistance, but the shots hadn't been noisy enough to attract attention, and this part of the lot was never busy in the afternoon. Everyone from the firm who used it was already back from lunch and wouldn't be out and about until well after six o'clock, which was also the time grocery shoppers would arrive in droves. For now, the smattering of early-bird customers were using spaces much closer to the market.

After a few more deep breaths, Suzannah managed to steady her hands, but still she wasn't dialing the phone. Not yet. Not until she knew what she was going to say.

*Hello, police? A man who looks exactly like my client just tried to kill me....*

She couldn't make that call. Not yet, at least. Not until she had discussed it with Justin.

*Then call him,* she advised herself, but again her fingers wouldn't dial the number. And again she knew why.

What if Justin didn't answer? Would that mean he wasn't there? Or he was taking the puppy out for a walk? Or he was in the bathroom? Or maybe just that he was following *her* instructions not to answer her phone?

And if he did answer, what if he then insisted on calling 911 before she was ready to face the police and their questions?

"Where's the wipe-off board when you really need it?" she asked herself unhappily. "You need a list of suspects who might want to impersonate Justin, either to hurt you or just to make you afraid of your own client. And you need to put Justin himself on that list or you're an idiot. Because that man really did look like him."

*But he didn't act like him. Because Justin Russo would never shoot you. He has no reason to shoot you! Even if he's been lying to you and he really did kill Gia, you're on his side. You've been one hundred percent loyal. Never questioned his innocence, not even for a second...*

Now she really didn't have a choice but to question it. Because someone had just tried to shoot her.

Heaving a miserable sigh, she stuck her phone back in her purse, then struggled to her feet. Still shaky, she managed to salvage the sack of puppy food from the soaking wet grocery bags before throwing them and their tainted contents into a nearby trash can, all the while keeping one eye on the roof of the parking structure. Then she wiped off her car with a beach towel she kept in the trunk, and after a long, wary glare to ensure that her assailant had indeed fled the scene, she put her Lexus into gear and departed, as well.

"Jeez! We were just about to send out a search party, weren't we, Murf?" Justin scolded her from the living room as he jumped to his feet and switched off the television. "You want me to go down to the car and get the stuff?"

"This is all I have." Suzannah held up the bag of

puppy food, then walked into the kitchen and dropped it on the counter.

"You're kidding? You really *are* tough. Food for the dog but none for the humans?"

Scooping up the puppy, who had been nipping at her heels, she murmured, "Something happened, Justin."

He stared for a moment, then whispered, "Shit" and walked over to her, cupping her chin in his hand, then staring directly into her eyes. "Are you okay? Was it some sort of accident?"

When she bit her lip, his gaze went steely gray. "Talk to me. No, wait." He took Murphy from her and deposited him in his box. Then he was back, resting his hands on her shoulders. "You okay?"

"I'm fine now," she murmured, trying not to notice how safe his touch made her feel. It would be so easy to let him take care of her. To melt against him, admitting how frightened she had been, how glad she was to be in his arms.

Shaking off the dangerous impulse, she told him quickly, "Someone took a shot at me. I don't know if they were trying to kill me or just scare me—"

"A *shot?* You mean, with a gun?" His left hand cupped her chin again, almost roughly this time. "When? Where? Are you okay?"

"I'm fine. They missed me. On purpose, I think." She pulled free and tried to smile. "They killed the root beer, though."

"Someone takes an effing shot at you and you're cracking jokes?" His eyes narrowed. "Are you in shock or something? What did the cops say? Were there witnesses? Why didn't you call me right away? Jeez, Suzannah, you could've been killed."

"Tell me about it." She bit her lip, pleased with his incoherent, frustrated-hero reaction. It was perfect. If she had needed any more reassurance he wasn't the man in the bomber jacket, this was it. "The good news is, I think he missed me on purpose. The bad news is…well, obviously he used real bullets."

Justin eyed her in frustration. "Something's not tracking. How do you know he missed you on purpose? He got the root beer, which presumably was nearby. Right?" He interrupted himself to ask, "We're sure it was a 'he'? Not a woman?"

"We're sure." She touched his cheek. "Sit down, okay?"

"Nope. But you should." He pulled her by the hand to the couch, and once she had settled down, he retrieved Murphy and deposited him in her lap, instructing the puppy with a wry smile, "Protect her, stupid. That's your job. *My* job, too. Apparently we suck."

Suzannah cuddled the ball of fur and was touched when the puppy licked her face gently as though sensing how confused and vulnerable she felt.

Justin planted himself in front of her. "If you don't want to go over it again, I can get the details from the cops. I should do that anyway, actually. Do you have the investigating officer's number handy?" Before she could respond, he interrupted himself to ask, "Why didn't someone call me? You told them I was FBI, right?"

"I didn't call the police. I wanted to talk to you first."

He stared, his expression blank for a second before

becoming completely incredulous. "You left the scene? To talk to *me?* I'm flattered, I guess, but—"

"The shooter impersonated you. I think he missed on purpose. I think he *wanted* me to call the police." She bit her lip, then explained, "They keep trying to frame you, right? Well, this was part of that. *That's* why I needed to talk to you first."

Justin came over to the sofa and sat next to her, draping his arm around her shoulder and giving it a squeeze. "Suzy? Are you in shock?"

"Cut it out." She wriggled away, genuinely smiling for the first time since she spotted the shooter on the rooftop. "Pay attention."

"How does someone impersonate me?"

"By wearing a jacket like yours. And hiding his hair with a baseball cap. And he covered his face, too. With binoculars. Things like that."

"Maybe you should just start at the beginning."

She nodded, then told him the whole story, complete with exploding root beer.

"So?" His tone was gentle. "You got rid of the evidence? Threw it away? Why?"

"Because…well, because there would have been questions. The shooter wanted the evidence to lead the cops to *you.* To further discredit you."

"I hate this asshole," Justin whispered. "He could have killed you. And for what?"

"He never intended to hit me."

"Maybe not, but what if he had miscalculated? No one's *that* good a shot." He cocked his head to the side. "Can you describe the weapon?"

"It was long and black. And it made more of a popping sound than a real blast."

"Like an air rifle?"

"I think it was too short to be a rifle. Although it was longer than the guns I've seen on TV."

"Was it fitted with a silencer?"

"How would I know?" she demanded. "It looked dangerous, so I hit the dirt."

"Smart move." Justin squeezed her shoulders again. "We need to call the cops right away. I understand why you protected me, but it's not necessary. There's no way they'll believe I took a shot at you. What would be my motive?"

"That I was getting too close to the truth? Figuring out that you really *did* kill Gia? We know that's not true, but they don't."

"Interesting theory, but it doesn't hold up. I'm a great shot. If I wanted to hit someone, I would. And no way would I let the target get a look at me first. I'm a professional. So they'd realize it couldn't have been me."

"True, although they might think you *wanted* me to survive and *wanted* me to see you. So I'd corroborate your story that someone was trying to frame you." She laughed self-consciously. "I guess you're right. The police probably wouldn't have held you for long. But I didn't want to take the chance. Period."

"Suzannah," he said firmly, "don't let loyalty to me override common sense. You *have* to report this. If you don't, I will."

Stroking his tensed jaw, she murmured, "This is my decision. To postpone reporting it until I've completely thought it through. That's better than lying, isn't it? Which is what you'll force me to do if *you* report it."

Justin rubbed his eyes, repeating unhappily, "I *hate* this guy. He killed Gia and he could've killed you too. I swear, Suzy, I never would have dragged you into this case if I'd known there was any chance they'd come after you. It's nuts!" He jumped up and began to pace. "I always made fun of SPIN for insisting on anonymity for the spinners, but now I get it. Guys like me can't have women like you in our lives. It makes us vulnerable and it puts *you* at risk."

"I think you're overreacting."

He shook his head. Then he admitted, "You're right about one thing. They've got no reason to actually kill you. They wanted to turn you against me. They figure if you told the judge you were scared of me, then he'd throw me in jail for sure. That would get me off their trail. Maybe permanently, because my career would be toast."

"But it didn't work," she reminded him. "I'm not going to tell the judge. And the good news is, we now have a little more information about the man who killed Gia. For one thing, like you said, we know it *was* a man. There's no disguise in the world that could make Mia look that much like you. So if she's involved, she's got a male partner. And he's fairly tall and well built."

Justin's scowl faded. "True. And we also know it's not Charlie Parrish. He's medium height at best. And slender. You're sure from the angle you saw him that it wasn't a small man?"

"Pretty sure." She eyed him hopefully. "What about Derek Seldon?"

"A definite possibility. His hair is curly and black, but the hat took care of that. And he's older than I am, but at a distance he could pass for my age. I'd be shocked if he could pull it off mentally, though. He didn't seem like the type. And I don't remember seeing anything in his profile about any expertise with guns."

"That's a good point," Suzannah mused. "About his having the guts, I mean. How many guys—well built or not—could impersonate someone in public and then fire a weapon at another human being? It would take nerves of steel and training or experience, right?" She gave him a teasing smile. "Do you know what that means?"

"That you think it was me?"

"No, silly. It means I might just be ready to buy into your foreign-agent theory. A professional spy who wants our government secrets and targeted Masterson Enterprises as the perfect source. I'm not quite sure why he's still at it, given the fact that the company's reputation has been trashed by all the scandals. But maybe he hopes the government will start contracting with them again if he can pin everything on you and the Angel."

"Yeah." Justin nodded intently. "That makes sense. Good old Agent X, right?"

"Except it wasn't really Night Arrow he cared about. Just government secrets in general."

"Don't kid yourself. He wanted Night Arrow. I'll bet it still kills him that Masterson Enterprises lost that contract and he'll have to settle for other, less exciting projects if he manages to get control of the company someday."

Suzannah laughed. "I guess it's a good thing you're such a fanatic on the subject. It made you tenacious about your investigation, and now it turns out you were probably right."

"Probably?" he asked with a challenging smile.

"Let's just say we need more proof. For one thing, we need to check out every single guy Mia has had anything to do with for the last few years. It's possible Agent X planned to use her to infiltrate the company after he got Gia out of the way."

"I've already done that," Justin assured her. "But you're welcome to look at my notes. Maybe you'll find something I missed. And we can't completely dismiss Derek yet either. He could be in league with the shooter."

"I'd like to interview him. Do you think he'd agree?"

"He cooperated in the past, but just to provide background on the history of Masterson Enterprises. If he realizes he's a suspect, he might not be so eager." Justin pursed his lips. "One thing was clear. Derek has wanted for years to reunite his half of the old company with Masterson's. And he's got the money to make it happen."

"And enough to hire someone—a professional, I mean—to kill Horace and Gia? And then to take a fake shot at me?"

"Yeah, he's got enough for that." Justin's eyes flashed with steely-gray determination. "Looks like we've got our work cut out for us, counselor."

"I'll say one thing for being a skinny heiress—it'll get you some first-class dates," Suzannah told Justin as she closed the last Mia file and pushed it away. "Royalty, rich guys, movie stars, rodeo hunks—she's had quite a time since she came home. And I can't even imagine what Gia's dance card looked like. She was an heiress plus she had a forty-inch chest to go with her twenty-inch waist. They must have been lining up for her."

"She didn't socialize the way Mia did. She was more fragile. Sweeter. A little lost despite all the money and power."

"Sweet? She turned her back on her own sister," Suzannah reminded him, then she held up her hand to ward off any further defense of Gia. "I know, I know. She was a great gal deep down inside. Spare me."

He laughed. "If I didn't know better, I'd think you were jealous."

"Of what? She only cuddled with you because your body reminded her of Daddy's."

"Ugh, I'm begging you. *Stop* saying that."

Suzannah laughed as she began clearing away the remnants of their dinner, which had consisted of pizza and salads. "Too bad the root beer got shot. I was really looking forward to those floats."

"Don't remind me," Justin muttered. "Wait till I get my hands on that jerk."

"It's a good thing Murf will be here to protect me tonight," Suzannah said, scooping up the sleepy puppy and burying her face in his fur.

"And just in case he needs backup, I'll stick around, too."

She looked up, surprised and slightly embarrassed. "That's not necessary."

"You think I'm going to leave you here with a can of mace and a puppy after what happened today?"

She grimaced. "I don't think it's a good idea for you

to stay, Justin. For one thing, the judge might ask me where you sleep at night. He's just enough of a creep to do that, you know. Plus, the authorities—local and federal—might still be watching us. It would look bad." She gave him a halfhearted smile. "It's sweet of you to offer, but I think you'd better go."

"If the judge asks, you'll tell him I slept on the sofa. If they want to believe we're fooling around, it won't really matter where I spend the night. They'll think we're doing it during the day, right? And anyway, fuck 'em. It's none of their business."

She chewed her lip, then told him bluntly, "I still think you should go. It's cleaner. More professional. I've got a reputation to protect, and honestly I feel perfectly safe. If anything happens—the slightest noise or whatever—I'll call you right away. How's that?"

"I'm staying," he said with a cheerful shrug. "If you're worried about your honor, lock the bedroom door. Murf and I will camp out here and watch the game. Right, boy? Unless—" The agent's smile faded. "Unless you're afraid to have me here. Is that it?"

"Of course not."

His expression was grim, as though all the strain from the past few days had finally caught up with him. "I'd never hurt you, Suzannah. But if you don't feel safe with me here—if that's why you want me to go—"

"Justin..." She locked gazes with him, wanting to reassure him but also understanding that he needed more than platitudes. He needed to be sure that *she* was sure.

And he wasn't the only one who would eventually ask her such questions. Noelle would ask—in fact, she'd have a fit if she heard Justin had spent the night when there was any chance at all he might have been the shooter. Suzannah's parents would be aghast, too. So would anyone else who cared about her.

So she forced herself to maintain eye contact while she worked it through her brain, her heart and her gut. And to her relief, all votes were in Justin's favor, so she exhaled sharply and walked over to him, slipping her hands behind his neck and pulling his head down for a long, reassuring kiss.

His hands gripped her waist, drawing her body against his as he returned the kiss with hungry, almost overpowering intensity. Then his arms surrounded her, hugging her close. Protecting her. Banishing the specter of the assault.

She hadn't realized until that moment how much she needed this. Needed *him*. And so she clung to him, kissing him mindlessly, allowing him to own her, at least for a few moments.

Then she remembered who he was—who *she* was—and she forced herself to step back from him, then eyed him sternly. "I don't want to hear another word about it. Agreed?"

He nodded, his blue eyes blazing, his hands hanging uselessly at his sides.

"Good, then I'm going to bed. The sofa folds out, and there's bedding in the trunk, so make yourself comfortable. You and Murf can play or watch TV. Just try not to make a mess. And FYI? I *am* locking the bedroom door. So…" She strode across the room, pausing in the doorway long enough to say, "Good night. I'll see you both in the morning."

\* \* \*

As soon as the bedroom door was closed, she leaned against it and shuddered in confused disbelief. She hadn't intended to kiss him—not tonight, not ever—but the situation had more or less demanded it. How else could she have reassured the poor guy so effectively?

*And it was definitely effective,* she mocked herself. *Nice going, Eve.*

After her bold claim that she was the perfect lawyer for Justin because of her ability to resist him, she had practically attacked him. And from the responses of his body—his arms, his mouth, his eyes—she knew he had been wanting to grab her and devour her from the moment he first heard about the shooting.

And she had wanted it, too.

The strain of the last few days—first with Judge Taylor and then with the bullets whizzing by her head—had caught up with her. Delayed stress reaction, driving her into his arms. A client's arms! But not just any client. A trained professional with a gun. She had craved that sense of absolute security. And if that need had mingled with repressed sexual attraction—just for a moment or two—she wasn't going to beat herself up over it.

She could just imagine what Noelle would say about all this, but almost as quickly as she picked up the phone, she reconsidered sharing the day's events. As confident as Suzannah now was that Justin wasn't the shooter, she couldn't expect her overprotective friend to accept that assessment so easily. It was better not to mention the shooting yet and to let Noelle assume that Justin had gone back to the hotel.

She still made the call, but only for a quick Sperminator update.

"Any chance you two will patch things up?" she asked her friend casually.

"We'll see. It'll take some serious groveling on his part," Noelle predicted. "And I said a couple of things that were a little harsh, so I might have to apologize, too. But him first. I miss him a little, but I don't think he's Mr. Right or anything, so..." She cleared her throat. "What about *your* new guy? Has he been putting the moves on you?"

"No. He flirts a lot, but that's just his style. He gave me a puppy—don't ask me what I'm going to do about *that,* but..." Suzannah laughed self-consciously. "It's going well. He's innocent, so my job's pretty easy."

"A puppy?"

"Remember the one I told you about? At the cleaner's? I mentioned it to him, and the goof went and got him for me. Obviously I'm not ready for a dog. I'll probably send him with Justin when he leaves. But meanwhile it's kind of fun. He's so cute."

"The dog? Or the client?"

"Very funny."

"What about the presentation?"

"The what?"

Noelle snorted. "Earth to Suzannah! You're leaving for Hawaii on Sunday. I thought the fate of the Twelve-Year Plan was riding on how well you did at the conference. Has this guy changed all that?"

"Of course not. I can give that speech in my sleep, I know the subject so well." She scowled, admitting that Noelle had hit a nerve. "I'll work on it tomorrow."

"Unless you're too busy playing fetch with your client," Noelle said, her tone teasing. "Remember, I talked to him on the phone. If he can be that charming long-distance, I'm guessing he's deadly at close range."

*Deadly at close range...*

Suzannah winced.

"So?" Noelle asked. "Do you want to go out? It's still early. We could catch a movie. Or I could just pick up evil sweets and come over to meet the puppy."

Suzannah faked a yawn. "Let's do it tomorrow, okay? I'm beat."

"Sure." Noelle's voice warmed. "Just be careful over there, will ya? We're giving this Russo character some slack because he's a sexy FBI agent, but the truth is, he's also a murder suspect. Right?"

"Right."

"We'd feel pretty stupid if it turned out he really did shoot that rich girl. Maybe you shouldn't let him hang around your apartment so much."

"He's harmless."

"Yeah, right," Noelle drawled. "Anyway, get some sleep. I'll call you tomorrow about that movie. Nighty-night, Suzannah."

"Nighty-night," Suzannah replied without thinking. It was only after she had hung up that she realized why the endearment bothered her.

"Nighty-night" was the reassuring little bedtime phrase Suzannah's grandmother had used to comfort them both during their childhood. They rarely said it these days, and she suspected Noelle's use of it was a sign that her friend was worried about her.

*We'd feel pretty stupid if it turned out he really did shoot that rich girl....*

Suzannah now knew that Noelle would make a huge deal out of the shooting. She'd think Justin was dangerous, when the truth was just the opposite. Somehow Justin was the one in danger here, not just of being framed or convicted but maybe something worse. And for some cosmically screwed-up reason, it was up to Suzannah to make sure everything turned out okay.

A burst of playful barking from the other side of the door made her sigh, but she resisted the temptation to rejoin her rambunctious houseguests.

Because somebody had to be the adult. Which meant she had to stop feeling sorry for herself over the shooting. And she *definitely* had to stop lusting after Justin.

The first step, she knew, was to get a good night's sleep, so she climbed into bed and instructed herself to think about something restful.

*Hawaii, for instance. You'll be there in less than a week! Too bad Justin can't come, too, but they probably don't want him leaving the state. Plus, he'll have to watch Murf. Plus, well, you know what would happen....*

She half expected to dream about herself and Justin having hot sex on a secluded beach, but a more familiar sight was waiting for her as she dozed off, and she almost groaned in her sleep from frustration.

Again? Why tonight? She hadn't really screwed anything up, had she? Wasn't that usually when they appeared?

But there they were. The Inquisition, as she had dubbed them over the years. Five somber accusers seated in a row across a table from Suzannah, who was fumbling with a stack of papers that kept sliding to the floor.

Ordinarily the panel would have been interrogating her about the defects in her high school record. But tonight they were wearing judicial robes, which didn't make any sense, given the usual context of this dream.

And worse, one of the inquisitors looked just like Judge Taylor!

"So, Suzy e-lawyer," he was saying, his scowl deep and familiar. "Any chance you're competent today?" Eyeing her nightshirt, he added contemptuously, "Didn't they teach you how to dress in law school?"

"I'm sorry, Your Honor. I didn't know you'd be here."

"Where is your client? Didn't I order you to watch him? But you didn't, did you? And now he's dead."

*"What?"* Suzannah felt her stomach cramp. "He is not!"

"If you had taken biology when everyone else took it, you'd be able to recognize a dead body," a woman on the panel said with a sneer. Then she pointed to a corpse that was covered by a white sheet on a nearby stretcher.

The patient's face wasn't visible, but Suzannah knew instinctively that it was a man—a *dead* man. And despite a sense of foreboding, she insisted, "That can't be Justin."

"See for yourself," the judge ordered her. Then, with a maniacal flourish, he grabbed the sheet and ripped it away, revealing a bloody, mangled corpse.

## Chapter 6

"Hey, Counselor. How's the presentation coming?"

"Great, thanks," Suzannah answered without looking up from her laptop. "Find anything in that box of letters your friend sent over to you?"

"Not yet."

She gave him a quick sympathetic smile, then quickly lowered her eyes back to the computer screen, wondering how she was ever going to make it through the day. And even if she did, there was her girls' night out with Noelle to worry about.

An endless parade of nightmares had left her completely drained. First Justin had been mutilated. Then he had been the mutila*tor*, wielding a black machine gun, an evil grin on his face. Then he had been dead again. By morning, she truly wasn't sure which was worse—evil Justin or dead Justin. But either way, she had found herself dreading another day with him.

Fortunately a messenger had knocked on the front door while Suzannah was still in bed, and by the time she had dressed and joined her houseguest, he was eagerly sorting through a box of documents. He explained that Charlie Parrish's mother had found some letters in a basement cupboard and had turned them over to the FBI, where one of Justin's buddies had discreetly made these copies.

Suzannah had seized upon the opportunity to suggest that they work separately for a change, citing her need to make some progress on her Hawaiian speech. She had expected Justin to protest, but he had surprised her by agreeing almost too readily. She decided not to analyze the reaction, just to appreciate it, and while she chatted with him lightly from time to time, she remained as disengaged as possible.

The puppy wasn't quite as easy to discourage, and after a while Suzannah just gave in to him, cuddling him on her lap as she made notes on her computer. It was amazing to her how much comfort his sloppy kisses and adoring stare could give her, and she warned herself not to get too attached. She still hadn't decided whether to keep him and suspected he was better off without her anyway. Once the case was over, Justin and Murphy could and would disappear from her life and she'd get back on track. Noelle was right about that at least—neglecting the Twelve-Year Plan at this point, almost ten years into it, was foolish, especially considering she didn't have a new plan to take its place.

Out of the corner of her eye she saw Justin wander

into the kitchen, where he began making sandwiches. That was a good sign. She had made it through the morning at least. In fact, a glance at the clock showed her it was already one o'clock. She wondered if she dared take a nap. She definitely needed one after her sleepless night.

Murphy seemed to have the same idea, she noted with a smile as he began snoring loudly. Careful not to disturb him, she moved him onto the pillow in the box that had become his unofficial doghouse. "Nighty-night, Murf," she whispered. Then she returned to her seat, rubbed her eyes and turned her attention back to the laptop screen.

"So?" Justin carried a platter filled with peanut-butter-and-jam sandwiches over to the brass trunk between the sofa and the chairs. Then he sat next to Suzannah. "Want to talk about it?"

"My presentation?"

"Come on, Suzy." He pushed the save button on her keyboard, then moved the computer onto the trunk. "Something's been bothering you all day. Let's hear it."

Before she could invent an excuse, he suggested, "I know I come on too strong sometimes. If you're upset about the kiss—"

"I'm the one who kissed *you*, remember?"

"It felt pretty mutual." He rested his arm on the cushion behind her shoulders. "I know you didn't want our relationship to go in that direction—"

"It was a platonic kiss," she reminded him weakly. "My way of showing you I wasn't afraid to let you stay here."

"I guess we define *platonic* differently."

"Justin—"

"Shh." He touched his finger to her lips. "It was a great kiss. But the point I'm trying to make is, you don't need to worry about it."

"I know. But thanks."

"So?" His eyes clouded. "You're upset about something else? That's what I was afraid of. You looked like shit this morning, comparatively speaking. I wanted to believe you couldn't sleep because you were having hot thoughts about me, but that's not it, right? So…"

She grimaced, knowing that he wasn't going to let it go, so she decided to give him some—but not all—of the information he wanted. "I had nightmares. Not that it's any of your business."

"About what? The shooting?"

"I guess so. It was a little more oblique. Judge Taylor was yelling at me, accusing me of not taking care of you. And you were dead." She didn't have to pretend to shudder. "It was awful. And I must have had it five or six times, all with different gruesome variations."

He squeezed her shoulders gently. "You should have woken me up."

"I had a suspicion you and I defined *platonic* differently, so I didn't dare," she quipped. "But it was nice knowing you and Murphy were out here. And *really* nice knowing you weren't dead."

"Better dead than guilty though. Right?"

"Don't be silly."

"Admit it, Suzannah." His tone had grown solemn. "Something happened yesterday. To you *and* to me. We had to confront our worst fears."

The observation surprised her. "What are you talking about?"

"You trusted me right from the start. Instinctively. Even though you aren't a fan of instinct or spontaneity or impulse. If you had been wrong—if I turned out to be a murderer—your whole self-image would have crumbled. You'd be just like your parents—an impulsive, self-indulgent screwup."

She couldn't help being fascinated by the bizarre theory. "That's my worst fear?"

"Absolutely."

"And? What's yours?"

His voice grew hoarse. "That I can't have a meaningful relationship. With a woman, I mean. As more than a distraction."

"That's silly. You and the girl in the envelope—"

"Yeah. *There's* a healthy relationship," he drawled. Then his eyes clouded. "I meant what I said yesterday. I'm glad now that SPIN demands anonymity. It probably keeps Essie safe. Plus, I always knew she wanted someone more solid than me, so I never really saw it going any further than just cyber-friendship. But with you, I started believing I could have it all. A girl to work with. To trust with my secrets. My life. Even with the no-sex policy temporarily in place, it's been amazing."

Suzannah didn't dare show how deeply he had touched her, so she arched an eyebrow and repeated weakly, "*Temporarily* in place?"

"Man, I love it when you do that."

A shudder of confusion shot through her body, and

she decided they need a quick change of subject. "You know what you need, Justin?"

"Oh, yeah. Definitely."

"Be serious. You need a twelve-year plan of your own. Something to transition you from your life of danger and bachelorhood to something more domestic. But you don't really have twelve years—you're thirty-four, right?—so maybe a three-year plan."

"Three years?"

She took a second to study his handsome face and toned body before answering. Did she dare encourage this guy to settle down? Didn't the women of the world need him?

But he wasn't just a hunk. He was a fine man, with noble, loving tendencies, so she told him softly, "I know you like spontaneity, but some things in life are just too important—and too fragile—to leave to chance. You need to make some gradual but important lifestyle choices. Start taking other assignments—less dangerous ones—occasionally. According to your file, you're as bad as my parents, never staying in one place for more than a few months. That has to change. You need to put down some roots. Become part of a community."

"When you describe it like that, it sounds kinda dull."

Suzannah rolled her eyes. "Obviously you're not ready yet. You want all the fun of a relationship but none of the hard work. That's why your phone friendship with the spinner worked so perfectly for you. Ninety percent fantasy, with no strings attached."

"What about you? You're not exactly on a domestic track yourself," he accused her.

"Sure I am. The whole point of the Twelve-Year Plan is to get me into a high-paying corporate job with stable hours. Then I'll begin phase two—joining some clubs, buying a house, meeting solid guys, dating." She smiled. "I was supposed to get a dog and a cat in that phase, but if things work out for me in Hawaii—if I leave there with a job offer—then I'll keep Murf."

"Otherwise?"

"Otherwise, he's all yours."

"Man, you really are tough," he murmured. Then he flashed a provocative smile. "You know what *you* really need?"

"Good Lord, this should be interesting." She laughed in spite of herself. "What do I need?"

"A little Night Arrow. Come on." He stood, then gestured to her to do likewise as he walked over to the CD player. In an instant the air was filled with slow, sexy prom music. "You know the drill. This stuff is top secret. I can only discuss it under tight security measures."

"You already told me all about it," she reminded him with a wistful smile.

"Did I? Are you sure? Maybe I saved the best part for last."

Something in his tone implied he might actually be telling the truth. And even if he wasn't, she couldn't really turn down a chance to dance with him again. Life was simply too short—and too fragile, as she had learned in that parking lot—not to enjoy a little harmless body contact with a brave, noble hunk along the way. He had proven to her during their kiss that he wouldn't take advantage of her. And she had proven to herself that she wouldn't let things go too far. So...

Feeling slightly giddy, she stepped into his arms and they began to sway together. Then he murmured into her hair, "Did I tell you Night Arrow was the stuff of legends?"

She snuggled against him. "Uh-huh."

"Did I mention the magic potion?"

"Uh-huh."

"And did I tell you my how my friend Miranda tried it? And she claims it really worked?"

"Yes, Justin." Looking up reluctantly, Suzannah whispered, "You also said Miranda is a great shot, so she couldn't be sure it was the potion that made the arrow fly straight."

"But there's more," he said softly.

She stared into his blue eyes and felt her self-control begin to slip. "What is it, Justin?"

"The real miracle wasn't that the arrow flew straight. Miranda says it was much more than that. A sensation that she was in control of it. She could see it flying through the air, even though it was pitch-black outside. She could sense it. And she could sense her prey. His every move. She could even hear his heartbeat."

"No way," Suzannah protested. But she wanted to believe it. Wanted to be a part of it, if only because of the way it made Justin's eyes blaze when he talked about it.

"Miranda swears it's true. Of course," he added matter-of-factly, "she had just ingested a powerful hallucinogen, so that could have had something to do with it, too."

Suzannah smiled with delight and slipped her hands

behind his neck. "My God, you are so *freaking* adorable. I must have been crazy thinking I could resist you."

"You're kind of cute yourself," he admitted. Then he pulled her tightly against him and kissed her for a long, dizzying moment before asking, "Do you want to take it slow…?"

"Depends on what you mean by *slow*," she said with an amorous sigh. "Because I definitely want it to take all afternoon."

"Oh, yeah, it's gonna take a while," he assured her, dancing her over to the closed door between the living room and bedroom. Pressing Suzannah gently against it, Justin deepened his kisses. "I've wanted to do this since forever."

"Since Monday," she tried to quip, but she was getting too turned on to pretend any semblance of cool, so she let the words fade and just sifted her fingers through his thick, wavy hair, mindlessly enjoying the feel of his mouth devouring hers.

Justin's breath was growing ragged, and when he finally reached behind her to turn the brass doorknob, she was more than ready to head for the bed. Attacking the buttons on his shirt, she stripped it off him just as they tumbled onto the mattress. He immediately shrugged out of his shoes and jeans, as though suspecting she might change her mind. Instead she eyed his handsome body with complete approval, then pulled her sweatshirt and camisole over her head in one smooth, revealing motion.

Justin urged her back against the pillows while he knelt above her, his gaze fixed on her breasts. "I've got a confession to make," he told her, his eyes darkening to navy-blue.

"What is it?"

"I had a dream myself last night. About those beauties."

"Just my breasts?" she protested. "Where was the rest of me?"

"It was there somewhere, but these were definitely the stars. I was rubbing the Night Arrow potion all over them, and it was getting you off big-time. Me, too."

"Wait!" Suzannah leaned over the edge of the bed and opened the bottom drawer of her nightstand, searching for a party favor from a recent bachelorette party. Locating the tiny wicker basket covered with pink cellophane, she rejoined Justin, explaining as she unwrapped the package, "Noelle's cousin gave these out as wedding favors. I'm pretty sure…yay!" She handed him a bottle of massage oil.

"Man, you really *are* organized." He scanned the directions. "Safe for use on any body part. So what do you think? We can experiment on *me* first if you're concerned about side effects. I've got a body part that's dying to volunteer."

"Maybe later. For now, we're reliving your Night Arrow dream, remember?" Suzannah lay back against the pillows and pointed to her chest, then smiled hopefully.

"They're even prettier than they were in my imagination," he admitted as he coated his palms with oil. Then he covered her breasts with his hands and began to rub them slowly, sensuously.

Stabs of pleasure assaulted her, and when one of his hands traveled lower, across her stomach and then lower still, she wound her arms around his neck, pulling his mouth to hers for an appreciative kiss. "Yum. Those Masterson girls knew what they were doing when they chose you and Horace."

"You're killing me with that, you know."

She laughed and reached over to where the condoms had spilled from the basket onto the bed. Choosing a bright scarlet one, she explained, "Night Arrow red."

"Definitely heat-seeking," he agreed, watching her stretch it over him. Then, as soon as she had wriggled out of her jeans and panties, he pushed her back onto the bed and kissed her mouth while teasing at her with his fingers until she gave a moan of half appreciation, half complaint. More than ready and aching with frustration, she guided him into herself, gasping as he filled her with need so intense she was sure she'd die if he didn't satisfy it completely.

And luckily he did.

"Hey, sleepyhead."

"Hi." Suzannah smiled and touched Justin's cheek. "Is it still Wednesday?"

He laughed. "Yeah, but I know what you mean. That was really something. The best sex of my life," he added sincerely.

"I doubt that, but thanks." Suzannah sat up, conscious of his eyes on her naked body. "Did you get any sleep? Or am I the only one who conked out?"

"I got a little." He gave her a gentle kiss. "Relax. I'll go pick up something for dinner. And maybe a bottle of wine."

"We've still got those sandwiches," she reminded

him, looping her arms around his neck and pulling him back down to the bed with her. "We can live on those for days."

"They're stale. And you deserve a classy meal."

"I don't want you to leave."

He glared teasingly. "Someone has to be the adult, remember?"

The silly sentiment impressed her. "That's so sweet. I could use a day off."

"You definitely deserve it." He kissed her again, then rolled out of bed. "I'll be back before you know it."

"Check on the dog," she murmured, stretching her arms in a yawn. "He's been so quiet."

"That was a brilliant move on your part, giving him that ham bone."

Suzannah smiled. "I was saving it for soup, but keeping him occupied was a higher purpose. Otherwise all that scratching at the door might have wrecked your concentration."

Justin waggled an eyebrow. "I just figured something out. You know all that candy your parents gave you when you were a baby? I'll bet they were doing the same thing. Keeping you distracted so they could get it on without interruption. It must run in the family."

"Justin!"

"And they must've really gotten it on a *lot* if your first word was *candy*."

"Be quiet! My parents rarely if ever had sex. I'm quite sure of that," Suzannah told him with a pretend pout.

"Yeah, right. If your mom's anything like her daughter in the sack—"

"Hey! Didn't you say you were going to the store?"

He grinned. "Yeah, but I'll be right back. *Don't* get dressed."

She decided to put on shorts and a tank top, mostly because she wasn't used to being naked in front of a dog, much less a puppy that wanted to cuddle. Plus, it would be fun when Justin undressed her again. And it wasn't as if she'd gone overboard by putting on underwear.

"You've been such a good boy today," she complimented Murphy in a singsong voice. "Yes you have. I know it's crazy—I'm sleeping with a client, for the love of God. It doesn't get much crazier than that. But it can't go on much longer. He's got a case to solve, and I've got one to win, plus the trip to Hawaii coming up. So just be patient with us, okay?"

She threw a tennis ball across the room, and the puppy obliged her by fetching it. But instead of bringing it back to her, he ran under her bed and hid, a tactic that was his new favorite. Suzannah laughed as she tried to grab him, but he slyly stayed just out of reach. It was only when she pretended to ignore him that he came scampering out and the game began again.

It was fun in a mindless way, but she couldn't afford to be mindless for long. She had Noelle to deal with, for one thing. And in the long run, she also had to deal with this affair.

*And by "deal with it," I mean end it, she told herself sternly. Obviously not tonight. Or tomorrow. But once the furor dies down, sexually speaking, you definitely have to put an end to it. Luckily Justin won't be too surprised. And he'll probably be relieved.*

And meanwhile, she wasn't about to feel guilty over giving in to temptation. It had felt right. In fact, it had felt great.

*Best sex ever,* she admitted. *And a helluva a story to tell your granddaughters. Of course, in that version, Justin won't be FBI. He'll be CIA or MI6. And he'll beg you to be his woman, but you'll send him away, knowing he's too wild—and too important to the fate of the world—to be tamed.*

A knock at the door interrupted her planning, so she picked up the puppy and ran over to peek through the peephole, hoping it wasn't Noelle—although it would be kind of fun to tell her the news. What she really wanted to see was Justin holding flowers and champagne and so much food that he couldn't juggle it all along with his key to her place.

But it was a delivery boy from the Chinese restaurant down the street. The kid had been bringing food to her door for more than a year and usually looked bored to death, but today he actually appeared alert.

"Good thing I got dressed," Suzannah murmured to Murphy. "Justin must have sent the food ahead while he went to the liquor store."

Pulling open the door, she asked with a smile, "Did my associate pay you already? Or do I owe you?"

"He paid me. Gave me a big tip, too." The boy eyed Murphy with surprise. "You got a dog?"

"On a trial basis." She took the white bag of food from him. "Thanks a lot. See you next time."

"He said to tell you there's a note for you in the bag."

"Oh, really?" She felt her cheeks redden at the thought of what Justin might have written. Something naughty but in code—maybe about heat-seeking potions? "Okay, thanks. 'Bye."

"Yeah, see you later." The boy waved and sauntered down the hall.

"Do you know how long it's been since I got a love note?" Suzannah asked the puppy as soon as she had closed the door. "Go play for sec while I read it, okay?" Tossing the tennis ball to distract him, she dug in the bag and pulled out a folded piece of paper.

Recognizing his writing immediately from hours of poring over his case notes, she felt a tingle run through her before she even started reading.

Dear Suzie,
You've been great. I don't deserve you. And I can't stand the thought that I've put you in danger. So I'm going to handle things on my own for a while. I want you to stay in your apartment. Work on your presentation for Hawaii. I'll be in touch in a few days. Whoever took that shot at you is probably watching. Once they realize we're not hanging out together anymore, I'm hoping they'll back off. But if you feel like you need to go to the cops or the judge, then do it. I'll understand. I could use a few more days, but not at the expense of your safety. So do what you need to do. And try not to worry.
Fondly, JRusso

Suzannah shook her head, stunned and disbelieving. It didn't make any sense, so she forced herself to read it again.

But this time she sat down first.

"'Do what you need to do'?" she read aloud. "'Try not to worry'? Are you freaking *kidding* me?" A surge of anger coursed through her and she crumbled the paper into a ball. Then she growled his name. "Justin! I can't *believe* this."

Murphy jumped onto the sofa beside her and gave a worried whimper.

"That's right," she told the dog, pulling him into her arms and holding him close. "That bastard left us. Can you believe it? After pretending to care..." She buried her face in his thick, warm coat, refusing to give in to a wave of hurt feelings. "I must be the stupidest, *stupidest* idiot in the universe."

Setting the dog on the floor, she jumped up and began to pace. "He's so worried about my safety that he has to leave? But does he leave right away? Noooooo. He's gotta *nail* me first. What a jerk!"

She stormed over to the bay window and glared out, hoping he was down there, secretly watching, so she could give him the finger. "Thanks for making me feel like shit, Russo. Thanks a freaking lot. Now what? You think I'll just sit around and wait for you to come back? You're forgetting one minor detail. The judge released you into *my* custody. It's *my* ass that's on the line. *Sheesh*."

The phone rang and she dived for it, so anxious to give him a piece of her mind that her "Hello" sounded more like a threat than a greeting.

"Suzannah?" Noelle murmured. "What's wrong?"

"Oh. Hey…" She sighed. "I slept with him. And it gets worse."

"Uh-oh. I'm in my car. Want me to just head on over? I could pick up some food—"

"That's the good news. He left Chinese as a parting gift. So just come straight here."

"You make it sound like he's gone for good."

"Believe it," Suzannah confirmed sarcastically.

"You mean you're not even his lawyer anymore? That's good at least, right?" When Suzannah didn't respond, Noelle groaned. "I'm three minutes away. Hang on."

With Murphy jumping happily back and forth between her lap and Noelle's, Suzannah quickly filled her dark-haired, green-eyed friend in on all of the events leading up to "the dumping," as she had officially named it.

"I can't believe someone actually shot at you. With a *gun*."

"I know."

"And the guy looked like Justin? But you're sure it wasn't him?"

Suzannah nodded. "Justin Russo is a lot of things, and most of them are disgusting—*believe* me—but he's not a murderer."

"Why didn't you tell me about this last night?"

"I thought you'd do something crazy. Like call the cops and report it yourself."

Noelle nodded. "That sounds like something I might do. Okay, so go on. Get to the good stuff—no offense."

Suzannah sighed. "We were hanging out here, like

we've done for the last few days. Just innocently working. But at the same time he was flirting with me, like he always does. Then we started dancing."

"Dancing?"

Her cheeks began to burn. "It seemed harmless. He's got this theory that the music prevents any spies from listening to our conversation…. Okay, I knew it was lame, but it was fun, so I went along with it."

Noelle grinned. "Got it. What happened next?"

"We started kissing. That was a relatively new development, except for one platonic episode. But after that I pretty much threw myself at him and then we adjourned to the bedroom and had a great afternoon, if you get my drift. Then he went out to pick up dinner and never came back. But he sent a delivery boy with food and a note. Here it is," she finished, picking up the crumpled paper and handing it to Noelle. "Exhibit A."

Noelle's eyes scanned the page. "JRusso? Not Justin?"

"He signs everything JRusso," Suzannah assured her. "And it's not like this is a love note."

"It actually sounds pretty sincere," Noelle mused. "Like he went back into agent mode and realized your safety had to be the primary concern. I agree with that, by the way."

"If that's true, why didn't he disappear right after the shooting? Why wait until tonight, when—conveniently—he had just managed to get me into bed?"

"He's obviously a jackass," Noelle agreed. "That goes without saying. But still, he might have a point. Once the bad guys realize he's not hanging around here anymore, they'll think you two lovebirds had a falling out—which is truer than they know—and they'll leave you alone."

Suzannah rolled her eyes. "I still think it's too convenient. Plus, wasn't I safer when he was here to protect me? It doesn't ring true. He may tell himself he's worried about my safety, but let's face it—he just didn't want to deal with the aftermath of the sex. Right?"

Noelle shrugged. "You know him better than I do. Is that his style?"

"Hmm...let's see... We had sex. Five minutes later, he ran out the door. Didn't even say goodbye. Just sent a delivery boy with a kiss-off note. So yeah, I'd say it's his style."

"Speaking of sex..." Noelle grimaced but still dared to ask, "How was it? I mean, he sounded pretty hot on the phone. And you made him sound like a stud. So? Did you at least...you know...get in touch with your inner slut?"

Suzannah laughed in spite of her foul mood. "My inner slut? That's a new one. And the answer is, oh, yeah. Several times. And it had this intense, self-sustaining, blockbuster quality. Very cool, as he would say."

"Excuse me?"

Suzannah nodded. "I don't give him much credit for the first one because I was so keyed up from all the flirting and dancing, a eunuch could've gotten the job done. But after that..." She sighed with exaggerated appreciation. "He was like one of those guys who blow up buildings. They know just where to plant all the charges, then set them off with perfect timing so it blows up and collapses into itself all at the same time."

Catching her friend's incredulous expression, she added with a laugh, "Too much information?"

"I'm officially *not* giving you any more sympathy about this," Noelle assured her.

"Unless he gets me disbarred?"

"Could that happen? Really?"

"I doubt it," Suzannah admitted. "As long as he doesn't leave the jurisdiction and as long as he's back in time to go to court with me on the twenty-second, I'm probably safe. After that, I assume he'll let me withdraw as his lawyer, and it'll all be over except the sugar bingeing."

Noelle patted her arm. "In his own feeble way he's just trying to protect you. Once he slept with you, he cared more about you than ever. And he figured the best thing he could do for you was to stay as far away as possible. So he went back into agent mode."

Suzannah shook her head.

"Come on. I know the note was a burn, but if he had tried in person to convince you to let him back away, for the sake of your safety, you wouldn't have agreed to it. Right? You were so into being his lawyer—admit it, 'cause it's true. And you were into him personally, too. So he did what he thought was best."

In her heart Suzannah suspected her friend was right. Justin was trying to be noble. Failing miserably, of course, but trying nevertheless. "I still think it works for him, sex-wise. He got to have some fun, then didn't have to deal with the consequences. What did he think? That I'd be demanding? Clingy? Freaking goo-goo-eyed? *Sheesh.*"

"I doubt it. In fact, maybe he thinks he did you a favor. Let *you* off the hook."

"Hmm." Suzannah nodded. "Interesting. Go on."

Noelle laughed. "He knew that once the slutty glow wore off, you'd be kicking yourself for sleeping with a client. You'd want to find a way to break it off. To restore some distance."

"And now there's plenty of distance? Nice theory."

Noelle smiled triumphantly. "In his own jackass way he did the right thing. He ended the affair quickly, like ripping off a bandage. And he made you safer, so you wouldn't be a target of his enemies anymore."

"Ugh, I hate it when you're almost right."

Noelle studied her intently. "So? Are you going to do what he asked? Stay out of the investigation? Just lay low and concentrate on Hawaii?"

Suzannah nodded. "Like I kept telling him, I don't need to solve Mia's murder. I only need to establish reasonable doubt, and that's already in the bag. But I'll probably set up a meeting with Derek Seldon anyway. Just as a way of corralling loose ends."

"Derek Seldon?"

"He's Mia Masterson's old boyfriend. The one whose father nailed Horace's wife and started all the trouble. Derek wants to own Masterson Enterprises, so he has a couple of possible motives. I'd like to eyeball him, just in case...." She bit her lip. "Actually, I just want to ask him if he's seen Justin. Because I'm pretty sure that's where Justin plans to go next."

"Oh, my God. Let me guess. You want to eyeball him to see if he might have been the shooter? Are you *nuts?*"

"Justin says no way could Derek have pulled that off, and I trust his instincts when it comes to human nature. Apparently Derek's very reserved and cautious. If I make an appointment, I'll be perfectly safe. I just like tying up loose ends, like I said. Then I'll concentrate on Hawaii until Sunday."

"You can't meet with a suspect alone. But maybe I could go with you—"

"I'll be fine." Suzannah gave her friend a reassuring smile. "I'm guessing Justin might keep an eye on me anyway, so I'll be safe."

Noelle was silent for a second. Then she murmured, "You really think he's watching over you from a distance? Wow. It's almost…"

"Don't say it," Suzannah warned. "It's annoying, not romantic."

"Do you think he might be outside right this minute?"

"I hope so, 'cause I intend to keep flipping him the bird through the window every couple of hours."

"He probably thinks the guy who shot at you might try again." Noelle frowned. "You don't think he's using you for bait, do you? Pretending to leave? So they'll think you're unprotected and try again?"

"I don't think so," Suzannah said slowly. "But then again, I don't really know the guy very well. *Ugh*, just when I thought he couldn't sink any lower. Using me for bait would *really* suck."

Noelle nodded. "We'd definitely have to castrate him then. But we can't convict him without evidence. And we don't *have* any evidence. So maybe we should just drop it for the time being. Talk about something else."

"Like Steve?"

"Lord, no. Let's just watch TV or something. And after that, I'll spend the night. It'll give me and Murf a chance to bond," she added, scooping up the puppy and nuzzling him as she spoke.

"That's sweet but totally unnecessary. I'm fine. Plus, Justin might come back."

"So what? I'd love to tell him what I think of him."

"Get in line," Suzannah said with a laugh. "But I'd rather not have any witnesses when I strangle him. Plus, you get up at five, right? That would seriously annoy me." Her tone softened. "You're a pal, but really, I'll be fine. Just stay and watch TV for a while, like you said. We'll make popcorn and watch *Highlander*."

"Which one?"

"Technically there can be only one. But since you're being such a good friend, and I've got both copies, we can watch the other one."

"We'll watch them both," Noelle insisted. "Then we'll let Murf choose the best one. Deal?"

"Yeah." Suzannah gave her friend a wistful smile. "That sounds pretty good."

"It'll be okay, you know?" Noelle patted her arm. "And meanwhile, at least you got laid. That's gotta count for something, doesn't it?"

Suzannah burst into laughter. "So much for sympathy."

"Like I said, you don't *get* any sympathy. Blockbusters? Buildings blowing up? *Sheesh!* Just go make the popcorn, will you?"

## Chapter 7

Derek Seldon turned out to be a *lot* more attractive than Suzannah had expected. She had seen some pictures, all of which had shown an aristocratic man with black hair and a guarded smile. But in person, he had something more—a sexy charm that bordered on true charisma.

The fact that he had taken her call in person the day before had already given her a glimpse of his warmth. Upon hearing that she was Justin Russo's attorney, he had insisted that he wanted to accommodate her, but his calendar was full, so would she be so kind as to wait another day and to join him for breakfast at his estate on Friday?

Suzannah had actually been pleased with the delay, mostly because she had hoped Justin would contact her in the meantime or better still, realize the error of his ways and come back to the apartment. But she never heard a word from her errant ex-lover. Instead she took the puppy to a vet for a checkup and shots, then spoiled him the rest of the day, using his occasional naps to prepare for her trip to Hawaii.

Her bruised ego healed fairly quickly, and her anger faded, but still, Justin's absence rankled her. He was so sure he was protecting her from the shooter, but what if the bad guys went after *him* instead? She had no way of knowing where he was or if he was even alive. She had located his cell phone number among the papers he had left scattered on her kitchen table, but all attempts to contact him rolled over to voice mail. His car was no longer parked behind her building, and she quickly learned that he hadn't been back to his hotel since late Tuesday morning—right before he'd brought Murphy home. The very day on which someone had shot at her.

"Your house is much better guarded than the Masterson place," she told Derek as he led her into a sunroom overlooking a rose garden. "I went there a couple of days ago. With Agent Russo. To interview Ms. Masterson. I only saw one guard the whole time, and he wasn't exactly Rambo-esque. But you've got burly guys everywhere."

"I take security very seriously," Derek admitted. "In addition to a priceless art collection, I keep valuable jewels on the premises. We had an intruder just last night, in fact. He got away, but not before one of my guys got a piece of him."

"Did you report it to the authorities?"

"Of course. It would be foolish not to report a crime, don't you think?"

Suzannah winced.

"So how was Mia holding up?"

"Hmm? Oh, you mean when I went to her place? She was a little worried about security herself. Which is understandable under the circumstances."

Derek shook his head in apparent sadness. "I wonder how much more stress she can take."

"Because of her sister's death so soon after her dad's?" Suzannah asked, eyeing him intently.

"And even before that, her life was a mess. As I'm sure you know."

"Right." She tried for a casual tone. "It's amazing that she and Gia were able to put the past behind them."

"That surprised me, too," he admitted, "given how deep the rift was. Gia and Horace treated her so shamelessly."

"Sounds like you really cared about her," Suzannah murmured.

"Does that surprise you?"

"No, but…" She smiled in apology. "I guess those of us on the outside always assume when the super-rich get together that it's a mixture of business and love."

He gave a wry smile. "That's an interesting way to put it. And I suppose there's something to it. I loved Mia, but I also knew she was Horace Masterson's daughter. I had long dreamed of reuniting the two halves of the company my father helped establish. So I suppose it's fair to say that I was aware of the business aspect of the courtship." He gave a slight nod. "Thanks for being so honest. It's refreshing."

Suzannah smiled. "My pleasure."

"And I suppose it works both ways?"

"Hmm?"

"A beautiful young attorney representing a playboy federal agent. Don't you and Russo ever mix business and pleasure?"

She felt her cheeks redden. "Wow, I didn't see *that* coming."

"Shall I answer for you? You're a professional. You're also a decent human being. So even if you are having a dual relationship with him, you have nothing to be ashamed of."

"Is this where I say 'touché'?" Suzannah quipped. "Or is a simple 'I apologize' enough?"

Derek leaned forward. "No need for that. You're just doing your job. And quite well, I might add. Especially considering you're outside your usual venue, isn't that so? I'm told you prefer contracts to criminals. Even handsome playboy ones."

Suzannah laughed warily. "You've done your homework. And you're absolutely right. I was dragged into this case kicking and screaming. If I hadn't been convinced that Agent Russo was innocent, I would have found a way out of it. But as it is, I'm okay with it for a change of pace."

"Innocent? In the sense that he didn't do it at all? Or that it was justifiable self-defense?"

"He didn't do it at all."

"Then who did? Charlie Parrish?"

Things were moving a little too quickly for Suzannah, so she decided to slow them down. "You tell me. Who's your number one suspect? Aside from my client, that is."

Derek gave an appreciative chuckle. "Considering that I'm on the list or you wouldn't be here today, I'd say that's a loaded question. But the answer is simple. It was Parrish. The so-called Angel. I'm almost sure of it. Do you want to know why?"

Suzannah nodded, impressed by his straightforward response.

"I went to the hospital the day Horace had his massive stroke. The day the doctors said he was a vegetable. I'll never forget the moment when Gia stepped up to a microphone and told the media that she would never, *ever* pull the plug. Not if Horace lived to be one hundred and ten. Not if she bankrupted the company providing for his care." He cleared his throat, then continued. "I'm told that that videotape made the Internet rounds, viewed by fanatics like Parrish. Given his strong belief in allowing souls to move on, I imagine Gia's manifesto must have turned his stomach. I wouldn't be surprised if he didn't make *two* vows that day—to free Horace and to kill Gia."

"I'd like to see that videotape," Suzannah admitted.

"I'm sure I can arrange for a copy. My IT folks are the best. And I have contacts with the local TV station, as well. Surely they have it in their archives."

"Thanks."

Derek cocked his head to the side. "Is there something else you want to ask me?"

"Not really. Not on the record, at least. I just can't help getting the feeling that..." Suzannah took a deep breath then blurted, "You're still in love with Mia, aren't you?"

He surprised her by chuckling. "Would it matter? She moved on, Ms. Ryder. And after a few years of trying to reconnect with her, I moved on, too. Somewhat less successfully, but I still had to try. There's nothing worse than being the only party in a love affair who's actually in love."

*I know the feeling,* Suzannah assured him silently.

And Derek seemed to sense her thoughts, because his attitude grew perplexed. "Somehow I got the impression that you're too—what's the expression...goal-oriented?—to allow yourself to get hurt."

"I beg your pardon?"

He flushed. "No offense intended. My attorneys told me that you have an outstanding reputation—at your firm and beyond—of single-minded devotion to your craft. Almost to the exclusion of a social life."

"That's a pretty accurate description of me ninety-nine percent of the time," she assured him.

"It describes me well, too." He paused, then suggested carefully, "Would you like to come work for me?"

Her jaw dropped.

"You're surprised? Why? E-contracting is your specialty, isn't it? And it's the number one priority of my legal office. Add to that the fact that you're gutsy and smart. And prettier than any attorney I've ever seen."

"And I represent the man who might have killed the sister of the woman you might be in love with."

Derek chuckled. "Excellent point. A little convoluted but excellent. And the answer is, I believe I can overcome that obstacle if you can."

When Suzannah hesitated, he said lightly, "Why

don't we drop that subject for now? Once the trial is over, we'll see where we're both at."

She felt disloyal even thinking about such a possibility, but reminded herself that Justin would surely move on after the trial. Why shouldn't she?

*Unless Derek's the bad guy*, she reminded herself, but that possibility was seeming more remote by the minute. For one thing, he was much, much richer than she had realized. He surely didn't need Masterson Enterprises enough to kill for it. And he didn't seem disposed to killing for Mia either—he was far too stable and practical for that sort of mindless romanticism.

Standing, she reached for her purse, then extended her hand to him in farewell. "Thanks for seeing me, Mr. Seldon. And for being so cooperative. And, of course, for the yummy food."

"My pleasure. I'm selfishly glad Agent Russo didn't come with you." Derek pursed his lips, then added pointedly, "He went with you to interview Mia. But not here. Any particular reason?"

"I felt I needed to come alone. For a variety of reasons." Suzannah returned his stare calmly for a moment before smiling and adding, "I think I made the right choice. Goodbye, Mr. Seldon—"

"Derek."

She nodded. "Goodbye, Derek. Thanks again for everything."

She had planned on hitting the grocery store on the way home, but after the feast Derek had supplied, she knew she wouldn't be hungry for hours. And she needed to check on Murphy, whom she pictured sad-faced and whimpering by the front door.

*Or you're afraid to park in your space ever again,* she challenged herself sternly. *Is that how it's going to be? You can't go to the store or to work because you think someone will take a shot at you?*

She needed to confront that fear, but she also needed to be smart about it, because the shooter was still out there somewhere. And if her theory was wrong—if he hadn't missed on purpose—then he might be planning to try again.

But if he had been watching her closely, he'd know that she and Justin weren't hanging out together anymore. If so, she was safe from him, and it was Justin who was in danger.

*Don't worry about that! Justin's got a gun. And he's trained to take care of himself. He'll be fine. And so will you. So just suck it up and stop at the store before the noontime rush.*

She was tempted to park in a space close to the market, just to test the waters, but forced herself to drive deeper into the lot and pull her car into the spot assigned to her.

The one with the root-beer stains on the pavement.

*Root beer, not blood, so get over it,* she told herself with a shaky smile. Taking a deep breath, she opened the car door and stepped out, looking first at the roof of the adjoining parking structure, then slowly turning a full three hundred and sixty degrees, scoping out the area.

No Justin impersonators anywhere, she decided with relief. In fact, the only other human in sight was a gangly boy in ragged jeans and a parka who was collecting grocery carts that had been abandoned in various parts of the lot.

She walked toward him, calling out, "I'll take one of those," refusing to admit that she wanted the company, not the cart. Did she really think this kid could protect her from an armed killer?

Then, to her amazement, the kid turned out to be armed himself! He pulled a snub-nosed pistol from the waistband of his jeans and warned her unhappily, "Don't move. Don't scream. D-don't do anything. Or else."

Terrified—not just by the déjà-vu quality but by the fact that the weapon was only inches away this time—Suzannah held up her hands like a hostage in a 1950s bank robbery as she struggled to control the pounding of her heart. "Okay, steady. We're good here. Right? You want my purse? It's all yours. And this is your lucky day because I've got two hundred dollars on me. So just settle down. Okay?" She took a deep breath, then forced herself to note that her latest assailant seemed as terrified as she was. He was also older than she had first thought. And there was something familiar about his face—

"Charlie?" she murmured, disoriented.

"Keep your hands up! Shit! I was hoping you wouldn't recognize me. Now I've gotta do something. Don't say anything. Let me think."

Unnerved again, Suzannah tried for a calming tone. "You're here for a reason, right? And I don't think it's to shoot me. So you must want to talk to me. Right?"

Encouraged by his silence, she continued. "We can't just stand out here like this. Someone will see us and call the police. So let's go sit in my car. Okay?"

He licked his lips, then nodded. "Yeah, that makes sense. But don't try anything. I'm the one with the gun. Remember that."

She could see he was scared to death, and while she knew she was in some measure of danger herself, she also knew this young man didn't want to kill her. He was an angel of mercy—a soft-hearted, misguided, well-intentioned crazy guy. Which meant that, for the moment, the most important thing was to steady his nerves so that the gun wouldn't go off accidentally.

"Lower the gun a little. And I'll lower my hands. That way we won't look so suspicious. Then we'll go back to my car. I'll sit in the driver's seat. You can sit behind me or next to me. Wherever you feel most comfortable."

"Yeah, that's good. Thanks." A shy smile turned his plain face into an appealing one. "I knew you'd be smart. That's why Agent Russo chose you for his lawyer. But I didn't know you'd be so nice." He closed his eyes for a second and murmured, as though suddenly and completely exhausted, "What a relief."

"Why don't you just start at the beginning, Charlie?" Suzannah advised when they were safely settled in the front seats of her car. "But first, I'm going to drive to the far side of the lot, okay? Just so none of my friends walk by unexpectedly and recognize me."

"Yeah. That's smart."

She gave him a sympathetic smile, knowing that he wasn't feeling very smart himself at the moment. As she started the engine and drove slowly away from the store and her office building, always mindful of the gun in his hand, she murmured, "What was your plan, anyway? Obviously you don't want to hurt me. Did you want information about Agent Russo?"

"I need a lawyer."

"Ooh..."

"I want to turn myself in. So they'll stop saying I killed people I didn't kill. But I need to be smart about it or I'll get the electric chair or something. So I want a smart lawyer. Like you."

"I understand." She pulled the car into a spot under a tree, then turned off the engine and faced him squarely. "The problem is I'm already Agent Russo's lawyer. It would be a conflict of interest for me to represent you."

"Why? Do you think he killed that girl?"

"No."

"Then we're both innocent. So where's the conflict?"

She smiled. "If I were representing you, I'd try to make the jury think Agent Russo did it. And if Agent Russo goes to trial, I'll try to make the jury think *you* did it."

"But I didn't. I swear."

"I believe you." She was dying to ask him if he was also innocent of Horace's murder, but the ethics of the situation confounded her, so she reminded him, "I'm not your lawyer. I can't be. Which means if you say anything to me, it's not privileged. Do you understand what that means, Charlie? When Agent Russo talks to me, I have to keep it all secret. But anything *you* say, I can repeat to him. Or to the cops."

"That's not fair. We're both innocent."

She licked her lips. "How can you be so sure about him?"

Charlie shrugged. "My mom said he treated her respectfully when he came to the house asking about me. She trusts him and she's a really good judge of character. Maybe if you ask him, he'll say it's okay to represent me and him at the same time. If it's okay with him, can you do it?"

She reached across and touched his hand. "There's another problem, Charlie. I haven't ever handled a murder trial before. I haven't even handled a speeding ticket. You'd be much better off with an experienced attorney. I can recommend one, actually. How does that sound?"

He hung his head, clearly dejected. "You think I'm a serial killer, don't you?"

"No. Not really. I mean..." She grimaced. "You thought you were doing the right thing. I understand that."

"They asked me to do it. *All* of them. They asked me to free them and I did."

"Okay, okay."

"It's not murder if they ask you. It's not murder if they're helpless and miserable and begging you to set them free."

"Okay, Charlie. Just settle down, please? You're scaring me a little."

"I am?" His eyes filled with tears. "I'm sorry. I wouldn't hurt you. I didn't hurt that Gia girl or her father—just the people who were really dead already and *begged* me to help them."

Suzannah caught her breath. He was saying he hadn't killed Horace Masterson. Which meant Justin had been right all along. She couldn't wait to tell him!

"I think my friend Tony can help you, Charlie. He's a terrific lawyer."

"But I want you!"

"I know. And maybe once Agent Russo is cleared I can associate with Tony. But for now, the best I can do is call him and ask him to meet with you." She patted his hand again and insisted, "It's good advice, you know. Please take it?"

"You trust him?"

"Completely. He's an experienced defense attorney and a wonderful man."

Charlie stared directly into her eyes. "Will he believe me when I tell him those people spoke to me? Asked me to free them?"

"He'll believe that you're trying to tell him the truth. And he'll probably ask you to talk to some doctors to confirm it."

"I've already talked to a doctor. And he believed me."

"That's great, Charlie. That's just the kind of witness you'll need. What's his name?"

"No way. Our conversations were confidential. I want them to stay that way." The young man's shoulders slumped. "When I first started hearing the voices, I went to him for help. He believed me, but he tried to stop me for my own good. I'm not going to ruin his career."

"Even if he *wants* to help you?"

"He does," Charlie admitted. "He tried calling me after the last—well, you-know-what. But I didn't call back."

"Why not?"

"Because it's not fair to him. He shouldn't suffer for my mistakes."

"If you don't want him as a witness, your lawyer will respect that," she promised. "But he'll still want to talk to him. What's the doctor's name?"

Charlie hesitated, then murmured, "It's Dr. Schuler. But don't tell anyone."

"Do you have his phone number?"

"Not anymore. I don't want lawyers calling him and scaring him." Charlie's eyes clouded. "I guess I'll have to talk to the new doctors. But...what if they don't believe me?"

"They will."

"Do *you* believe me?"

"That you heard those patients ask you to kill them?" She bit her lip. "They were in comas, so I guess you're saying they contacted you by ESP or something?"

He nodded. "I heard them just as clear as I hear you right now."

"But you didn't hear Horace Masterson?"

"I didn't need to *hear* him. He left written instructions. I thought about trying to help him, but Dr. Schuler told me not to."

"Okay. That's fine. I'm just going to take my cell phone out of my purse now and call Tony. Okay?"

"No. No calls. Like you said," he murmured unhappily, "you're on Agent Russo's side. Not mine."

"That's right. That's why you need Tony."

"I need to think about this. I need to be smart. I'm so tired," he admitted, "but I have to be smart."

Suzannah nodded sympathetically. "I'll give you my card. When you've thought it through, call me. I won't say anything to Tony just yet, okay?"

"That sounds good," he murmured.

"When you're ready, though, you need to meet with him alone. Then you can talk freely. It'll all be privileged, like we talked about earlier." She sighed. "The sooner the better, Charlie. You understand that, don't you?"

"Yeah. My mom says the same thing. She's the one who found out where your office was for me. But don't get her in trouble for talking to me without telling the cops, okay? She's a good person. Too good sometimes."

"Like her son."

He seemed confused for a moment, then flashed a tremulous smile. "Thanks for saying that."

Suzannah resisted an impulse to pull him into a hug and thereafter to drive him home so he could have a hot meal and sleep on the sofa with Murphy licking his face. He needed someone, but she couldn't be that someone.

*Plus, he has a gun,* she reminded herself. *Your first priority has to be getting away from him. So focus on that.*

"Can I reach in my purse to get my business card for you?"

He nodded wearily. "Will you ask Agent Russo if it's okay with him for you to be my lawyer, too? If he says yes, then maybe the judge will let you."

"I couldn't do a good job for you and for him at the same time."

"But will you ask him?"

Suzannah hesitated, then nodded as she handed her card to him. "I'll talk to him about it. In the meantime, you'll think about Tony. Talk to your mom about him, okay?"

He agreed, then with a quick glance around the

parking lot, he hopped out of the car and disappeared in the direction of the parking structure.

*Okay, Agent Russo,* Suzannah told her ex-lover ruefully. *It's officially time for me to track you down.*

"Who's the best doggy in the whole world? You are, that's who!" Suzannah scooped up Murphy and cuddled him close. "Did you miss me? Here..." She set him down and rolled a tennis ball across the floor. Predictably he grabbed it in his mouth, then raced into the bedroom for his favorite hiding place.

"Murf! Come out, please? I've got so much to tell you," she wheedled. "I met Charlie Parrish at gunpoint. And he says he didn't kill Gia. And I believe him."

When the puppy barked from under the bed, she laughed. "I know what you're thinking. Once again, I should have called 911. But you're wrong. If I call the cops, they'll ask me where Justin is. And then he'll be in big trouble. So we can't call them.

"What we need to do is find your daddy. Right away. I already called his hotel and left a message for him to pick up some root beer—get it?—just in case he shows up there. And I'm thinking of calling the girl in the envelope, too, although that's a little riskier. But meanwhile, in case he's watching the building, let's signal him, okay?"

She dragged one of her floor lamps over to the bay window and turned it on. "I know it's goofy, but it should catch his attention," she told the puppy, who had finally come out of hiding. "Hopefully he won't be stubborn about this and will come home."

Pouring some dog food into a bowl, she sat beside Murphy on the floor and laughed when he began gobbling up his lunch. "I didn't tell you the best part, Murf. It's not just the Angel of Mercy we've got on our side now. We've got his freaking shrink, too. A man named Dr. Schuler. We need to track him down. Since Charlie's from Nevada originally, we'll try there first, but we'll also try California and Oregon. How many Schulers can there be? I *want* this guy. Of course, he'll claim all his conversations with Charlie are privileged, but I want to talk to him anyway. Charlie needs him and so do we. Because he's a witness who can testify that Charlie didn't kill Horace. And if Charlie didn't do it, then it's easier to prove that someone—probably Agent X or Mia—tried to frame Justin. See? We're so lucky! Now if only he'd come home."

She grimaced, admitting that seeing Justin again would have its awkward aspect. But much more awkward for him than for her. And she needed someone to talk to more than she needed to be hurt and angry.

Again she thought about the SPIN girl—the one Justin claimed was brilliant at figuring things out. It would be such a relief to dump this into her lap for a while. The spinner cared about Justin, so she could be trusted to do the right thing.

"But Justin should make that call. Not us," she told Murphy firmly. "Remember what he said? He's gotten her into trouble before. What if we got her fired? That would be nuts. And what if she decided to follow her agency's rules? She'd report my meeting with Charlie to the authorities and maybe even tell them that Justin's AWOL. I doubt it, but I'm not ready to take that chance. Are you?"

When the puppy climbed into her lap and licked her cheek, Suzannah gave a victorious laugh. "Then it's settled. We'll try to find Schuler on our own first while we wait for Justin to come home."

As it turned out, there were a lot more Schulers around than Suzannah had predicted, not to mention more than one way to spell the name. After two long, frustrating hours of dead ends and answering machines, she was ready to give up. She had left dozens of messages but had a feeling she'd get no response. Or she'd hear from them what she'd heard from the offices she had managed to reach—that they had no patient named Charlie whom Dr. Schuler had been trying to contact.

Meanwhile, there had been no word from Justin either.

Frustrated, Suzannah walked over to the kitchen table and opened his briefcase. The unmarked manila envelope was right on top. Breaking the seal, she examined the contents—a single piece of paper with a phone number scrawled across it in blue ink.

No name. But Suzannah remember it clearly.

S-3.

Aka, the spinner.

Suzannah drove slowly down the winding, tree-lined street known as Sea Shell Drive, hoping to spot one of Noelle's landscaping trucks, which were white with a dark green logo consisting of meandering vines and the words *Designs by the Yard*. None appeared, but she did find an imposing three-story brick home set back far from the street. The front yard was in the early stages of remodeling, with all of the former lawn and other vegetation stripped away, leaving only a pair of stately maple trees. Trenches for sprinklers had already been dug, and forms for a tiered walkway were in place, presumably built by the wiry young men Noelle kept on her payroll.

A sturdy sign sporting the telltale logo confirmed that this was the right project, but there was no sign of Noelle anywhere, and Suzannah grimaced in frustration. She needed a puppy sitter but had been unable to reach her friend by phone. And the thought of leaving Murphy with a total stranger, such as one of her colleagues from the law firm, had bothered her for multiple reasons. But "S-3" had made her a plane reservation for four-forty, so she had to move quickly.

She had liked the spinner immediately and had respected the fact that they couldn't say much to one another over the phone, given the fact that Suzannah had called on "an unsecured line." Fortunately S-3 had explained that she wasn't in Washington but rather was having her calls routed to her at SPIN's Los Angeles office. Suzannah could be there in less than an hour by plane. And just to be on the safe side, the spinner had sent her boyfriend's home address to Suzannah's work e-mail account, which *was* secure, so that they could meet there, away from prying eyes. In addition to the plane ticket, a rental car would be arranged for Suzannah, courtesy of the federal government.

"Come on, baby. Let's go find Auntie Noelle," Suzannah cooed, picking up Murphy with one arm while grabbing his cardboard box with the other. There was no sign of life in the front yard, so she wandered around back and was frustrated when there was no one there either.

"Hey, is that a dog?" a squeaky voice asked from behind her.

Suzannah turned to stare down at an adorable brown-haired child who couldn't have been more than four years old. "It sure is," she told him. "His name's Murphy. What's yours?"

"Sam."

She smiled, loving the fact that such a little boy could have such a grown-up name. "I'm looking for a friend of mine, Sam. She usually works here."

"They all go-ed home. Prob'ly for nap time."

"Probably." She leaned down to allow him to pet Murphy, who was struggling to get free. "I think Murf likes you. Want to hold him for a sec?"

She placed the dog in the boy's arms, laughing when Murphy went into his usual face-slobbering routine.

Then a voice from out of nowhere boomed, "Are you stalking me, Ms. Ryder?" and she stood up straight, dropping the cardboard box in the process.

"Judge Taylor! Good grief, this isn't *your* house, is it?"

"Mine is two doors down," he explained. "I see you've met my grandson."

She bit her lip, finding it impossible to believe that sweet little Sam could be related to the Jailor. "I was just looking for my friend Noelle. She owns the landscape company that's redoing this yard."

"Grandpa?" Sam asked, sitting down and corralling the puppy in his lap. "Can your friend and her dog come over to our house?"

Suzannah smiled. "Sorry, sweetie, but I've got to find my friend. She's going to babysit Murf for me."

"Can't *we* do it? Grandpa? Please?"

"Sure, why not?" Judge Taylor gave Suzannah a smile that seemed surprisingly needy. "It would be fun for Sam. And a break for me. My daughter left him here for a week, but I ran out of ideas after a day. A puppy might be just what we need for a few hours."

"It would be longer than that, sir. And I couldn't impose. Really."

*"Please?"* Sam begged. "I'll take good care of him. He can have my food and everything."

"Don't worry, Ms. Ryder. I won't bite unless he bites first."

"That's funny, Your Honor," Suzannah murmured. "But it could be ten o'clock or even later before I get back."

"I'll be up. Lucky for you, I've got perpetual insomnia."

*So that's why you're so cranky all the time,* she accused silently. Resisting an urge to suggest he try sleeping pills for the sake of the local bar, she forced herself to consider his offer. After all, she had a plane to catch, and the judge's grandson was bonding nicely with Murphy right before her eyes.

"Are you sure, sir?"

"It's settled," he replied gruffly. "Believe me, you're doing *me* a favor. Not vice versa. I need a reprieve from Sam's incessant questions. Not that I don't love watching him," he added quickly. "I'm just not very good at it."

Suzannah wanted to say something reassuring, but the idea of Taylor the Jailor as anyone's playmate was simply too absurd, so she settled for saying, "I really appreciate it. And here—" she rummaged in her purse for a pad and pen "—I'll leave you Noelle's number. If Murf gets on your nerves at all, just call her and she'll come get him. And I'll leave my cell number, too. Don't hesitate to call. And you should give me yours—"

"You're worse than a new mother," he protested, but still he obliged her by scribbling down the requested information. "It's going to be fine, Ms. Ryder."

"I know, sir. It's just...well..." She lowered her voice and reminded him, "You know how you are. A little grouchy, no offense."

He surprised her by laughing. "I'll try to control myself. And speaking of self-control, why isn't Agent Russo watching the dog for you? Or are you two going out together?"

"There, you see?" she complained. "You're implying he and I are going on a hot date, when the truth is there's some very, *very* important investigative work to be done on his defense."

"My apologies," the judge told her with unexpected sincerity. "I didn't mean to discuss the case. That wasn't my intention." Motioning toward Sam and Murphy, who were romping across the lawn together, he sighed. "Look at them."

Pleased, Suzannah nodded. "Okay, sir. Thanks again. And remember to call those numbers if you need help. I'll be back as soon as I can."

As promised by S-3, a rental car was waiting for Suzannah when she arrived at LAX. Following the spinner's e-mailed directions, she drove to a modest neighborhood, puling up in front of an attractive cottage on a street lined with palm trees and basketball hoops. Before she made it halfway up the walkway, a pretty blonde in jeans and a white T-shirt burst through the front door and ran toward her, her blue eyes sparkling. "Suzannah?"

"Hi." She regretted wearing her boring gray suit and sensible shoes, especially since S-3 wasn't wearing any shoes at all. "Thanks for seeing me on such short notice."

"You're just like Justin described you. Of course, I had a sneak peek because of that press conference you did a few weeks ago. Nice spin control."

"I guess you'd know about that," Suzannah said with a laugh. "Do they really call you a spinner?"

"Yep, but my friends call me Kristie. Come on inside. Will's not here, so we've got the place to ourselves."

The sound of a barking dog contradicted the statement, and Kristie laughed. "That's Nugget. I put him in the backyard so he wouldn't maul you. With kisses, I mean."

"I should have brought my puppy. They could have played."

"I wish I'd known. He's not in a kennel, is he?"

Suzannah winced. "Believe it or not, I left him with the judge who's handling Justin's case."

"The *Jailor?*"

"It's a long story, believe me," Suzannah drawled.

Laughing, Kristie led her up the steps and into a dining room that had been converted to an office. "I work here a lot. Have a seat. And forgive me, but I'll burst if you don't tell me what's going on, so..." Her eyes were now dancing. "What's up?"

"A lot, actually. But I've been rehearsing a speech, so if you don't mind?"

"Be my guest. Sit. Talk. But most of all," the spinner added softly, "trust. I'm not sure why you're here, but I'm sure you were right to come."

Suzannah gave her a grateful smile. "Justin told me to call you in case of emergency. If I was feeling scared or worried or something like that. He also told me that you could get in trouble for helping us. That he's gotten you in trouble before. So I'm really sorry, but the truth is, I need to find him right away and I didn't know where else to go."

"You aren't in touch with him?"

She grimaced. "Hard to believe, I know. He took off without giving me any way to reach him. And I really need to find him, because I met the Angel of Mercy today."

"Yowza! In the flesh? The whole world has been trying to find him! How'd *you* manage to do it?"

"*He* found *me*. And he was armed but not dangerous. Kind of pitiful, really. He wanted me to represent him."

Kristie exhaled slowly. "Okay, let's rewind this a little. You don't know where Justin is? But you're sure he's okay?"

"He took off the day before yesterday. And he left me this note." She produced the crumpled sheet of paper. "Supposedly he did it for my benefit. Because someone took a shot at me the other day, so he decided I was safer with some distance between us."

The spinner's eyes widened. "Someone? Do we have any theories about who?"

"Sure. Whoever shot Gia Masterson took a shot at me, too. But my best guess is they missed on purpose." Noting Kristie's confused expression, she quickly filled her in on the details.

"Wow, our first solid proof that Justin was really framed. That's kind of a relief."

Suzannah cocked her head to the side, honestly surprised by the statement. "Wasn't his word enough?"

"Truthfully? Nope." When Suzannah gasped, Kristie explained quickly, "I never thought Justin did it on purpose. But part of my job is to analyze human behavior, and frankly guys get so caught up in their professional image, even the best of them—and I mean the *very* best—will cover up mistakes if they feel their reputation is on the line. So when all evidence pointed to Justin shooting that girl in self-defense but he insisted otherwise, well…"

"Wow." Suzannah leaned back in her chair, wondering whether she had made a big mistake. She had expected to find Justin's friend. His supporter. Not a skeptic who thought him capable of lying to cover up a justifiable homicide.

"You're shocked? A year ago I would have been, too. Think what you want," Kristie told her sadly, "but believe me when I say I adore Justin Russo. And I'd do almost anything for him. But—" she shrugged "—he's not perfect."

"Amen to that." Suzannah laughed self-consciously. "It's actually hilarious that I'm defending him. I mean, I think he's innocent, but I also think he's a louse."

Kristie winced. "Uh-oh. I had a feeling once I found

out how pretty you were that he'd mess things up that way. So? How bad was it? Did you two actually...?"

Suzannah nodded. "Then he went out for Chinese food and never came back."

"Ouch."

"Needless to say, he's a dead man. But I really want to clear him first, and now I think I can. It's not just the Charlie Parrish sighting, although that's huge. It's the fact that Charlie told me he has a psychologist who knows the whole story. A man named Schuler." She leaned forward eagerly. "My dream is that Schuler can help us prove Charlie had nothing to do with Horace Masterson's murder."

The spinner pursed her lips. "It would be in his patient's best interest to do that, so who knows? We psychologists are a loyal bunch. But in any case, having Charlie should be enough, right?"

"I don't have him. I had to let him go—the gun, remember? But he'll call me soon. I'm sure of that. And when he does, I want Justin to be there."

"I'll help you find him," Kristie promised.

"Without getting into trouble? Because Justin was really sensitive about that."

"I know. I felt awful the last time we talked. Like I had withdrawn my support from him at the very time he needed it most." She reached for Suzannah's hands and squeezed them. "That's why I'm so glad you called. And the good news is I can brief my boss about all this right away. There's no conflict at all. He'll understand completely and he'll really want to help."

"He sounds nice."

"Cute, too. You're sitting in his house."

Suzannah burst into laughter. "I guess I was worried for nothing."

"Not really. I'm on probation—in more ways than one. And Justin's usually as much a rogue as I am. Believe me, Director McGregor will be as happy as I am to hear he didn't kill Gia Masterson. Now the question is, who did?"

"Right." Suzannah cleared her throat. "Did you just say you're a psychologist?" When Kristie nodded, she gave her a hopeful smile. "That's great. Because I've been dying to get a professional answer to a hypothetical question. Okay?"

"Shoot."

The lawyer took a deep breath. "Imagine a dad and his two daughters. The dad is tyrannical. He's also a multibillionaire. One of the daughters crosses him, and he disowns her. Tosses her out on her ass, disinherits her, leaves her to the wolves, so to speak. And the remaining daughter sides with him, which means she becomes sole heiress to a freaking fortune. Years later, the dad has a stroke and becomes comatose, but even then the heiress shuns the outcast. Refuses to let her come home. Finally the sisters reconcile. My question is—" Suzannah leaned forward again "—is there any possibility the outcast is able to completely forgive and forget? Isn't it more likely that she harbors deep resentment? Forever?"

Kristie was about to answer, when the phone on the table between them began to ring, so she winced apologetically, then reached for the receiver. "This is S-3. Please identify yourself."

As Suzannah watched, the spinner's blue eyes widened. Then she murmured, "Oh, my God, what perfect timing! Guess who's here? No, don't guess, let me tell you. It's *Suzannah*. I know, I know. Isn't it great? Hold on, Justin. I'm going to put you on speakerphone."

## Chapter 8

Suzannah realized too late that while she wanted to *locate* Justin, she wasn't really ready to *talk* to him yet. Unfortunately she didn't seem to have a choice.

"He sounds raw," Kristie said and then, before Suzannah could ask what "raw" meant, the spinner pushed the speakerphone button and said brightly, "Justin? Go ahead."

His first word was guarded, like a schoolboy who had been caught smoking. "Suzannah?"

"Hi, Justin."

"So…" His voice was hoarse and ragged, just as Kristie had observed. "I'm glad you're there. I was going to ask Essie to contact you for me, but this is better."

"I'll bet," Suzannah drawled. "You don't sound too good, Justin. Are you okay?"

"Except for the pint of blood dripping down my throat, I'm fine."

"You're hurt?" Suzannah felt her pulse quicken. "What happened?"

"My face got into an argument with one of Derek Seldon's storm troopers, but I survived. My nose is busted, my jaw's out of whack and my eye socket has seen better days. But otherwise, I'm fine."

"How awful! Are you in the hospital?"

"A doctor buddy patched me up in his basement. He wanted me to get further treatment—see a specialist—but I wanted to push forward with the investigation. Turns out I was kidding myself. I'm just too messed up, even with all the painkillers he gave me."

"You sound exhausted," Kristie told him, her tone warm with concern. "Let me send a team to pick you up—"

"Not yet. I've got some favors to ask first. From each of you."

"Anything," the spinner promised.

"Thanks." His breathing was growing more labored with every word. "You're not gonna like this, Suzy—"

"Don't worry about me," Suzannah insisted. "And guess what, Justin. I have great news. Charlie Parrish made contact with me today. That's why I came to see Kris—I mean, S-3. He told me he didn't kill Horace Masterson. You were right all along, Justin, and now we have proof! Isn't that wonderful?"

"Proof? The word of a deranged serial killer?" he demanded, then he paid for the effort with a fit of coughing.

Suzannah and Kristie exchanged worried glances,

but before either spoke, he continued. "Of course he'd say he didn't do it. I'm just glad he didn't hurt you. Stay away from him from now on, understand?"

"He was so harmless it was heartbreaking," Suzannah assured him. "Things just look hopeless to you right now because you're hurt. But once you get some R & R, you'll see this is a positive development. Now we can focus our investigation—"

"Our investigation is over. I'm too messed up to go on. And the truth is...well, it's an effing relief."

"Okay, Justin," Kristie said softly. "Just tell us how we can help."

"Suzy?"

"Yes?"

"I need you to talk to Armstrong. Or maybe check with Johnson and Wiley first. Whatever makes more sense. Just see if we can make the same deal the D.A. offered before."

*"What?"*

His tone grew urgent. "They may insist on a slap on the wrist. Something like obstruction of justice. I'll agree to that as long as they agree to give me probation for it."

"What are you talking about? How did you obstruct justice?"

Kristie reached across the table and squeezed Suzannah's hand as she murmured, "What are you telling us, Justin?"

"I'll sign a statement that I did it but it was self-defense. Because...well, that's the truth."

Suzannah stared at the speakerphone, confused and slightly desperate. "What do you mean you did it? Did what?"

"She was going to shoot me, Suzy. I went for the gun and it went off. I couldn't believe it, it all happened so fast. And then all I could think was they'll take me off the case. Maybe they'll even drop the Masterson investigation completely and chalk his killing up to the Angel of Mercy. I couldn't accept that. I was still convinced Night Arrow was at risk." He paused for another fit of coughing, then whispered, "In my gut I thought I was doing the right thing. But I'm out of commission now. And maybe it's for the best."

Suzannah wasn't really listening anymore, mostly because none of what he was saying made any sense. Her focus was on the dining room, which had turned ice-cold. But she didn't reach for her suit jacket. She was numb. So numb she didn't even realize she was crying until she saw droplets of water actually hit the tabletop.

"I know I should've told you sooner, Suzannah. I'm sorry."

"You're sorry?" She batted away her tears. "*Sorry?* Oh, my God..."

"I did it for my country, Suzy. For Night Arrow. I don't expect you to understand, but—"

"Shut up!" She covered her face with her hands and instructed him unhappily, "Just let me think for a minute."

Kristie patted her arm. "I'm so sorry, Suzannah. Do you want to go in the other room and just...well, just be alone? I can get the rest of the details—"

"No, I'm fine." She sat up straight, her tears gone. "Start at the beginning, Justin. Why did Gia pull a gun on you?"

After a short, eerie silence, he explained. "We had dinner. And sex. But there was a lot of tension. She wanted me to end my investigation. She kept saying it was destroying the company, and that she was sure the Angel of Mercy killed her father. Finally I said we should stop seeing each other and she panicked. She told me she thought Mia did it. Killed Horace, I mean. And she said she couldn't blame her. That he hurt Mia so badly, so cruelly, that she wasn't responsible for her actions. She begged me to let it go. Reminded me that she, Gia, could have pulled the plug on the old man anyway, anytime she wanted. Then she offered me money—not to mention full-service sex for the rest of my life—if I'd pin the murder on Charlie."

He cleared his raspy throat, then continued, his words more strained than ever. "When I said no, she pulled the gun. Said she was going to tell the police that I tried to blackmail her. That I promised to drop the investigation if she gave me money. And that I threatened, if she refused, to frame Mia. It was ludicrous—I knew the Bureau would never believe such a stupid story—but she was going to go through with it. I could see that, too. So I dove for the gun and it went off."

"And you'll sign a statement to that effect?" Suzannah asked woodenly. "That's what you want me to tell Armstrong?"

"Right. Self-defense." His voice broke. "My career's over. I know that. I took a gamble, thinking I could prove that whoever killed Horace was going after Night Arrow. And I would have succeeded if I hadn't tangled with Seldon's security guard."

"Night Arrow?" Suzannah almost growled the words. "I knew you were obsessed, but my God. Is that *all* you care about? Never mind," she interrupted herself. "Don't answer that."

"You never understood," he told her, his voice resonating with the pure, fanatical devotion she had heard so often. "It's so much more than just a science experiment. It's a true miracle. Anyway...Essie?"

"Yes, Justin?" Kristie asked.

"When I said I wanted a favor from you too...well, that's it. I know I'm finished at the Bureau, but with your connections, I was hoping you could get me a job on the project. Either directly or through whatever subcontractor they hire to provide security." He gave a self-deprecating laugh. "I think I've proven I'll move heaven and earth to protect it."

"Oh, my God," Suzannah said again, disgusted but also depressed. "You sacrificed your career—your happiness?—for a half-baked legend?"

"You don't understand. But S-3 does. Right, Essie?"

The spinner bit her lip. "We're all excited about Night Arrow, Justin. But I never realized how much you...well, I guess that doesn't matter now."

"Will you help me? No one has stronger ties to the project—or connections right up to the President—than you do. Make them understand, okay? I can be valuable to them. It's something I believe in. Maybe the *only* thing I believe in anymore, professionally speaking."

"I'll do my best."

"Suzy? I need you, too. Talk to Armstrong for me, okay? Get me a good deal. I'll contact SPIN again in a couple of days to see if it's safe to turn myself in."

The thought of going to Armstrong and then to the

judge made Suzannah's head throb. What would she say? How much would she need to tell them, not just about Justin but about her own foolish trust of him?

Then the worst of it hit her right between the eyes, and she demanded frantically, "Oh, my God, Justin. Was it you? Did you *shoot* at me?"

Kristie gasped. "Oh, no."

Suzannah closed her eyes. "Justin?"

"You weren't in any danger," he told her firmly. "You've seen my file. I'm a great shot, especially at close range. I'd shoot my*self* before I'd take a chance with your life."

As Suzannah listened, dumbfounded, he continued. "I thought you'd call 911. You'd describe the guy, and of course they'd question me, but no one would believe it really was me. I had no motive. I figured that once the D.A. heard about it, he'd finally accept the fact that someone was trying to frame me—"

"You shot a gun at me?" Suzannah interrupted him.

"Only because I was confident I wouldn't hit you."

"Justin?" Kristie murmured. "You know I love you like a brother. But still..." Her tone turned brisk. "I'll help you. You know that. But for the moment, maybe you should just get some rest. Call back later if you want. But for now, I want to talk to Suzannah."

"Essie—"

"I'm not kidding, Justin. I can't talk to you right now. And I won't ask Suzannah to either. It's too weird, at least for now."

"Forever," Suzannah corrected her quietly. "I'll do what he asks. Arrange a deal. Then I'm out of it."

"I don't blame you for feeling that way now, Suzy," Justin told her. "But I have to believe that someday you and I—"

"If you really believe that," Suzannah told him through gritted teeth, "you're a bigger fool than I am."

"We're hanging up now, Justin," Kristie added.

"Wait, Essie! One more thing. It's important. It's about McGregor."

"Pardon?"

"Go ahead and tell him everything. I'm not asking you to keep this secret. I'd never put you in that position. Not over me. Not ever again."

"Thank you."

"Tell McGregor I'm going to turn myself in. He has my word. But if he and the Bureau will wait till Monday, so Suzannah has a chance to broker the deal, I'd appreciate it."

"Okay." The spinner's tone warmed a little. "Take care of yourself. Promise? Follow your doctor friend's advice. And call me in a day or two."

"Will do." He cleared his throat. "Suzy? Do you think you can arrange the deal before you leave for Hawaii? Or will we have to wait—"

"I'm not going to Hawaii until this is resolved," Suzannah said, speaking to Kristie rather than to Justin. "I'll do my best to reach Armstrong this weekend, but at the worst, I'll have something hammered out by Monday afternoon. Justin can call you for an update then." Ignoring his attempt to thank her, she murmured, "Maybe I'll just get myself a drink of water, if you don't mind?"

"Help yourself," Kristie told her. "I'll be there in a minute."

Managing a grateful smile, Suzannah left her purse and briefcase on the table and hurried into the kitchen, where she splashed cold water on her face. This nightmare still seemed unreal. And impossible. And yet things were already falling into place.

*Right from the start, it was all about Night Arrow for him. Even the lovemaking. It was part of the dance. Part of the foreplay. It's what turned him on. And meanwhile, you were so distracted, first by the judge, then by the prospect of representing a sexy federal agent, then by his eyes....*

She sank into a chair and buried her face in her hands, mortified and brokenhearted and furious beyond belief.

*Even when you saw him pull out a gun and shoot at you! How stupid can you get? Remember how he reacted when you got back to the apartment? He tried to talk you into calling the police. Because that's what he wanted! That was his plan, but he didn't know that you were so stupidly, stupidly hung up on him that you couldn't suspect him of such a thing even if you saw him do it with your own two eyes.*

"Hey." Kristie draped a quilt around Suzannah's shoulders, then sat across the kitchen table from her. "I'm so sorry."

"Yeah. Me, too." She tried to smile. "I feel like someone punched me in the stomach."

"I think someone did."

Suzannah nodded. "I hope you told him to get to a hospital. He sounded like he was on his deathbed."

"He said he's got painkillers and fresh bandages. He wants to stay under the radar until the deal is set. I guess I don't blame him for that. It's going to be a nightmare when this breaks. His career has been so perfect up till now."

Suzannah sighed. "I know. I read his file. And I heard the dedication and pride in his voice when he talked about the case. I don't think I imagined that. I just didn't understand where it was coming from. Even though," she smiled wryly, "he told me often enough. Night Arrow, Night Arrow, Night Arrow! He was like a broken record."

"We were all excited about that project," Kristie said, shaking her head sadly. "My boyfriend and me, our friends who first uncovered the research and Justin. The five of us talked about it on a conference call one night like kids around a campfire. But I guess for Justin it was more mesmerizing than I realized. I never could have predicted this."

"But you did," Suzannah reminded her. "Right before he called, you told me straight out that he might have lied about killing Gia." Her hands clenched into fists at her side. "But me? I never *once* questioned his story. Not even at the beginning. And even when I saw him shoot at me with my own eyes, I immediately assumed it was someone pretending to be him."

"He can be very convincing. And he was—is—your client."

"He's your close friend—almost like a brother to you. But you still asked questions."

"True," Kristie murmured. "But then again, I've never been in love with him. That's a little different."

Suzannah opened her mouth to protest, then just shrugged her shoulders. What was the point in disputing it? She wasn't ready to concede that her feelings for him had been anything approaching actual love, but she *had* been smitten. There was no denying that.

"You'll get through this, you know. And someday you'll forgive him. Trust me on that because I've been there. I know all about it."

"You're nicer than I am," Suzannah assured her. "I'm glad you were with me when he dropped his little bombshell. Anyway…" She took a deep breath, then stood up. "I'd better get going or I'll miss my plane. I'll keep in touch."

"Are you okay driving yourself to the airport? We could change your flight and you could stay—"

"I've got to pick up my dog. And I probably need the time alone. But thanks."

Kristie walked her into the dining room, where they gathered up her things before heading for the front door. "Keep in touch. You can call me anytime, day or night, even if you just need someone to talk to."

"I'll be fine," Suzannah assured her. "Give me a couple of days to contact Armstrong and make the deal. I'll check in Sunday evening no matter what. And thanks again." On impulse, she gave the spinner a quick hug. "I see why you mean so much to him."

Kristie eyed her with concern. "None of this is your fault. You know that, don't you?"

"Don't worry," Suzannah promised with a halfhearted smile. "I plan to blame *him* completely."

* * *

By the time her plane landed, Suzannah's head was swimming, mostly because she had spent the entire flight identifying all the clues that should have alerted her to Justin's deception. As it turned out, there were dozens of them, mostly centered around Night Arrow, but those were the forgivable ones. The ones related to the shooting incident were the ones that really hurt, even though she had to admit those grocery bags had been at least three feet from her—probably more, considering the fact that she had already taken her dive toward the pavement by the time the shots were actually fired. So Justin was probably right—even on his worst day, he wouldn't have come within inches of hitting her.

And as far as hurting her emotionally was concerned, he had been so confident he'd solve the case. He'd find the superspy, foreign-agent, Night Arrow-stalker he was so sure killed Horace and he'd pin the blame for Gia's death and Suzannah's near miss on that guy, too. And the whole world would believe him and praise him, and Suzannah would forever adore him, and Night Arrow would be safe.

Then he hit a wall. Or more accurately a fist. She wondered what the D.A. would think about that. Or maybe Justin didn't plan on admitting he had tried to break into Derek Seldon's house. She should have asked him whether it was okay to tell them about his injuries and how he got them.

*You had other things on your mind. Take Kristie's advice and give yourself a break. And don't worry about what to say to Armstrong. There'll be time for that tomorrow. Tonight, just go home and sleep it off.*

But first she had to pick up Murphy, so as soon as she was outside the airport, she dialed the judge's number.

He answered on the first ring. "Ms. Ryder, I presume?"

"Hi, Your Honor. I just landed. Give me twenty minutes and I'll take Murf off your hands." Striding toward the short-term-parking lot, she asked, "How did he do?"

"He and Sam had a ball. They're sound asleep, curled up together like littermates."

"Oh..." She bit back a sigh that was inches away from a sob. "How cute."

"There's no sense waking them up. Pick the dog up in the morning. Or Sam and I can drop him off at your place if that's better for you."

"What?" Suzannah bit her lip, surprised by how much she had been looking forward to holding the puppy in her arms. His fur would be so soft, so comforting. He'd lick her face and stare adoringly into her eyes and make her feel loved, not to mention needed.

"They wore each other out," the judge was telling her. "I wish you could have seen it."

"Me, too."

"Anytime you need him watched this week, just let me know. It's been a godsend for me."

"Actually..." She had reached her car and began to rummage for her keys as she pictured what Saturday was going to be like, trying to arrange meetings with Johnson and Wiley and thereafter with Armstrong while also preparing for her trip to Hawaii.

And then there was the trip itself! For some strange reason, she had assumed Justin would come home in time to stay with Murphy. That was a laugh! Of course, she could always ask Noelle, but even at its quickest, the trip would take close to three days, right smack in the middle of the landscaper's important design project.

And a kennel was out of the question, especially when a warm, loving, kid-filled environment was available.

"I have some errands to run tomorrow," she murmured finally. "So if I could drop him off for a few hours, that would be terrific. And then there's the infamous e-presentation in Hawaii. I was originally supposed to leave Sunday, but now I'm thinking Monday night at the earliest. So if you and Sam are really available—"

"You'd be doing me a favor, believe me. Just leave Murphy here tonight, too. You can run your errands first thing in the morning, then come and get him after that."

She grimaced but nodded. "That makes sense, I guess."

"Good." He chuckled. "You should have thought it through, Ms. Ryder. A young, ambitious attorney at your stage of a career doesn't have time to raise a puppy alone. I can see why you couldn't resist Murphy, but you should have thought it through."

"You're right, Your Honor."

"If you decide you can't handle it and want to find him a good home, my daughter and Sam would be thrilled to have him. They've got a big backyard, and she's home all day—"

"He already has a home," Suzannah interrupted, and to her embarrassment, her voice cracked with emotion. "Thanks, anyway, sir."

The judge was silent for a moment. Then he asked, "Is everything all right?"

"Everything's fine. Thanks. I'm just exhausted. So

thanks for keeping Murf overnight. I'll—I'll call you first thing in the morning. How's that?"

"Get some rest," he urged her. "Things will look better after a good night's sleep, you know."

"Thanks, Your Honor. Give Murf a pat for me, okay? And if he seems to be missing me, just tell him nighty-night. He—he really likes that."

The first two nights after Justin's disappearance, she had slept on the living room couch, supposedly because it enabled her to hear Murphy if he whimpered from his box in the kitchen. The truth was more depressing—she hadn't wanted to revisit "the scene of the crime," even though she had changed the sheets and destroyed all other evidence of their afternoon of lovemaking.

But she couldn't go on sleeping on the sofa forever, so tonight she forced herself to go to bed, remembering only too late that there was another reason to avoid it—the nightmare.

Except Judge Taylor didn't seem so scary anymore. And Justin bloody and mangled? Well, that had turned out to be prophetic. The only difference was she no longer cared. Not about him nor about the Angel of Mercy nor her reputation nor the trip to Hawaii nor even the Twelve-Year Plan. All she really wanted was for this awful day to be over, even though she knew in her gut that the next two days were going to be even worse.

Talking to Noelle might have helped, but as Suzannah stumbled around her apartment at dawn the next morning, she reminded herself it wasn't a prudent option. Sharing confidential information with her best friend had rarely presented a problem—she trusted her implicitly—but news of Justin's guilt was simply too sensitive.

And on a more practical note, if Noelle ever realized Justin had been the one who'd shot that gun at Suzannah, well... That information was a little too volatile to share. Depressing, too, especially since Noelle's own romance seemed to be back on track, at least according to the message she had left for Suzannah about her "Sperminator relapse," which was the reason Suzannah had been unable to reach her the previous afternoon.

All of Justin's files, along with his briefcase and duffel bag, were still in the kitchen, but Suzannah wasn't ready to deal with them yet either, so she just sipped her morning coffee in the living room and watched the clock until it finally hit eight. Then she punched the judge's number for a Murphy report. Predictably Sam and the dog were already outside playing in the judge's "very safe fenced backyard."

Feeling relieved yet lonely, she thanked him again, then dialed a more difficult number—that of Aaron Johnson. When she only reached his message service, she tried John Wiley, who answered on the first ring and explained that Johnson had gone home to visit his wife and kids for a long weekend.

Wiley assured her that he was "at her service," so she arranged to meet him at a nearby coffee shop, where she quickly and dispassionately outlined the situation, carefully omitting the fact that her own client had tried to kill her and that, rather than calling the police, she had responded to the assault by sleeping with the assailant.

To her surprise, the attorney reacted with grace and sympathy. "I'm sure the deal will go smoothly, Suzannah, so try not to worry. I'm just sorry you've been thrown in the middle of this. It wasn't fair of Russo or the judge or, quite frankly, me and Aaron to let things get this out of hand."

"You're being so sweet. After the awful things I said to you. I was so arrogant, when all along you were right about Justin."

"Actually..." Wiley shrugged his shoulders. "Aaron and I had a long talk after you left that night and we decided you were right. We *were* jealous of Russo. Not because of his success with women," he added quickly, "but just generally, because the guy had so much going for him. His record *is*—well, was—outstanding, and he was so nonchalant about it. I guess men want their heroes to have more—well, more substance, for lack of a better word."

Suzannah sighed. "He has substance in his own way. I still believe he only lied about killing Gia because he wanted to continue the investigation. It wasn't to protect his reputation. He was convinced someone was trying to get their hands on secret government research conducted at Masterson Enterprises. He lied for his country and it backfired. On all of us."

"Maybe so. You know him better than I do." Wiley flushed. "I didn't mean anything by that."

Suzannah smiled. "Don't worry. As it turns out, I did sort of fall for his routine, just like you guys predicted. But no harm done, right?"

Wiley was silent for a moment. Then he suggested,

"You've got your conference in Hawaii to deal with. Why not let me handle things with Armstrong from here on out? I'm ninety-nine percent sure she'll go along with Russo's proposal—he signs a statement admitting to killing Gia in self-defense and to obstructing justice, the D.A. moves to dismiss the murder charge and recommends probation to Judge Taylor."

"And then?" Suzannah bit her lip. "Is there any chance the FBI will be lenient, too? In light of his amazing record of service? If there's some way we can help with that, I'd like to."

"It's hard to say. Even if they don't can him outright, they'll never trust him alone in the field again. Maybe they'll find something else for him to do. But my guess is they'll ask for his resignation, and he'll give it. Then he'll get some sort of consulting job. He'll land on his feet," Wiley added firmly. "Guys like that always do, so don't worry about him. He doesn't deserve it. Not after what he did to you."

"I'm fine. And I promised Agent Russo I'd be involved in any negotiations with the prosecutor. If we could do it together, that would be great. I know I'm an albatross," she said with a wry smile, "but I'm a quick study and highly motivated to get this settled."

Wiley seemed about to argue, then just shook his head and pulled his cell phone out of his jacket pocket. "Okay, then, if you're sure. Let's get this show on the road."

Jan Armstrong turned out to be a kind, intelligent, reasonable woman, only too happy to agree to a tentative bargain. She explained that the district attorney knew about the meeting and had asked her to proceed, but he would need to review the information and make the final decision, which he'd certainly do by Sunday night. Assuming Justin showed up on Monday morning to sign on the dotted line, the D.A. was confident they could appear before Judge Taylor that same day so that Suzannah could catch a plane Monday evening.

She could just imagine how the judge would react when he learned that her "errands" had revolved around a plea bargain for her client. At least he'd finally understand why she sounded so scattered every time she called to check up on Murphy, which was nearly every hour.

She was about to make another such call—this time to arrange the actual pickup of the puppy, since the plea bargain seemed acceptable to everyone—when Jan Armstrong suggested they have a drink together. Wiley begged off, and Suzannah was pretty sure she knew why. He thought she needed to talk to a woman—to cry on her shoulder—and since all of these negotiations were still confidential, he thought Armstrong was the only female shoulder available.

"I'll bet this isn't part of your usual job description," Suzannah joked after they had settled into a booth in a Mexican restaurant across from Armstrong's office. "I must seem like such a basket case, but I promise I'm not. I just have a lot on my mind. Because of the conference. Everything's so jammed, time-wise."

Armstrong eyed her sympathetically. "Criminal defendants are almost always guilty. And they're usually the scum of the earth on top of that. But Russo takes the cake. The way he roped you into this was unconscionable. The rest of us—me and my boss, Wiley and Johnson—we're used to a certain level of slime. We *chose* this line of work. But you... The guy was such an asshole to drag you into it just because he knew he could use your history with the judge to manipulate him."

"He wanted to solve Horace Masterson's murder."

"Give me a break." Armstrong scowled. "You don't have feelings for him, do you? Because that would make you an enabler, not to mention a doormat, and you don't strike me as the type."

Suzannah gave a rueful laugh. "I just want to make sure we all despise him for the right reasons. That's my last official act as his attorney."

Armstrong laughed, too. "Good. You're my hero, you know. The way you stood up to Taylor the Jailor—it was amazing. Did you see that vein in his neck bulge every time you hit him with a zinger?"

"I wasn't trying to zing him. Just to survive."

"Well, you really got him. And we all secretly applauded, because he's given us so much grief."

"He's not so bad," Suzannah murmured.

"You're enabling again."

"Right." Suzannah tried to smile. "It's a new habit, and one I plan to shake. It's just been so bizarre."

"That's an understatement. Remember when Russo defended you? That was actually pretty cool." Armstrong assumed a deep voice and intoned, "'Your Honor, I'm going to have to insist that you treat my attorney with respect.' Man, I wish some gorgeous guy would do that for *me* some day."

"Now who's an enabling doormat?"

The prosecutor grinned. "I guess he got to all of us. All the women, I mean. That's his MO right? And he's *sooo* good at it." She rolled her eyes. "Too bad he's a creep. But no lasting damage, right? Just five days out of your life shot to shit."

"Six days," Suzannah corrected. Then she laughed at herself and agreed, "But like you said, no permanent damage done."

No permanent damage...

"But the temporary damage is a bitch," she told herself when she finally made it back to her apartment later that afternoon.

She was glad she had resisted the urge to drown her sorrows in anything stronger than cola during the heart-to-heart with Armstrong. It just would have made her feel worse, assuming that was even possible. And as much as she had appreciated the prosecutor's genuine offer of friendship and sympathy "off the record," Suzannah didn't need a friend right now. She needed some sleep and some way to blot out all memory of Justin Russo.

She had barely had time to change her clothes when the phone began to ring. The sound caused her to jump, and she finally realized how raw her nerves had become. The thought that it might be Justin or Charlie or Doctor Schuler or even Armstrong saying that the deal had fallen through...

But it was Judge Taylor telling her that he and Sam were going to take Murf for a walk and didn't want Suzannah to worry. She heard herself assuring him that it was fine. That she'd contact him in a few hours to arrange to pick up the puppy. But she knew in her heart that it might not be true. Every hour that passed brought her closer to the moment when she'd have to admit that the responsible thing—the *adult* thing to do—was to let Sam keep the dog. It was best for everyone, especially Murphy, wasn't it?

"You need to get out of this funk," she warned herself aloud after she hung up the phone. "What if that had been Charlie? Or Schuler? What are you going to do about them?"

She hadn't revealed any of that information to Wiley or Armstrong, on the theory that it was really Justin's place to make such decisions. But if the Angel of Mercy appeared out of nowhere again, maybe even at Suzannah's front door, she needed a game plan.

She also needed Murphy there, she decided unhappily. Even if he was better off with Sam, he was Suzannah's dog, and she needed his unconditional, slobbery love. She wanted to curl up with him on the sofa and be miserable for the rest of the day and long into the night.

*Hypocrite. You want to curl up with Justin,* she taunted herself. And it was true. She even wished he had left behind his bomber jacket so she'd have something to cuddle close. Something soft and warm that smelled like him.

"Armstrong's right! You're an enabling doormat. Snap out of it." She strode over to the things he had left behind, namely stacks of folders and papers, which she began shoving into his briefcase. When that was full, she reached for his empty duffel bag and opened it wide, ready to stuff it, too, and then to toss all evidence of his existence into her laundry closet. He could come and collect it while she was in Hawaii.

*Because luckily,* she drawled to herself, *he has a key. Sheesh! You really were his sex slave, weren't you?*

The duffel bag, as it turned out, wasn't completely empty. There was a long white envelope in it with Suzannah's name scrawled in big blue letters across the front.

She stared at it, confused and angry.

"What now, Justin?" she demanded. "What more could you possibly have to say? Let me guess. You really *are* in love with Mia, like she claimed? Or Gia's death wasn't really self-defense?"

She was tempted just to throw the envelope away unopened. Or to make Noelle come over and pre-read it for her. But her fingers were already loosening the flap and pulling the folded piece of paper out, so she just prayed that it wouldn't be more bad news—or worse, some sort of half-assed love letter. Then she took a deep breath and began to read.

Dear Suzy,
If you're reading this, something must have gone wrong. Maybe I'm even dead. Whatever it is, I know you're blaming yourself, but I'm begging you not to. You've been so great. So amazing. I had no right to involve you in this, but selfishly I still believe that meeting you—dragging you into my life—has been the best mistake I ever made. I'm crazy about you and I know you have feelings

for me, too. But if it all went south, you have to move on. Don't try to solve the case or find my killers or anything like that. Talk to S-3—she'll help you through this. Then move on, either with the Twelve-Year Plan or something even better. And meanwhile, forgive me and believe me when I say you changed my life.
Love, Justin

Suzannah sank to the floor and wrapped her arms around her knees, then slowly, rhythmically began to rock back and forth.

"What are you *doing* to me?" she moaned. "Can't you just go away? This is nuts! How can you sound so sweet? So sincere? How can you sign *this* note 'Love, Justin' but the other one 'Fondly, JRusso'? You wrote this one *before* we slept together. You went from 'love' to 'fondly' *after* that?"

Her voice grew strident. "And *I* went from Suzy with a *y* to Suzie with an *ie*? *After* we slept together? When everyone knows Suzy with a *y* is ten times more intimate?"

Pulling her purse off the table, she located the crumpled note, laid it out flat on the floor and put the new note beside it. Then she forced herself to study them closely, and as she did so, her heart began to pound.

*Love, Justin*
*Fondly, JRusso*
*Suzie*
*Suzy*
*If you're reading this, something must have gone wrong. Maybe I'm even dead....*

"He didn't write both of these notes," Suzannah told herself warily. "The penmanship's the same, but this one—the Suzy one—is so clearly Justin. And the other one... Why would he spell your name two different ways? Why would he sign one Justin, then revert back to JRusso after you *slept* together?"

Jumping up, she began scanning every document in his briefcase that contained his signature. There it was, again and again. *JRusso... JRusso... JRusso...*

"Because these are all official forms or professional correspondence. This is his standard signature. If someone who only knew him in his professional capacity wanted to forge a note from him, they'd copy his handwriting and his signature."

It seemed far-fetched yet possible, and she realized that she had been aching for just that—a possibility that this nightmare was a mistake. That he hadn't betrayed her, hadn't shot at her, hadn't killed Gia.

*If you're reading this...maybe I'm dead...*

"Not dead," she whispered. "Not necessarily. You went out for Chinese food. That's the last certain contact I had with you. They were waiting for you. Grabbed you, forged the note and then..."

She grimaced. "Who made the call? It sounded like you, but how clever of them! With a supposedly broken nose, a raw throat and hopped up on pain killers, we'd never notice if the voice wasn't exactly right."

She began to pace. "Think, Suzannah. Why would they do all of this? Just so you'd tell the prosecutor Justin confessed? Is that what this is all about?" She recoiled from that thought, knowing that their next step would then be fiendishly simple. They'd kill him and arrange for his body to be found—a car accident or maybe even suicide, with a note declaring he couldn't live with what he had done to his career.

"It can't be true," she told herself frantically. "It's way too elaborate if that's all they want from it. Why drag Kristie into it, for one thing? And all that crap about Night Arrow! Why did they bother with that if— *Oh!*"

She stopped pacing and stood perfectly still, forcing herself to understand. To put it all together. Hearing the impostor's words again, spoken in a voice filled with devotion to a crazy South American legend. It had sounded so familiar at that moment because the speaker, whoever he was, had shared her client's obsession to such an amazing degree.

"Oh, my God, Justin," Suzannah whispered, her voice choked with desperate admiration. "You were right all along. It was *always* about Night Arrow."

## Chapter 9

"Mmm... Whoever invented make-up sex was a genius."

Director Will McGregor chuckled as his girlfriend and favorite employee stretched in exaggerated satisfaction. "Sometimes I think you start fights just so we *can* make up."

Kristie pulled the covers up to her neck. "Careful, handsome. You did a good job apologizing. Don't blow it now."

He laughed again. "Since we're handing out compliments, you did a good job, too. By telling me all about your conversation with Russo and his attorney yesterday, instead of handling it on your own, you convinced me you've turned over a new leaf in the by-the-book department." Licking his lips, he added softly, "You really surprised me with that."

"Well, I didn't want you to fire me and then resign," she quipped, adding more sincerely, "I love my job. And I love you. Even more importantly I *trust* you. That's why I told you about Suzannah's visit. And Justin's confession." She shook her head slowly. "It was so awful, Will. For everyone involved."

"I'll bet. On the other hand, life goes on, right?" he asked, trying for a casual tone.

"Hmm?"

He cleared his throat. "Remember the first time we were together in this bed? I reached like this—" he leaned over the edge of the bed to open the drawer of his nightstand "—then I pulled out a gun. Tonight I thought I'd try something more romantic."

Retrieving the ring box he had hidden earlier that evening, he handed it to his pretty bedmate. "So?"

"Omigosh! You're going to propose naked?"

"Is that a problem?"

"No. I kinda like it." She licked her lips, clearly dying to open the box but restraining herself. "Go on."

McGregor's heart pounded as he studied her trusting expression. "In some ways, I feel like I should be doing this over the phone. That's how I fell in love with you. Your sexy laugh. Your crazy, brilliant ideas…" His voice failed him unexpectedly. "You owned my heart from that very first conversation."

"And you owned mine," she whispered, wrapping her arms around his neck, welcoming his kiss.

It would have been the perfect romantic moment if Nugget, a usually well-behaved dog, hadn't started barking ferociously from the backyard.

Kristie gave a playful laugh. "He wants us to stay on task. This is supposed to be a marriage proposal, not a roll in the hay."

"Right." McGregor opened the box and pulled an exquisite emerald-cut diamond ring from its nest. "What do you say, Goldie? Will you marry me?"

"Oh…" Her blue eyes glistened. "I love it. I can't imagine a more perfect moment—" Her expression soured as the doorbell rang, accompanied by another spate of frantic barking by Nugget. "*Sheesh!* Now what?"

"I'll get rid of whoever it is," McGregor told her, trying not to let her see that his instincts had gone on full alert.

*Old habits die hard,* he reminded himself as he pulled on jeans and a white V-neck undershirt. There really wasn't much danger in his life these days—not like during the old undercover capers that had been the hallmark of his career.

This was probably a neighbor. Some kid whose basketball had jumped the fence. It was still early by polite-society standards, so no one would expect that they were getting McGregor out of bed.

Unless, of course, they knew Kristie was visiting.

Resisting an impulse to stop at the hall credenza to grab a small pistol—a remnant of his agent days—McGregor nevertheless eyed the umbrella stand in the foyer, ensuring that his baseball bat was in place, before he swung the front door open.

He wasn't expecting a pretty blond stranger dressed in jeans and a pink sweatshirt. But *she* was clearly expecting him, because she thrust her hand forward and said with apologetic confidence, "Director McGregor? Sorry to bother you, especially at dinnertime. But I'm Justin Russo's attorney and I really, *really* need your help."

Punchy from her long drive, Suzannah had to force herself not to notice how attractive this very rumpled, five-o'clock-shadowed Will McGregor was. After a week of Justin's golden glow, she had forgotten how sexy meat and potatoes could be.

*Lucky Kristie...*

As if hearing the silent tribute, the spinner peeked around from behind her boyfriend and exclaimed, "Suzannah? Good grief, is everything okay?"

Suzannah winced, realizing from Kristie's outfit—a man's tailored white shirt over bare legs—that she had interrupted more than supper.

"Come in," McGregor was insisting. Then he glanced pointedly at the white pickup truck parked at the curb, its landscaping logo brightly illuminated by a street lamp. "You didn't drive three hundred miles to get here, did you?"

"It's a long story."

"You must be exhausted, poor thing." Kristie grabbed her by the hand and pulled her into the house. "Do you want some coffee? Did something else go wrong? Did you hear from Justin again? Because I haven't heard a thing—"

"Let her get a word in, Goldie," McGregor advised, chuckling.

"Sorry." The spinner touched Suzannah's cheek. "Is it worse? Or better?"

"It's...well, it's different, that's for sure. And I don't

really know where to start, but—" Suzannah eyed them hopefully. "Is there any chance your agency recorded that call we got from Justin yesterday?"

"Sure. They record all of them," McGregor told her. "We can get you a transcript if you want."

"All of them?" She exhaled sharply. "So it's possible you could compare the most recent one with a call that Justin made at some other point in time? The farther back, the better."

"What would we be looking for?"

"To see if the voice patterns match." Suzannah smiled self-consciously. "You must have that capability, right? I mean, even if someone's injured or has a sore throat, you could see if the patterns matched. Couldn't you?"

McGregor and Kristie exchanged worried looks, then the director suggested, "Why don't we all sit down? You must be tired, Ms. Ryder. And hungry, too, I'm guessing. You've been under tremendous stress—"

"It wasn't Justin," she said, looking him directly in the eyes, then moving her gaze to the spinner's shocked expression. "I'm sure of it. I just need you to do the comparison so *you'll* be sure, too."

McGregor pursed his lips, then nodded. "I'll make the arrangements right away. Goldie, why don't you and Ms. Ryder get comfortable in the living room? Visit for a minute or two." He gave Suzannah an unexpected grin. "But don't spill the details until I get back. I don't want to miss anything."

She laughed with relief. "I'll try to restrain myself."

As McGregor disappeared through the kitchen door,

Kristie pulled Suzannah over to the sofa. "Sit. Talk. Tell me how you're so sure it wasn't Justin."

"Your boyfriend asked us to wait. He's really nice, by the way."

"And he's not just my boyfriend."

"Right. Your boss, too. Lucky you."

"Boyfriend, boss. And now this." Kristie wagged her hand in Suzannah's face, playfully showcasing a small but dazzling diamond.

"Oh, no! *Please* tell me I didn't interrupt the freaking marriage proposal! I'm so, *soooo* sorry."

"That's okay. It makes for a better story years from now. Especially if what you're saying is true." The spinner's voice grew soft with hope. "Tell me why you think it was someone else."

"You're the spinner," Suzannah reminded her. "You tell me."

Kristie hesitated, then nodded. "Okay, I'll give it a try. Hmmm... For one thing, he said he wasn't going to turn to me to solve his problems anymore. But then he called *me,* not you, the first time something went wrong."

Suzannah tried not to laugh as she watched the gears turning in her new friend's brain. "That's a pretty good one. What else?"

The spinner bit her lip, then admitted, "Justin Russo would never fire a loaded gun at an innocent woman, much less one he cared about. He'd never take that kind of chance."

"Okay, they're working on it," McGregor interrupted from the doorway. Walking over to the coffee table, he set down a tray with three bottles of beer and two cans of cola, then settled into an overstuffed chair. "We'll have the results in a few minutes. Meanwhile, why don't you start from the beginning, Ms. Ryder?"

"Call her Suzannah," Kristie scolded him, then she turned to their guest. "We're dying here, so *please* tell us where you got this idea."

"He left me another note. I didn't find it till this afternoon, but he must have written it Tuesday or Wednesday. Before we had...well, sex." Suzannah gave McGregor a sheepish wince. "You know all about that, right?"

He nodded. "What did the note say?"

Suzannah pulled it out of her purse and handed it to him. "It sounds like him. Much more than the other note—the kiss-off one—did. And look how he signed it—*Love, Justin*."

Kristie reached over and took the note from her fiancé. "Love, Justin? But the other note...?"

"*Fondly, JRusso*," Suzannah confirmed, passing the crumpled page to the spinner for comparison.

"*After* sex, he's suddenly back to JRusso?"

McGregor eyed them as though they'd lost their minds. "I'm assuming there's more than just this?"

Suzannah gave him an encouraging smile. "In the kiss-off note, I'm Suzie with an *ie*. But in the pre-sex note, Suzy with a *y*."

"You lost me."

Kristie laughed. "Don't you see, Will? Suzy with a *y* is much more intimate."

He scowled. "Sorry, but I'm still gonna need a little more."

The spinner laughed again, but this time her heart

clearly wasn't in it. "The more I think about it, the more I actually *don't* want to believe it, Suzannah. Because if someone has been impersonating him—forging notes and mimicking his voice—then the next step is too awful to think about. You see that, don't you? Now that he has quote-unquote confessed, they'd want to finish the job. Kill him so he can never set the record straight." She patted her guest's arm. "I know you're mad at him, but it's better if he's guilty and alive than innocent and dead. Right?"

McGregor's cell phone rang, and he flipped it open and had a short conversation that ended with, "Stand by. We may need to move fast on this."

Then he closed the phone and announced quietly, "Russo didn't make that call."

An eerie silence filled the air, with even Suzannah feeling a tremor of shock. She had been almost sure, yet until this moment there had been the chance, however slight, that he was okay.

*Guilty but alive,* as Kristie had so succinctly put it.

"Suzannah isn't crying," the spinner noted to her fiancé. "That means there's more. That means there's hope."

"There's always hope," he murmured, his eyes warm with sympathy as he looked from one Justin admirer to the other. "But we need to be realistic. Like Kristie said, once they got you two to believe his confession on Friday, the smart move was to kill him. The good news is, they need to make it look like he died instantly. As a suicide or an accident. Either way, it would be over for him quickly and with a minimum of pain." He cleared his throat and insisted, "I promise you they'll pay for what they've done. No one kills an FBI agent and gets away with it."

"You're assuming their only goal is to frame Justin for Gia's murder," Suzannah protested.

"What more could they want?"

"Night Arrow. Remember?" She flashed a confident smile. "I agree, at some point they'll kill him. But the longer they keep him alive, the longer they can learn to imitate him. Not just his voice but his manner. His bearing. His facial expressions. They can drug him and extract information as it becomes necessary. So—" she exhaled sharply "—I think he's still alive."

McGregor cocked his head to the side. "You're saying they want to infiltrate the Night Arrow project by impersonating Russo? That's pretty far-fetched. The guy has a very distinctive face, at least according to most women I know." He caught himself and added quickly, "Sorry. That was a stupid thing to say."

Kristie leaned across the table to grip McGregor's arm. "The man on the phone claimed to have a broken nose and a smashed eye socket. I think she's right, Will. The old Justin *was* recognizable. But now? I myself could probably be fooled, and I know his face by heart from designing identities for him. There'll be bandages, and even when those come off—" She jumped up, as though unable to contain herself any longer. "It's so simple! I can't believe I missed it." She beamed in Suzannah's direction. "You're miles ahead of us, I can see that in your eyes. So tell us."

"Yeah," McGregor interrupted. "It's still not making sense to me. They can't just find a guy who looks like Russo, with or without a smashed face. They'd need surgery, which takes time. Leaves scars. And the impostor's body would have to match, too. Height, weight, stature."

"*Now* who won't let her get a word in edgewise?" Kristie demanded.

Suzannah sighed. "It's fun watching you go through all the same steps I went through. But I have the advantage. For one thing, I *saw* the bad guy, remember? The day he took a shot at me from that rooftop. It fooled me for a minute. He was wearing a jacket like Justin's and he had the same body, same stance. Apparently he had been practicing already."

Kristie clapped her hands. "Of course!"

Suzannah gave McGregor a reassuring smile. "Don't worry. There's more."

"Good."

She reached into her purse and pulled out a handful of photos from Justin's files. "Take a look at the Masterson clan."

Kristie and McGregor spread the pictures on the coffee table.

"Wow, I knew those sisters were supposed to look alike," Kristie said. "And a lot like their mom. But this is just amazing."

"We'll get back to that," Suzannah promised. "But for now, look at the one of Horace and Julia on their wedding day. Note their body types in particular. When Justin and I went to question Mia—the younger daughter—she literally threw herself into his arms. And they looked just like Horace and Julia. Except, of course, Justin's face was different."

"Are you following this, Goldie?" McGregor muttered.

"Not really," the spinner admitted. "But I'm sure we will eventually. Go on, Suzannah."

"Okay." Suzannah took a deep breath. "After I compared the two notes and decided someone was trying to impersonate Justin, I had the same reaction you did. That it would be impossible to find someone who looked enough like him, unless by some miracle he had a bunch of look-alikes in his family tree, the way the Masterson girls did. Then I remembered the guy who took a shot at me. Same body as Justin. Which meant he had the same body as Horace, see?"

McGregor winced. "You're saying Horace Masterson is still alive?"

"No, no. I'm saying there's a guy running around with the same build as Justin and Horace. The body type that Mia Masterson can't get enough of."

When McGregor and Kristie just stared, Suzannah laughed in frustration. "I keep forgetting you don't know the Masterson saga as well as I do. Those sisters were Elektra-fied, if you get my drift. Huge complexes when it came to earning, losing and otherwise engaging Daddy's love. If someone wanted to infiltrate the family as a way of getting their hands on the company, the quickest way would be to seduce one of the daughters. I think that's how the impostor first entered the picture. Justin and I call him Agent X—a foreign agent or some sort of broker of government secrets."

She took a deep breath, then continued. "Justin suspected from the start that the Angel of Mercy didn't kill Horace. Agent X did. If I'm right—and you'll see that I probably am—Agent X looks like Horace, probably through a combination of natural body type and plastic surgery. He used that resemblance to seduce Mia when she was in exile at her cousin Cynthia's house in Boston. There was Mia—a spoiled yet penniless outcast. And suddenly she could have it all—sex with her daddy look-alike, the money, the company—and revenge. I'm guessing she didn't know—maybe still doesn't know—that Agent X was after government secrets. She just thought he was helping her get back what she had lost."

"You're saying he had plastic surgery once to look like Horace. And now again to look like Justin?" McGregor asked skeptically.

"I think so. Or it's possible that the body type was enough to seduce Mia, especially since—"

"Especially since Agent X is a natural mimic," Kristie interrupted, her blue eyes dancing. "We have a couple of them on our payroll, Suzannah, and they're absolutely amazing. If this man was able to *sound* like Horace and had the goods, body-wise, the face would have been overkill. So I'll bet he didn't get surgery the first time. Just imitated Horace's manner."

"You're right," Suzannah admitted. "The face would have been too creepy. Not subtle enough for Agent X."

Kristie smiled. "But this time—to impersonate Justin— he needs the face, too. So he got plastic surgery as soon as he realized Justin's investigation had ruined Masterson

Enterprises's chance of getting Night Arrow. Then all he had to do was find a way to take Justin's place."

"I have a question, Suzannah," McGregor interrupted. "Why are you so sure he seduced Mia at her cousin's house? Wasn't that years ago? Isn't it more likely that he did it recently? Especially if his motive was to get at Night Arrow?"

"Will's right," Kristie said. "None of us knew about Night Arrow back then, much less that Masterson Enterprises would have a chance at developing it."

"Agent X didn't know about Night Arrow in those days," Suzannah agreed. "He just wanted access to Masterson Enterprises in general. Because of the string of top-secret projects they were constantly handling. He was willing to be patient. To wait years, if necessary. Then Night Arrow came along and he got sloppy."

The spinner's brow furrowed. "You said Agent X gave Mia a way to get revenge, which I assume means he killed Gia and Horace for her, right?"

When Suzannah nodded, Kristie jumped up and started to pace. "You were asking me about this on the phone, right before Justin called. You wanted to know if Mia could ever have really forgiven Gia for siding with the dad against her. For taking all the money for herself and tossing Mia out into the cold."

"Right. It never made sense to me. From the beginning, everyone—Justin especially—kept talking about how genuinely close Gia and Mia were after their reconciliation. Everyone said that they truly loved each other. That Mia could never have harmed Gia. But I kept saying that Mia was the obvious suspect in Gia's death because there was no way she could have ever forgiven her big sister for the way she treated her. Or for stealing all their father's love, not to mention millions of dollars, from her."

"So you think she just pretended to love Gia? To reconcile with her after Cynthia was killed in an accident? Oh! *That's* it, isn't it? You think Agent X killed Cynthia to engineer the sisters' reconciliation!"

Suzannah grinned. "He engineered the reconciliation all right, but not the way you think."

"Huh?"

She sighed. "Even though I didn't really believe Mia could forgive Gia, I had to admit when I met her I thought I sensed some genuine, heartfelt grief. Like she had just lost the person she cared most about in the whole world."

"Oh. My. God."

Suzannah nodded, pleased with the dazed look on the spinner's face. She remembered having that same feeling in her kitchen six hours earlier, when she had thought about the thread of plastic surgery that ran through this entire case. Not just Agent X making himself look like Justin but Gia going to such great lengths so that she *wouldn't* look like her mother. Or like her sister.

Or like her cousin Cynthia. The only person in the world who had loved and cared for Mia in her time of need. The girl whom Mia had proclaimed to be "exactly" like Julia Masterson.

"Look at this picture," Suzannah suggested, handing McGregor a shot of Julia with her two daughters and her niece.

"It's uncanny," he murmured. "I've never seen such a strong family resemblance."

"Gia had plastic surgery so that she wouldn't look like those women anymore."

"And then Cynthia had the exact same plastic surgery—at Agent X's urging—so that she would look like the *new* Gia," Kristie said with a flourish. "Right?"

"Right. It wasn't Cynthia who died in that car wreck three years ago. It was Gia."

## Chapter 10

"Omigosh, Suzannah," Kristie said, her eyes shining. "It all makes perfect sense. There was never any reconciliation. Just a substitution. Agent X knew that with Horace in a coma, there wasn't anyone who would catch the difference between Gia and Cynthia after the surgery. He got Cynthia into position and got at least limited access to Masterson Enterprises in the process. Then he waited for Horace to die so that Cynthia, posing as Gia, would inherit everything."

"He was a patient man," Suzannah repeated. "He could have asked Cynthia to use Gia's power of attorney to have the old man taken off life support, but that might have raised eyebrows, especially given Gia's proclamation that she'd never pull that plug. So he waited. But then Night Arrow came along—a project that fascinated him so completely he *had* to have it. So he got a little sloppy, piggybacking on the Angel of Mercy killings to get rid of Horace for good. Then Cynthia, posing as Gia, inherited Masterson Enterprises. And he controlled Cynthia."

"But because of Justin's investigation, Masterson Enterprises lost Night Arrow."

Suzannah nodded. "So Agent X looked for another way to get his hands on Night Arrow. He studied the confidential information that was supplied to Masterson Enterprises when they were preparing their bid."

"And that's how Agent X knew that Justin and SPIN were intimately involved with the project," McGregor guessed. When Suzannah and Kristie looked surprised, he grumbled, "I'm not a complete moron, you know. I'm beginning to catch on."

Kristie laughed. "I'm still a little fuzzy around the edges myself. Not about the surgery—I *love* that part. But the motives..."

Suzannah nodded. "It's possible Cynthia was motivated by greed. After all, she wouldn't have gotten anything from Horace as Cynthia. But as Gia, she became a rich woman. Unfortunately, once the government pulled Night Arrow from Masterson Enterprises, Cynthia was worth more dead than alive to Agent X. As a murder victim, she became his ticket to posing as Justin and infiltrating Night Arrow."

"I almost feel sorry for her," the spinner mused.

Suzannah nodded. "I think she genuinely loved Mia. Justin kept saying how sweet she was. And how unhappy, which fits. Especially if she helped kill her own cousin, then had to live with the guilt."

"Not just with the guilt. With these ginormous boobs," Kristie noted, tapping a photo taken of Gia postimplants. "I'll bet Agent X wishes he could have seduced *her* instead of Mia."

"Actually…" Suzannah grimaced. "Justin told me the two girls liked ménages à trois. So maybe Agent X had a little something going with Cynthia, too."

McGregor stood up, his expression businesslike. "You'll have to walk me through this another dozen times later. But for now, the important fact is we know the caller wasn't Russo. And if there's any chance he's still alive—"

"He is. They'll keep him alive until the last possible moment," Suzannah told them confidently, just as she had told herself for the whole ride to Los Angeles. Justin had to be alive, because if he wasn't—

"Things have changed now," McGregor reminded her gently. "They must realize that you're onto them. That *we're* onto them."

"Maybe not. Once I realized what was going on, I stopped using any of my phones. That's why I didn't dare call you or buy a plane ticket on my credit card. Or anything. I used my cell phone once—hoping it *was* tapped—and called the guy who's watching my dog. I told him I was stressed out, so I was going to spend the night at a girlfriend's house. Then I went to my friend Noelle's house and parked out front and went in. I snuck out the back and borrowed one of her trucks and used an alley to get out of the neighborhood. Then I drove straight here, paying cash for gas. I'll drive home, too, and park in the back. They'll never know I left."

McGregor and Kristie seemed amused by the elaborate scheme.

"You've got natural spinner tendencies," he told Suzannah.

She shook her head. "Thanks for the compliment, but my nerves couldn't survive much more than this. It's really a relief to be able to dump it on the two of you."

"Our pleasure," Kristie murmured. "I just wish I had figured it out myself. Justin's one of my closest friends, yet I was so willing to think badly of him."

"You were gun-shy because of your experience with Ortega," McGregor consoled her. "And those mimics can be pretty convincing."

"But Suzannah figured it out. Because she knew in her heart he was innocent. And she's only known him for a week."

"Well, to be fair," Suzannah reminded her softly, "I'm in love with the guy, so…"

"Oh!" Kristie strode over to her and pulled her into a hug. "Don't worry. We'll find him."

Suzannah backed away, smiling gratefully. "How?"

"We'll check medical facilities, for one thing. The fake Justin told us he hadn't gone to the hospital, but he might have been lying. Assuming Agent X has had plastic surgery and is still recovering, there should be a record somewhere." To McGregor she added, "We'll need to get Cynthia's medical files. And send someone to the area of Boston where Cynthia and Mia lived during the exile. Maybe the same surgeon who worked on her did Agent X. They need to look for some sort of private nursing facility, either here or in New England."

Suzannah bit her lip. "I just remembered something Mia said. That they have an infirmary on the Masterson estate." Her pulse began to race. "I'll bet that's where they're holding Justin."

"We'll check it out," McGregor promised.

"I want to be there when you do it," Suzannah told him.

McGregor stared down at her, his expression sober. "I could give you a lecture on leaving this to the professionals, but I recognize that look in your eye. It's the same look my fiancée gets when she's about to play superwoman. So I'm going to bypass the lecture and give you the cold, hard facts." His tone softened. "If Russo is alive, it's because they don't realize yet that we're onto them. They'll be watching you. You need to go back to your girlfriend's house and wait, just like you planned. Tomorrow morning, go home. Then wait some more."

She winced but nodded.

"Do you really understand? If you show up at the Masterson estate on some pretext, they'll know. Then they'll kill him and maybe you, as well. So give us time to get a warrant and do it right."

Suzannah scowled. "You don't need a warrant. This is a matter of life or death. Exigent circumstances, right?"

"So we storm the place? No surveillance? No plan? Just wild gunplay?" Before she could respond, he assured her, "My best spinner will plan this op, and it will be executed as rapidly as possible. That's Russo's best hope."

Suzannah glanced at Kristie, who smiled in sympathy. "Will's right. I know it's torture to just sit by and do nothing, but that's what Justin needs you to do.

Convince Agent X that you're still feeling hurt and betrayed, still pursuing the plea bargain, still anxious to get to Hawaii."

"I understand."

Kristie gave her shoulders a gentle squeeze. "If SPIN hasn't gotten results within twelve hours, we'll hijack a helicopter and go in ourselves. With Uzis. Okay?"

"Dammit, Goldie," McGregor muttered, but Suzannah could see he was trying not to laugh.

She felt a stab of longing, seeing them tease one another and remembering such moments with Justin—sexy, playful exchanges that were contentious yet filled with gentleness and respect. If only she had appreciated him when it had counted. If only she had known right away what it had taken her two days to realize.

And now that she knew the truth, she was aching to do something—anything—to save him. But she also knew that McGregor and Kristie were right. All she could do to help him now was a big, fat nothing.

"I've got something that'll make you feel better," Kristie announced with a mischievous smile. Then she dashed out of the room before anyone could respond.

Suzannah glanced at McGregor, who grinned. "Should be interesting. I'll go set things in motion while you two plot the overthrow of the world."

"It's so beautiful."

"It's Night Arrow," Kristie explained, her voice hushed.

Suzannah felt an inexplicable thrill as she examined the spinner's treasure—a nine-inch wooden replica of an arrow with a glistening obsidian tip. The guide feathers were black, as well, but the shaft was a deep red.

"My friend Miranda made it. It's supposed to bring me good luck. I want you to borrow it until all of this is over."

"Thanks." Suzannah smiled. "Justin would love this."

"Miranda made one for him, too. But she wanted to wait and give it to him in person. And she will," the spinner predicted confidently.

"What did she use to make the shaft red?"

"She kept one tiny vial of the potion for herself. That's a secret, by the way. *Don't* tell Will."

"I thought you were turning over a new leaf."

The spinner eyed her with pretend exasperation. "They pay me for my instincts. And every once in a while, my instincts tell me to break a rule. So sue me. Anyway..." Her tone grew more serious. "He's right in your case. Don't try to be a hero. Leave it to the professionals. That's what Justin would want."

"I know."

"It'll drive you crazy," Kristie predicted. "Luckily I can see you have more self-control than I would in your shoes. Still..." Her voice dropped to a whisper. "If you decide to do something crazy, call me for help, okay?"

Suzannah laughed. "I'm not going to do anything crazy."

"I know. But if you do, call. And keep this with you...." She reached into the overnight case that had sheltered the arrow and pulled out a tube of lipstick. "It contains a neurotoxin. See the nozzle? Point it at an assailant and twist the barrel."

When Suzannah just stared at it, the spinner said teasingly, "It's not like I'm offering you a gun."

"Right. *That* would be crazy." Suzannah studied the object cautiously. "I didn't realize SPIN was so covert."

"We aren't. I got this from an evil CIA officer."

"Pardon?"

Kristie laughed. "Her name was Jane Smith, and she was hot to recruit me. But then I uncovered what she was really up to, and she tried to kill me. And Will."

"Wow."

Kristie's eyes twinkled. "Obviously, we survived. And I ended up with this cool souvenir, so I can't really complain. Remind me to tell you the whole story someday."

"Definitely." Suzannah took a moment to stroke the Night Arrow shaft again, just for luck. Then she carefully placed both the arrow and the lipstick in her purse. "Thanks. I promise to get these back to you as soon as…well, as soon as we know he's safe."

Thanks to SPIN, Suzannah was able to fly rather than drive back home. They even arranged to have a truck waiting for her on arrival that was identical to the one she had borrowed from Noelle, right down to the logo.

"Just crash at your friend's house for the night. In the morning, go to your apartment," McGregor had instructed one last time as she was leaving. "We'll contact you the instant anything happens. Trust us. And give yourself a break. You did an amazing thing, figuring this out. The rest is up to us."

*In other words, don't help….*

It was completely contrary to every instinct in Suzannah's nature—both as the daughter of two impulsive, undisciplined parents and as the take-charge, hyperresponsible adult she had forced herself to become. She wanted to be there for Justin—her lover, her friend, her hero. And she *really* wanted to be there when Mia Masterson was handcuffed and stuffed into a patrol car.

*That unforgivable bitch,* Suzannah thought, fuming as she drove the deserted highway toward Noelle's house. *Throwing herself at him while secretly planning to steal his identity.*

Frustrated, she pictured Kristie and McGregor hard at work on three tracks—scoping out the Masterson house and grounds, checking out other suspicious medical facilities and identifying Agent X. The spinner had speculated that the CIA would have records about particularly talented mimics, and she hoped to find that one of them—a tall, lanky man in his early to mid thirties—had dropped out of sight approximately four years ago.

Meanwhile, SPIN would have someone watch Suzannah's apartment as well as Noelle's house. Not only did they want to protect Suzannah and her friend, but they hoped to intercept Charlie Parrish for his own protection if he came looking for an attorney again. For the same reason, Kristie would continue searching for Dr. Schuler, whom they guessed would be in danger, as well, if Agent X managed to find him first.

Meanwhile, Suzannah needed to behave as though nothing new had happened. As though she still thought the impostor's phone call had come from Justin. Still believed that he had confessed to killing Gia. McGregor and Kristie would do the rest. There really wasn't anything a lawyer could do anyway, was there? Aside from getting in the way and jeopardizing the whole operation?

She didn't even dare share the details of Justin's kidnapping with Noelle, whom she knew was dying of curiosity and probably worried to death. The information was simply too sensitive. But it would be difficult to remain silent when all she wanted to do was talk about Justin, preferably to someone who cared about him. Someone who could offer true reassurance. Comfort. Unconditional support.

Murphy!

That puppy adored Justin as much as Suzannah did.

And the judge had insomnia, so...

Smiling for the first time in hours, she changed course and headed for Sea Shell Drive.

As hoped, there were several lights on in the judge's house, both upstairs and downstairs, so Suzannah eased the truck up to the curb, then pulled out her cell phone, trying to imagine what she was going to say.

*I know it's three in the morning, Your Honor, but I was in the neighborhood and saw your lights....*

She grimaced, suspecting that Agent X was monitoring all her telephone conversations, both regular and cell. How else would he have known about her first trip to SPIN? Still, if he overheard *this* particular call, he'd hear a forlorn, brokenhearted lawyer who missed her puppy. Nothing to make him suspicious. In fact, the call would probably reassure the villainous bastard that Suzannah still believed Justin was a louse.

And so she took a deep, cleansing breath, then dialed the judge's number.

He answered on the first ring with, "Ms. Ryder? Is that you?"

"Hi, Your Honor. Sorry for the ungodly hour, but I've had such a rotten couple of days and I started missing the puppy, so I decided to drive over to see if you were up. I'm right outside your house. Do you think Sam would be awfully upset if I took Murf right now?"

"He's sound asleep and won't even know the dog's gone until morning," the judge assured her gruffly. "Come on and get him."

"Great. See you in a sec." Suzannah stuffed her phone and keys in her purse, then headed for the front door, half expecting Judge Taylor to dump the puppy into her arms and send her on her way. But he surprised her by opening the door wide and inviting her inside.

Then she reminded herself that she wasn't the only person in the world who needed someone to talk to. This man had spent the last forty-eight hours alone with a four-year-old and a dog. Plus, he had insomnia. All of which meant he was desperate for adult conversation, even with the attorney who usually set his teeth on edge.

"Murphy's in my study, Ms. Ryder. And very anxious to see you."

"I hope he wasn't any trouble."

"I'm too old to chase a puppy around," the judge confessed. "Especially since he keeps running up the stairs and hiding under my bed."

"Sorry, sir. Thanks for letting him off with a warning," Suzannah said with a smile, then she strode over to the cardboard box on the judge's desk and scooped Murphy up into her arms. Burying her face in his fur, she murmured, "Hey, sweetie. Did you miss me?"

He answered by covering her face with wet kisses, but she noticed he didn't have his usual wild-eyed energy. "Did we wake you up, Murf? Sorry. I just couldn't stay away a moment longer."

"So?" The judge motioned for her to sit down. "Do you want to tell me what's going on?"

"Hmm?"

"Where is Agent Russo?"

*Uh-oh...*

Taylor's tone softened. "Whatever it is, I can help. I'm a judge, remember? If he's in a worse predicament than we thought—if he's interested in making a deal, for example—I can be of assistance."

"That's so sweet of you," Suzannah told him, honestly touched by the sympathy behind his green eyes. "But Justin doesn't need a judge right now. He needs... Oh!" She gave a startled grin. "Actually, a judge is *exactly* what he needs."

"Oh?"

"We need a warrant, sir. Right away. I don't know why I didn't think of it sooner! You're *perfect* for this. It's been driving me crazy that I can't help, but now I can."

She imagined how surprised McGregor would be when he found out what she had done. He'd be annoyed, too, but she'd be quick to assure him that she wasn't planning on heading over to the Masterson estate alone. That would be crazy.

Tempting but crazy.

"It's three o'clock in the morning, Ms. Ryder. I'm in no mood to play guessing games. I want you to tell me what's going on. Why do you need a warrant?"

"It's complicated," she explained warily. "Before I say another word, you have to promise you'll keep what I'm about to say confidential. And I can't give you all the details—"

"You just expect me to hand over a blank warrant without knowing why you need it? What kind of judge do you think I am?" he demanded. "I need facts!"

The unexpected harshness of his tone seemed to shock the sleepy-eyed Murphy, so much that the frightened puppy bolted right out of Suzannah's grip.

"Goddammit!" Taylor shouted.

"Sorry, Your Honor! I'll get him." Suzannah raced after the dog, who was confirming his prior rap sheet by heading down the hall in the direction of an imposing wooden staircase.

"Ms. Ryder! Come back here!"

"Murphy!" Suzannah continued her chase, taking the steps in pairs, but the puppy stayed just beyond her grasp. Then he bounded toward a dimly lit room at the end of the second-floor hallway.

"Murphy Ryder! Come back here this minute!"

Suzannah could hear the judge calling her name, but she didn't dare return without the dog, whom she assumed was already headed for someone's bed. She only hoped that it was Sam's, not Judge Taylor's.

"Come on, Murf," she wheedled as she approached the doorway. "Let's go home and play with the ball. Remember the ball? Remember the ham bone?"

The puppy began barking excitedly, and she grimaced, recognizing the sound as his come-and-get-me call. Pushing open the half-closed door for a better view, she was chagrined to see that the room actually contained two beds—one giant four-poster affair and one made of cold white metal.

A hospital bed.

And worse, there appeared to be someone in it! Suzannah had assumed the judge lived alone and she wondered unhappily if this was a sick parent or sibling. In any case, it was someone who needed peace and quiet, not strangers and dogs running around in the middle of the night.

Mortified, Suzannah dropped to one knee and whispered in the direction of the stately mahogany bed, "Murphy, *please.* Come back here."

She didn't dare go into the room—it just didn't seem right—so she turned to face the judge, ready to apologize profusely, beg him to recover the dog and then promise to leave and never show her face on Sea Shell Drive again.

"Hey, Suzy," said a familiar voice from the shadows.

"Oh, my God..." Suzannah whispered. "How can this...? Justin?"

She was so amazed to see him standing there, she almost couldn't move. Then he gave her a wistful smile, and a burst of energy propelled her into his waiting arms.

"Oh, Justin! How did you find me? I was so worried. We *all* were."

"Everything's fine," he assured her, gripping her tightly with one hand while caressing her with the other, exploring first her neck and shoulders, then her breasts.

"Justin," she murmured, still giddy with relief but also anxious for answers. "How did you get away from Agent X? Did SPIN find you? At Mia's house, right?"

"Agent X?"

She thought she felt a tremor run through his chest. It was almost as if he was trying to suppress a sob.

Or was it a chuckle?

"Oh, God!" She wrenched herself free of the arms that she suddenly realized didn't feel familiar at all. Then she stared up in horror at the face she loved—a face now twisted into an unfamiliar and chillingly evil grin.

# Chapter 11

She stared at him, sickened but unable to look away. He had Justin's face, Justin's body, Justin's stance. "Oh, God…"

"Amazing, isn't it?" he agreed cheerfully.

Then a second figure appeared in the doorway, and Suzannah felt her stomach knot even tighter. "Judge Taylor? I can't believe you're part of this. How *could* you?"

"They have Sam," was his simple, mournful reply.

"Oh, no… No, Your Honor. Not Sam." Despair bubbled up inside her, but she fought it back the same way she intended to fight back—somehow, someway—against this unspeakable monster.

"Who *are* you?" she asked Agent X unhappily.

"I'll give you a hint. I'm not a psychologist, but I play one on the Internet."

"Schuler?"

"One of my many aliases. It'll do for our purposes. Unless of course you want to call me Justin."

*Justin...*

Miserable, she turned toward the hospital bed, knowing now who the patient was. She wanted to believe that the IV in his arm was solely to keep him sedated, but the bandages on his face told her another story. "What have you done to him?"

Schuler grabbed her by the forearm, preventing her from approaching the bed. "You'd better settle down, Suzy." His tone softened. "I had to break a few bones in his face to see how the swelling looked. So I could ensure my own residual swelling was consistent with being beaten by Seldon's guard." Looking down at her, he murmured, "So? How did I do?"

She bit her lip, wondering whether she dared let him know just how amazing the transformation was. The eyes were just the right shade of blue. The smile was eerily familiar. And Schuler was right about the slight swelling along his cheek and jaw—it was more evocative of an injury than surgery.

But it was the voice that was the real triumph. Every inflection, every nuance, right down to the hint of Wyoming. Even the choice of words was perfect.

She remembered Kristie's reference to natural mimics and wondered what the spinner would say if she could see *this*.

"It's my masterpiece," Schuler assured her proudly.

"With another week, it would have been completely undetectable. If only you had gone to Hawaii like a good little girl."

Before she could respond, he turned his attention to the judge. "You'll find a pair of handcuffs in the satchel on your bed. Immobilize Suzannah for me."

She gave the judge an encouraging nod. "Do what you need to do. He has no reason to kill us now. Right, Schuler? Your plan can't succeed. You can try to get away, but if they catch you, you won't want to have the murder of an FBI agent and a respected jurist on your tally, much less an innocent little boy."

He gestured to the judge, who had approached with the cuffs. "Behind her back, nice and tight. We don't want any heroics—not from either of you."

Suzannah winced as the metal cuffs bit into her wrists, but she reminded herself that what she had said was true. Killing them now didn't make much sense. So definitely no heroics.

Schuler gave her an encouraging Justin-like smile. "How did you discover the truth? Tell me and I might just let the little dog live."

"I'll tell you whatever you want to know," Suzannah promised. "Just let me check on Justin first."

"I'll ask his nurse if he can have visitors. Darling? You can come out now."

Suzannah turned around, her gaze trailing over the motionless body in the white bed and settling in disgust on Mia, who had stepped out of an adjoining bathroom. The heiress was dressed in black silk pants and a pearly white halter top and carried a small pistol in her right hand as casually as if it were an evening bag.

"Bitch," Suzannah muttered under her breath.

"I was just thinking the same thing," Mia assured her. Then she walked over to the bed and patted her patient's bandaged cheek. "I've been taking care of him personally. Sponge baths and designer drugs. Believe me, he's never had it so good, have you, baby?"

There was no response, and Suzannah's heart sank.

Schuler seemed to read her thoughts. "He's fine, Suzy. Just drugged to the gills, like Mia said. But resting comfortably, thanks to Judge Taylor. That bed belonged to his wife, and he apparently didn't have the heart to get rid of it when she died last summer. Go on. See for yourself how relaxed your client is."

Taking a deep breath, Suzannah crossed the room and stood by the bed, looking down at Justin, noting that his bandages were pure white—no leakage of blood, which she hoped was a good sign. His wrists were tied to the bed rails with thick fabric restraints, but the precaution hardly seemed necessary, given his glazed and unfocused eyes and slackened mouth.

"Justin," she whispered, her throat tightening. "I don't know if you can hear me but...well, I'm here."

She leaned down and kissed his lips, and for a moment his gaze seemed to grow clearer. More steady. And in that moment, all traces of blue vanished from his eyes, which turned to steel-gray as they stared up at her.

She forced herself not to react on the outside, but on the inside her heart did a cartwheel.

Because she knew that look. A look no impostor

could ever hope to duplicate. This was Justin Russo, hero. Protector of the innocent. He had saved little Lizzie Rodriguez and countless other persons. And now he was planning to save Suzannah.

*It's so sweet,* she told him in silent awe. *And so brave. But not very realistic. Just this once, you'll have to let SPIN do the rescuing. After that, you can have the job for as long as you want it.*

Murphy had been watching in silence from under the judge's bed but now barked impatiently at Suzannah, urging her to come play with him.

"Shut that mutt up," Schuler growled.

When Mia took a biscuit off the tray by Justin's bed and began walking over to the puppy, Suzannah demanded, "What's that? Leave him alone."

"It's harmless. I feed these to my babies before every plane ride, and they sleep right through. Your dog had one earlier and it worked well. I'd never hurt an animal," she added with a huff.

Concerned, Suzannah watched as Mia placed the wafer on the floor at the edge of the bed. Immediately Murphy grabbed it with his mouth and tugged it back into the shadows.

*It's for the best,* she assured herself nervously. *You don't want him in the mix when…well, when things start happening.* Turning to Mia, she forced herself to say, "Thanks."

The heiress pouted. "I didn't want to hurt Justin either, you know. We were just going to keep him drugged until Owen got that stupid Night Arrow. But now because of *you,* Owen says we'll have to kill you both."

"Suzy?" Schuler interrupted cheerfully. "Remember our bargain? I'd like to know how I gave myself away. For future reference."

She shrugged her shoulders as though it were the simplest question in the world. "In your note, you spelled Suzie with an *ie*. Justin calls me Suzy—with a *y*."

"That's nothing," Mia objected. "Just a stupid spelling error."

"No," Schuler corrected her. "Those minute details are the ones that really matter." He walked over to Suzannah and stared down into her face. "I can see it now. Suzy with a *y*."

She forced herself not to back away, remembering that with every passing minute the SPIN team was more likely to realize that Suzannah hadn't made it back to Noelle's house in a reasonable amount of time. They'd be looking for her as well as for Justin and Schuler.

Knowing Kristie, there was a good chance she'd remember that the puppy was staying with the judge, and they'd send a tall, strapping FBI agent with a huge gun and a suspicious mind to Sea Shell Drive. Meanwhile, every second that she could delay made rescue that much more likely, which meant she needed to keep these folks talking.

Forcing a sly, conspiratorial smile, she asked Schuler, "So how did *I* give *my*self away?"

"The littlest of all details," he said with a wink. "The puppy."

"Pardon?"

"After I called you and the spinner and confessed Justin's guilt, your heart was broken. You consoled yourself by checking on the little mutt's status every five minutes, as though he was all you cared about in the world. Then suddenly he didn't matter so much. Because your concern had turned elsewhere." Schuler pursed his lips and admitted, "It wasn't a fatal error on your part. I told myself that you might just be depressed. Wallowing in self-pity at your friend's home, wondering how you could have been naive enough to trust a con artist like Russo. But I needed to be absolutely sure, so I called your cell phone. Interestingly your phone returned a message that you were out of range. So I sent one of my men—his name is Bob, by the way, you'll meet him in a moment—I sent Bob to Noelle's house to look around. She was in the kitchen, but one of her trucks was missing. And you were nowhere in sight."

Suzannah felt her skin crawl at the very thought of thugs spying through her friend's windows.

Schuler continued. "I still wasn't sure whether or not you were onto us. But I needed to take precautions. For one thing, we couldn't stay at Mia's any longer. That would be the first place they'd look. Fortunately I thought of Judge Taylor—the one person you were sure to contact eventually. And someone you trusted implicitly." His smile widened. "I was sure you'd be more likely to confide in a judge than in Noelle and I was correct."

"So you threatened to hurt Sam. Where is he?"

"Safely sedated until morning. Cooperate, and he'll never know what happened."

Still anxious to buy time, Suzannah shook her head. "I still don't see why you brought Justin here. Once you had Sam, you must have known the judge would cooperate. You didn't have to be physically present for that."

"Didn't I?" Schuler scowled. "I've learned the hard way that I have to oversee every aspect of this venture or my incompetent associates screw it up. Starting with Cynthia. Or should I say Gia? She was supposed to convince Russo to close his investigation and go away with her on a long, luxurious vacation. That would have given us the perfect chance to make the switch—me for him. And it would have given more time for my surgery to heal. But she lost her nerve."

"She felt so terrible about letting you down that she shot herself," Mia told him sharply. "Stop being so critical of her."

For a moment, Suzannah almost felt sorry for the heiress, who didn't seem to suspect even for a minute that her ruthless lover had shot Cynthia to frame Justin. Apparently Mia had been brainwashed by a true professional.

*But I'll bet it didn't take much soap....*

"It wasn't just Cynthia who screwed up," Schuler was explaining to Suzannah. "If Mia here had done her job on Monday, luring Russo to her house *alone* so we could grab him, you wouldn't have become so involved. Wouldn't have known him well enough to figure things out. So you see," he added with a smile, "I didn't dare trust this phase to anyone else. I had to bring Russo here to keep an eye on him while also ensuring that the judge cooperated. Once he got the details from you, I could decide what to do next. If you knew that I used a fake voice but hadn't figured out about the plastic surgery, I could still impersonate Russo long enough to get Night

Arrow. But you're so clever," he added as though honestly fond of her. "You figured everything out."

Suzannah stared into the eyes that were just the right color but wrong in every other way. "Why are you telling me all this?"

"It's only fair. You've been my most crucial ally."

*"Me?"*

He chuckled. "My plan was foolproof right until Monday morning, when Russo's case was assigned to Taylor the Jailor. Then all was in jeopardy."

"Because if Justin was denied bail pending trial, you couldn't grab him and pretend to confess in his place?"

"Exactly. It was a miracle that you were in court that day. The one attorney who could take on the Jailor. You single-handedly saved my plan." He stepped closer and admitted, "Ever since that moment I've looked forward to showing up on your doorstep, battered and bruised, and having you nurse me back to health."

*Ugh,* she thought to herself. But aloud she forced herself to prolong the conversation. "I hate to admit it, but you're pretty amazing. The way you manipulated Charlie right from the start. And then when you made that phone call impersonating Justin. It was so convincing you even fooled the spinner, and she's a card-carrying genius. How did you get her number? Did you drug Justin and make him tell you?"

Schuler grinned. "Let me guess. You're stalling for time, hoping some knight in shining armor from SPIN or the FBI followed you here and will burst through the door at any moment?"

When she winced, he gave a playful shrug. "I suppose

it's possible. I have two men on patrol for that very reason. But the truth is, if there *is* such a hero, he thinks you're just visiting with the judge. If by some chance he decides to check, he'll knock respectfully at the door. And Judge Taylor here will tell him a convincing story. About how you asked to sit by Sam and Murphy's bedside for a few minutes to watch them sleep. But you dozed off yourself. Isn't that what you'll say, Your Honor? You're not going to disappoint me, are you?"

"I'll do whatever you say," the judge murmured.

Schuler smiled at Suzannah. "If the agent wants to see you with his own eyes, Judge Taylor will let him in. Then my men will kill him. So much for the rescue." He chuckled again. "Don't feel bad. You're an amateur at all this."

"No offense, Einstein, but you're not so good at it yourself," Suzannah retorted, relieved not to have to play along with him anymore.

"Ms. Ryder!" Judge Taylor's eyes as well as his voice pleaded with her to be quiet. "That's enough."

But Schuler waved away the protest. "I'm enjoying the spirited banter. I'm even tempted to take Suzy away with me instead of Mia, just for the conversation."

"What?" Mia glared.

"I'm joking, darling."

It was Suzannah's turn to laugh. "I'm not so sure about that. From the way he felt me up a few minutes ago, I'd say he's seriously missing Cynthia's implants."

*"What?"* Mia's eyes flashed as they fixed on Schuler. "I thought you said you preferred *my* body."

"And I do. This is simply another amateurish effort

on Suzy's part. Trying to drive a wedge between us." He reached for Suzannah's face and squeezed her cheeks roughly between his thumb and forefinger. "These tricks only work in movies, Suzannah. In real life, the more ruthless opponent always wins."

Suzannah pulled free but didn't respond. There was nothing left to say. Schuler was right. These tricks *were* amateurish—silly delays, pointless provocations—but they were all she had. Even if her hands were free, she had no genuine weapon to use against this monster. Not even her trusty mace. Or the lipstick tube containing the neurotoxin, which was in her purse in the judge's study.

"What exactly *is* your plan?" she murmured.

He gave a Justin-like chuckle. "In a nutshell? I'm going to shoot your hero. Then I'll shoot you."

"That's my favorite part," Mia interrupted with a smirk.

Schuler burst into laughter. "Is it any wonder I love this girl? Anyway, back to the plan. Mia and I will leave by the back door into the alley. If anyone comes looking for you, Judge Taylor will confess that he helped you sneak away through the back so that you could run off to the Masterson house and rescue Justin, whom you're quite sure is trapped in the infirmary." He grinned at Suzannah. "Your friend the spinner will believe that, don't you think?"

Suzannah wanted the mace more than ever now, just so she could squirt it into Schuler's smug face. He was so confident. Supremely *over*confident, really. He was so sure he was going to get away with this, thanks to the same arrogance that had made him believe he could actually impersonate Justin Russo, infiltrate a research facility and get his hands on a top-secret project like Night Arrow.

The thought jolted her, sending her back to the moment when Schuler had sounded the *most* like Justin—during the phone conversation when he had talked about Night Arrow. He had had that same reverent tone, the same fanatical interest.

*Night Arrow*...the project that inspired something close to madness. It wasn't nearly as practical as a gun or a neurotoxin, but it was a weapon nonetheless, wasn't it? And one that held enormous power if wielded just so.

If only she could take advantage of that.

Forcing herself to remain subdued, she admitted, "It's a good plan, Owen. Or Schuler. Or whatever your name is. But it's not a great one. With a great one, you'd get Night Arrow. Right?"

She licked her lips, enjoying the flash of frustration that contorted his handsome face. Then she locked gazes with him and said coolly, "Of course, if you're still interested, I've got a sample of the potion. Right downstairs in my purse."

## Chapter 12

"What are you saying?" Schuler asked, his voice hushed, as though not daring to believe Suzannah's claim. "You have Night Arrow? Here in this house?"

"Send Judge Taylor to his study to get my purse and I'll show you."

"Shut up!" Mia interrupted. "*Please*, Owen? Just let me shoot her."

When Schuler continued to stare at Suzannah, Mia's voice became a wail. "Can't you just forget about that stupid project? I *hate* it. We have twenty-seven million dollars waiting for us. Isn't that enough?"

Ignoring her, Schuler told Suzannah, "If this is another bluff to buy time, you'll be sorry." Pulling a slim walkie-talkie from the pocket of his bomber jacket, he barked into it. "Bob? Find Suzy's purse and bring it to me."

*Nice work,* Suzannah complained to herself. *You finally get a way to neutralize one bad guy, but you add an extra one to the mix. Let's hope Bob leaves quickly.*

"The sample in my purse is small. But S-3 at SPIN has a bigger one, plus a photocopy of all the research. She'll trade it for Justin and me, I guarantee you that."

"The U.S. government doesn't negotiate," Schuler countered. "If I thought that would work, I'd have tried it in exchange for Russo days ago."

"I'm not talking about the government. I'm talking about S-3, the infamous rogue spinner. Haven't you heard the stories?" She smiled at the flicker of acknowledgment in Schuler's eyes. "Did you know she was responsible for finding Night Arrow in the first place? That's why she has the sample and the research."

"I heard about that," he admitted. "But I had given up hope—"

"You can't just leave without it. Not when you're so close to succeeding. Make her an offer she can't refuse, as they say. Her old friend Justin. Her new friend, me. And a wealthy and important judge. She'll do it."

"Aren't you forgetting something?" Schuler demanded. "You alerted SPIN and the FBI. They're already looking for me."

Suzannah smiled reassuringly. "You and Kristie are both supersmart. You'll figure a way to make it work. Plus, even if the government found out what she was doing, they don't really think Night Arrow is valuable. They've all but determined it's a hoax."

Schuler licked his lips. "I've heard that, too."

"But Kristie knows better. Her friend used it once, and it worked. Just like all the stories say."

His eyes began to shine behind the blue contact lenses. "She told you that? That it works?"

Suzannah nodded. "The spinner has a theory that…"

"Finish that sentence!"

"She thinks it only works if you believe in it. I know that sounds crazy—"

"No," he interrupted. "I've always known that. It's what makes it so priceless. So unique. A true magical potion rather than just a formula."

Suzannah bit back a smile, loving the Night Arrow stupor that was going to be this guy's undoing. "Kristie showed me how it works. Uncuff me and I'll demonstrate."

"Owen, don't!" Brandishing her gun, Mia strode over to them. "She's lying, can't you see that?"

"If she's lying, I'll break her neck. But until we know…" Schuler turned Suzannah away from himself, unlocked the handcuffs, then spun her back and glared down at her. "I hope for your sake you're telling the truth."

A hefty, bearded man strode into the room at that moment, extending the purse toward Schuler while announcing, "I confiscated a can of mace, but otherwise it's clean. Except for a toy arrow."

To Suzannah's relief, Schuler motioned for her to take possession of the handbag. "Show me. *Now.* And no tricks."

She gave Bob a grateful smile, then took the purse and opened it wide. The lipstick was in plain view, but she didn't dare use it yet. It was better to wait and see if Schuler sent his thug away. The moment that happened, she'd spray Schuler with the neurotoxin, then dive for Mia and try to wrestle the gun from her. Hopefully, Judge Taylor would join in—and on the correct side. Then they'd free Justin, and he could take over from there.

But if Bob stayed, she knew that the lipstick wouldn't be enough. Even if she sprayed the bearded man and grabbed the gun from his hand, she didn't know how to shoot it. With her luck, she'd hit the judge or Justin!

*Just stall until Bob leaves,* she counseled herself. So she sank to the floor and motioned for Schuler to join her. "Let me show you. It's really amazing."

When the Justin look-alike knelt beside her, she pulled out Kristie's good-luck charm. "See? Night Arrow."

Schuler gasped. "Are you saying the actual potion has been applied to this replica?"

She nodded, exhibiting the arrow proudly. "When you stroke the shaft like this, you can feel the heat. Try it."

Schuler accepted it with care, then rubbed it lightly, as though caressing a priceless relic. "It's true. It feels warm."

"Owen," Mia pleaded. "We don't have time for this crap. We have to get out of the country right away."

"She's right, sir," said Bob. "I'll pull the car up in the alley while you take care of business here. You're still planning on having the judge cover for us, aren't you?"

Schuler gave Suzannah a conspiratorial glance. "How do you suggest I contact the spinner without alerting the FBI?"

"We can't do it from here." She struggled to keep her voice steady. "Bob? You go get the car. We'll get Justin on his feet somehow and bring him down with us. The judge will stay behind to cover for us if the feds come to the door. We'll find a motel room and call Kristie from there. I have her private line." She gave a weary sigh. "It would be better if Justin could make the call himself, but he's too out of it. Luckily I think the spinner and I have established enough of a rapport that it shouldn't be a problem."

Arching an eyebrow, she added firmly, "You need to let Sam go first, though. As a gesture of good faith. There's no way Kristie will go along with this if you've got a child captive. Where is he?"

"In the basement. Frightened but unharmed."

"Good. Leave him with the judge. That's nonnegotiable, understand? Murphy, too," she added, stealing a look at the puppy's slumbering form. He was out like the proverbial light but seemed to be breathing well, so she prayed he'd stay asleep for just a few more minutes.

She smiled up at Judge Taylor. "You'll cover for us, won't you, Your Honor? Even after you and Sam are safe? If you don't, these guys will kill me and Justin."

"I'll do anything you say," the jurist promised. "Just let Sam go first."

"No one will ever, ever blame you. You know that, don't you, sir?" she added softly.

He nodded.

"Don't try to be a hero. Just be a good grandpa and we'll get through this."

He nodded again, but the tear that slid down his face told her the whole story. He couldn't live with himself if anything happened to Sam. But if anything happened to Suzannah or, worse, if this vermin ever got hold of government secrets on Taylor the Jailor's watch... well, he couldn't live with that either.

She eyed him with stern compassion. "You need to trust me, Your Honor."

"I'll do my best," he replied.

"Then it's settled." Schuler stroked the Night Arrow replica one last time, then pulled out the walkie-talkie again. "Joseph? Bring the car around back. Quietly."

Suzannah grimaced, remembering too late that Schuler had *two* guys helping him.

*Bob wasn't enough? Now I've gotta neutralize Joseph, too?*

"Wait!" Mia was staring at Schuler as though he had lost his mind. "The kid is our insurance. You aren't really going to let him go, are you?"

The mimic tucked the Night Arrow replica into an interior pocket of his bomber jacket, then jumped to his feet and stared into his girlfriend's eyes. "To get the formula? Yes, for that I will let the child go."

Suzannah watched Mia's expression go from panicked to smug and knew exactly why. Something in the monster's expression had told her he had no intention of freeing Sam. Not now. Not ever.

But Suzannah also knew it didn't matter. If her plan didn't work—right here, right now—they were all dead anyway. So she forced herself to smile as she discreetly worked the cap off the lipstick. "You sound more like Justin than ever, Dr. Schuler. He would have done anything to protect Night Arrow. You'd do anything to get your hands on it. The resemblance between you two guys gets eerier every second."

"Thank you."

"Does that hospital bed turn into a stretcher? We need to get Justin down to the car, and he's in no shape to walk."

"Bob?" Schuler inclined his head toward the hospital bed. "Get him on his feet. The judge will help you carry him."

A thrill ran through Suzannah as Bob tucked his pistol into the back waistband of his jeans, then walked over to the bed and began loosening the restraints.

This was it. Justin would take care of Bob, with or without the judge's help. Wasn't that what the FBI agent had been waiting for? Lying there so silent, so patient, so still? Hoping she'd create an opportunity for him to do his thing?

Of course, it was always possible he had finally passed out from the drugs. But those iron-toned eyes had seemed pretty determined. And didn't his file tell the story of a man so strong, so fearless—so freakishly lucky—that he could defeat seemingly insurmountable odds? All he needed was a little help from Suzannah.

If her timing was right, this would be over in seconds.

And if her timing was wrong, it would be over even quicker.

Pretending to be concerned about Justin's wobbly condition, she kept her gaze fastened on the restraints. Bob loosened the first one but didn't remove it completely. Instead he reached across Justin's body and began working on the second one.

And Suzannah knew that Justin was doing the same

thing she was doing—calculating and recalculating, watching for the perfect moment to wrestle Bob onto the bed and reach behind him for his gun—

"Hey, boss?" said a new voice from the doorway. "I've got the car in the alley. What's going on?"

Suzannah groaned as the newcomer—a fellow twice as burly and three times as hairy as Bob—walked toward her. He wasn't holding a gun, but a partially concealed holster told her he had one handy.

Still, this could be the only opportunity they would have, so she made one last adjustment and prayed Justin would do the same. Then she jumped up and sprayed Mia in the face. As predicted by Kristie, the toxin took effect in a split second, and Suzannah grabbed the gun just as Mia's grasp released it.

Spinning toward the doorway, she fired at Joseph, who was just pulling his weapon. To her relief, he lurched backward, then slumped to the floor.

She was dimly aware of a ruckus in the vicinity of the hospital bed and had no doubt Bob had been neutralized.

Which left only Schuler. So Suzannah spun again to see that he had pulled a weapon, as well, and was leveling it at her.

"Don't be stupid," she warned, aiming Mia's tiny pistol directly at his forehead.

Schuler's mouth twisted into a cruel smile and he stepped forward, reaching for her with his free hand. Horrified, Suzannah tried to fire, but only a loud, ineffective click greeted her efforts as Schuler's hand grabbed her wrist. He pulled her roughly toward himself until her back was flat against his chest and the barrel of his gun was pressed along her cheek. Then he laughed victoriously.

"Let her go, asshole," Justin ordered from across the room.

Numb with a combination of fear and admiration, Suzannah gazed longingly in his direction. He looked so perfect standing there—so strong and steady despite his bandaged face—aiming Bob's pistol at Schuler as the judge fidgeted helplessly a short distance away.

"Careful, Russo," Schuler told him. "If you move, I'll shoot her. But if you cooperate, I'll take her as my hostage. Who knows? She might come up with another lamebrained plan to save herself." He chuckled as he added, "Unlike Mia's silly gun, this weapon holds eight rounds. Be sure to calculate that into your strategy."

"Shut up," Justin advised him, his steely gaze flickering momentarily toward the window as sirens began to scream in the distance. "You don't have much time, Schuler. If you want a hostage, take *me*. I'll get you out of the country. You've got my word on that. Just let these two go."

"And Sam," the judge added.

"Right. Sam, too."

"Or you could lay your weapon on the ground," Schuler countered coolly. "Now."

"That's not going to happen," Justin assured him. "You've studied my file enough to know that."

"I know all about you," Schuler agreed. "And about your hero father. He changed places with a hostage. And now you want that same glory for yourself. Unfortunately Suzy's more valuable than you are. So let's move on to plan B. Judge Taylor? Please get Joseph's gun out of his holster, then step between me and Agent Russo. Do it quickly or I'll make killing your grandson my very top priority."

When the judge didn't move, Schuler eyed him with feigned sympathy. "You can see how it is, can't you, Your Honor? Agent Russo won't shoot me. Not with Suzy at risk. So let's all just stop pretending. If you cooperate, Suzy and I won't stop at the basement to shoot little Sam on our way out of here."

The judge walked over to the dead man's body and retrieved the weapon, which he immediately trained on Justin. "I'm sorry," he murmured, moving to the center of the room.

The FBI agent looked right past him and told Schuler, "If you're smart, you'll let Suzannah go as soon as you're clear of the house. You've got nothing to gain from hurting her. And believe me, you don't want to be *my* top priority."

"I won't hurt her," Schuler replied, then he wrenched Suzannah harder against himself and backed out of the room and down the hall toward the top of the stairs.

Suzannah had no doubt that she was a dead woman. The only comfort was that Sam would probably survive. Despite Schuler's threats, it didn't make sense to stop at the basement just to kill the child.

But killing Suzannah? She was sure that this man—this Agent X—would make time for *that*.

Then he shocked her by murmuring, "As soon as we get someplace safe, you'll call the spinner. Agreed?"

"The spinner? You think she'll help you get out of the country?"

"She'll give me the potion and the Night Arrow files in exchange for your life. I'm perfectly capable of getting myself out of the country."

"The potion?" Suzannah couldn't believe her ears, and before she could stop herself she started to laugh. It was so absurd. So pitiful yet also so misguidedly devout. Almost mystical.

"Stop laughing!" he ordered her, clearly disoriented by her reaction.

A mixture of fear, hilarity and adrenaline bubbled over in Suzannah's system, and she whirled around, then reached into his pocket and pulled out the arrow, which she waved in his face. "This was supposed to bring me good luck. But because you're such a freaking fanatic, it's going to get us both killed."

"Give me that!" Schuler grabbed for the replica.

"You should have listened to Mia," she taunted, yanking herself free again, praying that Justin had somehow managed to subdue Judge Taylor and could now take a clear shot at Schuler.

But the mimic dived at her, propelling them both over the top of the staircase, and they fell, struggling and crying out as their bodies impacted the steps, their heads ricocheting off the walls. The silver barrel of the gun—still held by Schuler—glinted in the light of the entryway chandelier. But Suzannah was certain Schuler wouldn't fire at her as long as she was gripping the Night Arrow replica. He was simply too obsessed with the artifact to risk damaging it.

But his desire to preserve the arrow from gunfire didn't protect her from his huge hands, which encircled her neck and began to choke the life from her as soon as she hit the landing. "Give it to me!" he demanded furiously.

As she struggled, she felt waves of heat radiate through her palm and along her arm all the way up to her shoulder. For a moment she thought she was having a heart attack, but the sensation was traveling in the wrong direction—*toward* her chest, not away from it.

Then she realized it wasn't *her* heart that was at issue at all. It was Schuler's! She knew that because she could *hear* it, each beat sounding like an explosion in her ears.

She gasped for breath, her eyes staring at his jugular, which was protruding—and virtually glowing!—as he glared down at her. That spot was like a beacon, so mesmerizing she could almost smell the scent of his blood.

But the most overpowering sensation of all was the power that ran through her arm—so hot, so alive—and before she knew what she was doing, she had raised up the Night Arrow and plunged its obsidian tip deep into Schuler's throat, forcing the shaft through skin, through tissue, through muscle, until blood spurted freely from the jagged, gaping hole.

As the mimic's eyes widened with pain and shock, he lost his grip on her neck. Life gushed out of him, and he would have slumped over had she not been sustaining him, holding him up, impaled on the red shaft of the replica.

"Suzannah! Don't move!" Justin's voice boomed a split second before a shot rang out and a perfectly aimed bullet exploded through the back of Schuler's skull.

"Suzannah!" Justin rushed down the steps and yanked the bloody corpse off her, then he gathered her into his arms and began to croon. "It's okay, Suzy. He's dead. I promise. He'll never bother you again."

"I know," she told him, curling her arms around his neck and hugging him proudly. "I killed him before you did. But nice shot."

"*You* killed him?" Justin grinned through his bandages. "You must've bumped your head pretty hard if *that's* how you remember it. He was choking you."

"Check it out," she suggested.

He cocked his head to the side, studying her fondly. Then he turned toward his double's lifeless body and murmured, "What's that in his neck?"

"I'll give you a hint—your friend Miranda wasn't exaggerating."

He looked from the arrow to Suzannah, his expression confused. "You're kidding."

She laughed again as the sounds of pounding feet and loud shouts began to fill the air. "Looks like the cavalry's here. They need to find Sam right away."

Justin nodded, then brushed his lips across hers. "I'll take care of it. You wait right here."

"What about the judge?"

"He and Mia are a little tied up at the moment. And Murf's still sound asleep."

"He saved your life, you know."

Justin grinned. "With a little help from my lawyer."

Three men in jet-black SWAT gear stepped into view, their weapons trained on Justin and Suzannah.

"Don't move!" the apparent leader ordered them. "Okay, now. Slowly. Hands where I can see them."

Justin flashed a confident grin. "Hi, guys. Glad you finally made it. I'm FBI. Special Agent Justin Russo. I don't have my badge, but it can be easily verified."

Suzannah burst into helpless laughter.

"What's so funny?" the leader demanded.

"Even if he had his badge, the victim looks more like his photo than *he* does."

Justin laughed, too. "I can explain, guys—"

"Did you shoot this man?" the leader interrupted.

"Yeah, but he was already dead."

When Suzannah screamed with laughter again, Justin explained, "She's a little loopy. Hit her head a couple of times on the way down the stairs. But she's harmless. Deadly," he added with a grin, "but harmless."

"It's true, Officer," Suzannah insisted, trying for a more serious tone but failing miserably. "I killed Dr. Schuler first. And I *loved* doing it."

The SWAT leader was clearly not amused. Exhaling sharply, he turned to his team and instructed in a brisk, no-nonsense tone, "Cuff 'em both."

## *Epilogue*

"Well, here we are again," murmured Taylor the Jailor as he looked down from the bench. "Ms. Ryder? You look well, all things considered."

"Thanks, Your Honor. How's Sam?"

"He's fine." Taylor turned his attention to Justin. "Agent Russo, I'm glad you could be here this morning. I wasn't sure whether you'd be in surgery."

"It's scheduled for next week. After we get back from Hawaii."

Suzannah braced herself, imagining how the judge would react to news that she was vacationing with a client. But to her surprise, he simply said, "I wanted to be the one to formally dismiss the charges against you. After that, I'm taking a leave of absence, pending an inquiry into my involvement in your kidnapping."

"Oh, no!" Suzannah shook her head. "The cops understood completely, sir. You *had* to cooperate with Schuler to keep Sam alive. Are you saying the Judicial Council isn't convinced? Because we'd be happy to talk to them—"

"The Judicial Council isn't the problem," Judge Taylor interrupted her sadly. "*I'm* the one with questions about my competence. My judgment—or lack thereof."

Suzannah sighed. "We all need a little vacation, sir. But don't stay away too long."

"Yeah, and when you get back to work," Justin told him, "you might want to consider trying *not* to be such an effing—"

"Justin!" Suzannah elbowed him, then gave the judge an apologetic smile. "The doctors gave Agent Russo some powerful painkillers, sir. He doesn't know what he's saying."

The judge grimaced but nodded. "Let's get this over with then, shall we?"

"You almost got us both charged with contempt again, you know."

Justin grinned as he backed Suzannah against her car door. "But you rescued me again. I'm getting kinda used to that."

"Well, don't. Because next time, I want to be the rescu*ee*. I'm tired of doing all the work."

"Yeah? Let's see what I can do about that."

"If we don't hurry, we'll miss our flight," she warned, but when he started kissing her, she responded easily, still amazed that they were getting this reprieve before the swelling subsided and the surgeons could begin the delicate work of rebuilding his jaw, nose and eye socket. He would be on medical leave for at least ten weeks, and Suzannah had taken a corresponding leave of absence with her firm's blessing.

She needed the time, not just to play nurse/patient with him but to come up with a new career plan. Derek Seldon had reaffirmed his job offer, but considering his history with Mia, she wasn't sure that would make a lot of sense. Meanwhile, Will McGregor had asked her to consult with him on a SPIN legal issue, hinting that there might be a future for her there, too. And last but not least, she had promised to help Tony Moreno with Charlie Parrish's defense, and in the back of her mind she knew that had definite possibilities, especially since Tony had been trying to talk her into a partnership since the day they'd graduated from law school together.

"What're you thinking about, Suzy?"

She smiled. "We're on vacation. No thinking allowed, except for Wednesday morning when I make my speech."

"You'll get lots of offers after that," Justin predicted. "Then we can make our plans."

"Hmm?"

He gave a sheepish smile. "Remember what you told me? That I should develop a three-year transition plan into domesticity? Take less dangerous assignments, join some clubs, that sort of thing? I figure I'll use the medical leave for the transition—that's plenty of time.

And I've already alerted my supervisors that I want to be based in a permanent location to be determined after you and Murf decide where you're gonna be. I'm also willing to join one of those fantasy-football leagues. How's that?"

"It's a start," she said, amused and touched by the offer. "I'm going to try to change, too. To be a little less controlling—"

"Hell, no. I love it when you dominate me. Like last night," he added, his eyes sparkling.

"Last night," she murmured, re-aroused just by the thought of it. They had managed to have hours of careful but effective fun despite Justin's injuries and her mild concussion. "We've had some incredible experiences, all in one short week."

"You're not going to start raving about Night Arrow again, are you?" he asked with a teasing smile. "It's so hilarious that you're more of a fanatic about it now than I am."

"If you felt what I felt—"

"Give me a break," he said, laughing. "You were delirious from the bumps on the head."

"And Miranda was on drugs? That's why *she* felt it, too? What about the obvious explanation?" Suzannah demanded, vividly remembering her battle on the staircase. "Wouldn't it be amazing if it were true? That rubbing it on an arrow creates some sort of psychic connection between it and the archer?"

"It's a crock," he insisted. "But luckily Agent X believed it."

"You believe it, too. Don't try to deny it."

He grinned. "Did I tell you I had more Night Arrow dreams while I was unconscious after Schuler beat me senseless?"

"What kind of dreams? Oh!" Suzannah smiled with delight. "Was my whole body there this time or just my breasts?"

"The whole package, definitely. I'll give you a demonstration as soon as we check in to our hotel."

"Let's go, then. Noelle's waiting for us at the airport with Murf." She laughed lightly, remembering S-3's amazing success in finding them a flight that would accept a puppy, arranging to bypass any complications with Hawaiian quarantine, then moving Suzannah's reservation from a hotel room to a bungalow, complete with a housekeeper/dogsitter.

*And* a beachfront hot tub!

"We've got a few extra minutes," Justin murmured, stroking her face, then cupping her chin in his hand. "And I know exactly how I want to spend them."

Inspired—and suddenly in no hurry at all—Suzannah slipped her hands behind his neck and pulled his mouth down to hers for a kiss that was every bit as magical as Night Arrow itself.

It was a minimum-security facility, but this particular cell had all the bells and whistles.

*Sensible, given the identity of its occupant,* Max Overton decided as he allowed a huge guard to frisk him. *I wonder what they think they'll find on me? A gun? A bomb? If she wanted any of that, she'd have it already. It's been more than a year, and she's the best. Or at least she was.*

"I'm her attorney," he reminded the guard coolly. "Our conversation is privileged."

"Don't worry. We've got orders to give you complete privacy. You could even go conjugal if you like that type."

Overton frowned. "Was that a joke? Because I don't think a judge would find it funny."

"Sorry." The guard unlocked a heavy steel door, then stepped aside. "Her ankles and arms are restrained, but her hands are free if you want her to sign papers. Or whatever."

Overton nodded curtly, certain that the guard had been making another "conjugal" joke. Not that it mattered. If this buffoon only knew the true nature of the woman he was guarding, he'd never dare suggest such a thing.

Stepping into the brightly lit room, Overton smiled respectfully at the figure seated before him. She was dressed all in gray. Her russet hair was cropped short. She wore no makeup. Yet to him, she was the most breathtakingly amazing female he had ever had the privilege to serve.

"Have they been treating you well?" he asked as he seated himself across from her.

"Cut the bull, Max. Did they succeed or not?"

"They failed. Just like you predicted."

Her green eyes came to life. "They underestimated the spinner? I *knew* that would happen!"

"Not the spinner. They underestimated Russo and his defense attorney. It's a long story—"

"Spare me. I don't care what you *think* you know. It was the spinner. It's *always* the spinner. That's what I kept trying to tell them. I could supply them with her SPIN number and Russo's pet name for her—all the information they asked me for—but I warned them it wouldn't be enough." She leaned forward, her voice charged with excitement. "Are they ready to do it my way now? To strike her where she lives? That's the only solution, Max. Russo is an attractive aberration, I'll admit. But to outwit the spinner, you have to strike at the people she really loves."

"They see that now. And they're ready to give you whatever you need."

"Good." Jane Smith leaned back in her chair, her expression smug. "It's simple, really. But you have to get inside her head to fully appreciate it. I'm glad they see that I'm the only one who can do that. I've studied her for fifteen months, after all. She's my great white whale. I won't rest until I destroy her."

"Understood. Our associates will be pleased if you succeed. And ruthless if you fail."

"I only failed once in my entire life—the day I underestimated *her*. It won't happen again." Smith's face twisted into a vengeful smile. "I'll deliver the product one week after my release from this hellhole. Do we have any idea when that will be?"

"The wheels are already in motion," Overton assured her quietly. "It will happen within the month. And without advanced publicity, just as you requested. And in return?"

"And in return," she promised him, rising from her

chair and spreading her arms wide, then walking boldly to the middle of the room to demonstrate the ease with which she had freed herself from her heavy iron shackles, "I will deliver Night Arrow."

\* \* \* \* \*

*Yes! Kate Donovan has plans to continue her exciting S.P.I.N. stories. And, meanwhile, don't miss Kate's next thrilling adventure, part of the ATHENA FORCE continuity series. CHARADE Available in March 2007. Only from Silhouette Bombshell!*

*Set in darkness beyond the ordinary world.
Passionate tales of life and death.
With characters' lives ruled by laws the everyday
world can't begin to imagine.*

*Introducing NOCTURNE, a spine-tingling
new line from Silhouette Books.*

*The thrills and chills begin with UNFORGIVEN
by Lindsay McKenna*

Plucked from the depths of hell, former military sharpshooter Reno Manchahi was hired by the government to kill a thief, but he had a mission of his own. Descended from a family of shape-shifters, Reno vowed to get the revenge he'd thirsted for all these years. But his mission went awry when his target turned out to be a powerful seductress, Magdalena Calen Hernandez, who risked everything to battle a potent evil. Suddenly, Reno had to transform himself into a true hero and fight the enemy that threatened them all. He had to become a Warrior for the Light....

\* \* \* \* \*

*Turn the page for a sneak preview of UNFORGIVEN
by Lindsay McKenna.
On sale September 26, wherever books are sold.*

# Chapter 1

*O*ne shot...one kill.

The sixteen-pound sledgehammer came down with such fierce power that the granite boulder shattered instantly. A spray of glittering mica exploded into the air and sparkled momentarily around the man who wielded the tool as if it were a weapon. Sweat ran in rivulets down Reno Manchahi's drawn, intense face. Naked from the waist up, the hot July sun beating down on his back, he hefted the sledgehammer skyward once more. Muscles in his thick forearms leaped and biceps bulged. Even his breath was focused on the boulder. In his mind's eye, he pictured Army General Robert Hampton's fleshy, arrogant fifty-year-old features on the rock's surface. Air exploded from between his lips as he brought the avenging hammer down. The boulder pulverized beneath his funneled hatred.

*One shot...one kill...*

Nostrils flaring, he inhaled the dank, humid heat and drew it deep into his massive lungs. Revenge allowed Reno to endure his imprisonment at a U.S. Navy brig near San Diego, California. Drops of sweat were flung in all directions as the crack of his sledgehammer claimed a third stone victim. Mouth taut, Reno moved to the next boulder.

The other prisoners in the stone yard gave him a wide berth. They always did. They instinctively felt his simmering hatred, the palpable revenge in his cinnamon-colored eyes, was more than skin-deep.

And they whispered he was different.

Reno enjoyed being a loner for good reason. He came from a medicine family of shape-shifters. But even this secret power had not protected him—or his family. His wife, Ilona, and his three-year-old daughter, Sarah, were dead. Murdered by Army General Hampton in their former home on USMC base in Camp Pendleton, California. Bitterness thrummed through Reno as he savagely pushed the toe of his scarred leather boot against several smaller pieces of gray granite that were in his way.

The sun beat down upon Manchahi's naked shoulders, grown dark red over time, shouting his half-Apache heritage. With his straight black hair grazing his thick shoulders, copper skin and broad face with high cheekbones, everyone knew he was Indian. When he'd first arrived at the brig, some of the prisoners taunted him and called him Geronimo. Something strange happened to Reno during his fight with the name-calling prisoners. Leaning down after he'd won the scuffle, he'd snarled into each of their bloodied faces that if they were going to call him anything, they would call him *gan,* which was the Apache word for *devil.*

His attackers had been shocked by the wounds on their faces, the deep claw marks. Reno recalled doubling his fist as they'd attacked him en masse. In that split second, he'd gone into an altered state of consciousness. In times of danger, he transformed into a jaguar. A deep, growling sound had emitted from his throat as he defended himself in the three-against-one fracas. It all happened so fast that he thought he had imagined it. He'd seen his hands morph into a forearm and paw, claws extended. The slashes left on the three men's faces after the fight told him he'd begun to shape-shift. A fist made bruises and swelling; not four perfect, deep claw marks. Stunned and anxious, he hid the knowledge of what else he was from these prisoners. Reno's only defense was to make all the prisoners so damned scared of him and remain a loner.

*Alone.* Yeah, he was alone, all right. The steel hammer swept downward with hellish ferocity. As the granite groaned in protest, Reno shut his eyes for just a moment. Sweat dripped off his nose and square chin.

Straightening, he wiped his furrowed, wet brow and looked into the pale blue sky. What got his attention was the startling cry of a red-tailed hawk as it flew over the brig yard. Squinting, he watched the bird. Reno could make out the rust-colored tail on the hawk. As a kid growing up on the Apache reservation in Arizona, Reno knew that all animals that appeared before him were messengers.

*Brother, what message do you bring me?* Reno knew one had to ask in order to receive. Allowing the sledgehammer to drop to his side, he concentrated on the hawk who wheeled in tightening circles above him.

*Freedom!* the hawk cried in return.

Reno shook his head, his black hair moving against his broad, thickset shoulders. *Freedom? No way, Brother. No way.* Figuring that he was making up the hawk's shrill message, Reno turned away. Back to his rocks. Back to picturing Hampton's smug face.

*Freedom!*

\* \* \* \* \*

*Look for UNFORGIVEN by Lindsay McKenna,
the spine-tingling launch title from
Silhouette Nocturne™.
Available September 26, wherever books are sold.*

# Silhouette

# nocturne™

## Save $1.00 off

your purchase of any
Silhouette® Nocturne™ novel.

---

### Receive $1.00 off

any Silhouette® Nocturne™ novel.

**Available wherever books are sold, including most bookstores, supermarkets, drugstores and discount stores.**

Coupon expires December 1, 2006. Redeemable at participating retail outlets in the U.S. only. Limit one coupon per customer.

RETAILER: Harlequin Enterprises Ltd. will pay the face value of this coupon plus 8¢ if submitted by the customer for this specified product only. Any other use constitutes fraud. Coupon is nonassignable. Void if taxed, prohibited or restricted by law. Void if copied. Consumer must pay for any government taxes. Mail to Harlequin Enterprises Ltd., P.O. Box 880478, El Paso, TX 88588-0478, U.S.A. Cash value 1/100 cents. Limit one coupon per customer. Valid in the U.S. only.

5 65373 00076 2    (8100) 0 11265

SNCOUPUS

# Silhouette

# nocturne™

# Save $1.00 off

your purchase of any
Silhouette® Nocturne™ novel.

---

### Receive $1.00 off
any Silhouette® Nocturne™ novel.

**Available wherever books are sold, including most bookstores, supermarkets, drugstores and discount stores.**

Coupon expires December 1, 2006. Redeemable at participating retail outlets in Canada only. Limit one coupon per customer.

RETAILER: Harlequin Enterprises Limited will pay the face value of this coupon plus 10.25 cents if submitted by the customer for this specified product only. Any other use constitutes fraud. Coupon is nonassignable. Void if taxed, prohibited or restricted by law. Consumer must pay any government taxes. Mail to Harlequin Enterprises Ltd., P.O. Box 3000, Saint John, New Brunswick E2L 4L3, Canada. Limit one coupon per customer. Valid in Canada only.

52607136

SNCOUPCDN

# Silhouette
# BOMBSHELL

On their twenty-first birthday,
the Crosse triplets discover
that each of them is destined
to carry their family's legacy
with the dark side.

## DARKHEART & CROSSE

A new miniseries
from author

## Harper ALLEN

Follow each triplet's story:

*Dressed to Slay*—October 2006
Unveiled family secrets lead sophisticated
Megan Crosse into the world of
shape-shifters and slayers.

*Vampaholic*—November 2006
Sexy Kat Crosse fears her dark future as a vampire
until a special encounter reveals her true fate.

*Dead Is the New Black*—January 2007
Tash Crosse will need to become the strongest
of them all to face a deadly enemy.

***Available at your favorite retail outlet.***

www.SilhouetteBombshell.com

SBDTS

# Silhouette Desire

## THE PART-TIME WIFE

by *USA TODAY* bestselling author

# Maureen Child

Abby Talbot was the belle of Eastwick society; the perfect hostess and wife. If only her husband were more attentiive. But when she sets out to teach him a lesson and files for divorce, Abby quickly learns her husband's true identity...and exposes them to scandals and drama galore!

On sale October 2006 from Silhouette Desire!

*Available wherever books are sold, including most bookstores, supermarkets, discount stores and drug stores.*

**Visit Silhouette Books at www.eHarlequin.com** SDPTW1006

If you enjoyed what you just read,
then we've got an offer you can't resist!

# Take 2 bestselling love stories FREE!

## Plus get a FREE surprise gift!

**Clip this page and mail it to Silhouette Reader Service®**

| IN U.S.A. | IN CANADA |
|---|---|
| 3010 Walden Ave. | P.O. Box 609 |
| P.O. Box 1867 | Fort Erie, Ontario |
| Buffalo, N.Y. 14240-1867 | L2A 5X3 |

**YES!** Please send me 2 free Silhouette Bombshell™ novels and my free surprise gift. After receiving them, if I don't wish to receive any more, I can return the shipping statement marked cancel. If I don't cancel, I will receive 4 brand-new novels every month, before they're available in stores! In the U.S.A., bill me at the bargain price of $4.69 plus 25¢ shipping & handling per book and applicable sales tax, if any*. In Canada, bill me at the bargain price of $5.24 plus 25¢ shipping & handling per book and applicable taxes**. That's the complete price and a savings of 10% off the cover prices—what a great deal! I understand that accepting the 2 free books and gift places me under no obligation ever to buy any books. I can always return a shipment and cancel at any time. Even if I never buy another book from Silhouettte, the 2 free books and gift are mine to keep forever.

200 HDN D34H
300 HDN D34J

| Name | (PLEASE PRINT) | |
|---|---|---|
| Address | Apt.# | |
| City | State/Prov. | Zip/Postal Code |

*Not valid to current Silhouette Bombshell™ subscribers.*
*Want to try another series?*
Call 1-800-873-8635 or visit www.morefreebooks.com.

\* Terms and prices subject to change without notice. Sales tax applicable in N.Y.
\*\* Canadian residents will be charged applicable provincial taxes and GST.
All orders subject to approval. Offer limited to one per household.
® and ™ are registered trademarks owned and used by the trademark owner and or its licensee.

BOMB04 ©2004 Harlequin Enterprises Limited

# Silhouette BOMBSHELL

## COMING NEXT MONTH

### #109 DRESSED TO SLAY by Harper Allen
*Darkheart & Crosse*
On the eve of her wedding, trendy society-girl and triplet Megan Crosse found out about her mother's legacy as a vampire slayer the hard way—when her fiancé turned on her and her sisters, fangs bared! Now it was up to Megan to trade in her bridal bouquet for a sharp stake and hunt down her mother's undead killer....

### #110 SHADOW LINES by Carol Stephenson
*The Madonna Key*
Epidemiologist Eve St. Giles had never seen anything like it—an influenza outbreak that *targeted* women. But this was no natural disaster—someone was manipulating the earth's ley lines to wreak havoc. Could the renowned Flu Hunter harness the ancient healing rites of her Marian foremothers in time to avert a modern medical apocalypse?

### #111 CAPTIVE DOVE by Judith Leon
When ten U.S. tourists were kidnapped in Brazil, the hostages' family connections to high political office suggested a sinister plot to bring American democracy to its knees. Only CIA operative Nova Blair—code name, Dove—could pull off a rescue. But would having her former flame for a partner clip this free agent's wings?

### #112 BAITED by Crystal Green
Pearl diver Katsu Espinoza was never one to turn down an invitation to cruise on multimillionaire Duke Harrington's yacht. But when her dying mentor announced he was disinheriting his assembled family and making Katsu his heir, the voyage turned deadly. Stranded on an island in a raging storm, with members of the party being murdered one by one, Katsu had to wonder if she was next—or if she was the bait in a demented killer's trap....

SBCNM0906